STRANGERS

THE RECKONER

STRANGERS

DAVID A. ROBERTSON

HIGHWATER
PRESS

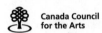 **Canada Council for the Arts**

We acknowledge the support of the Canada Council for the Arts, which last year invested $157 million to bring the arts to Canadians throughout the country.

Nous remercions le Conseil des arts du Canada de son soutien. L'an dernier, le Conseil a investi 157 millions de dollars pour mettre de l'art dans la vie des Canadiennes et des Canadiens de tout le pays.

HighWater Press gratefully acknowledges the financial support of the Province of Manitoba through the Department of Culture, Heritage, & Tourism and the Manitoba Book Publishing Tax Credit, and the Government of Canada through the Canada Book Fund (CBF), for our publishing activities.

HighWater Press is an imprint of Portage & Main Press.
Printed and bound in Canada by Friesens
Design by Relish New Brand Experience
Cover Art by Peter Diamond

24 23 22 21 20 19 18 17   1 2 3 4 5

Print   ISBN 978-1-55379-676-3
EPUB ISBN 978-1-55379-737-1
PDF   ISBN 978-1-55379-738-8

Library and Archives Canada Cataloguing in Publication

Robertson, David, 1977-, author   Strangers / by David Alexander Robertson.

(The Reckoner ; book one)Issued in print and electronic formats.
ISBN 978-1-55379-676-3 (softcover).--ISBN 978-1-55379-737-1 (EPUB).
--ISBN 978-1-55379-738-8 (PDF)

I. Title. II. Series: Robertson, David, 1977- . Reckoner ; bk. 1

PS8585.O32115S77 2017   jC813'.6   C2017-905166-0
C2017-905167-9

 HIGHWATER PRESS

Toll-Free: 1-800-667-9673
www.highwaterpress.com

DEDICATED TO MY KIDS.
ALL FIVE OF 'EM.
LOVE YOU GUYS.

"SHIT," ASHLEY WHISPERED.

The coyote strolled out from the woods and through the mist, towards him. Ashley looked around frantically, assessing if he could outrun the animal. He couldn't go backwards: Silk River was behind him, too deep and wide to be an escape route. The coyote shook its head. *Did coyotes do that?* Then the animal scoffed. There was no denying it. *It scoffed.*

"I can't even," the coyote said.

"Are you…" Ashley started, but the words escaped him.

"Going to kill you?" the coyote asked. "Going to chase you through the woods in some dramatic scene?"

"I…I…"

"Nah, not my style. I mean, that sure would make for an exciting start, though, wouldn't it?"

The animal waited for Ashley to respond, but Ashley was in a state of shock. He'd traded in his tense muscles, ready for fight or flight, for pale, clammy skin.

"But you have nothing to be afraid of, my young friend."

"You're talking. You were scoffing and now you're talking." Ashley pointed at the coyote, his index finger trembling.

"Well, yes. I scoff when appropriate, naturally. Right then you were figuring out if you could outrun me, if I were, in fact, here to kill you. Imminently scoff-worthy. Four legs good, two legs bad, am I right? Know what I'm saying?"

The coyote continued towards Ashley. At the teenager's feet, it casually turned into a man. He adjusted the lapels on his baby blue suit, straightened his top hat, and stroked the orange feather sticking out of its band. The man stood there, shoulder to shoulder with Ashley.

"Ashley, I presume," he said and extended a hand.

Ashley nodded and shook the man's hand weakly. "Yeah. Ashley. I'm Ashley."

"You can call me Choch."

"Choch."

"Ash," Choch said, "we're not going to get anywhere if you simply repeat whatever I say. You watch enough television to not get so enthralled by an anthropomorphic spirit being."

"An anthropo…po—"

Choch rolled his eyes animatedly as he interrupted, "—morphic, *really.*" Exasperated, he prompted Ashley with, "Mickey Mouse? Roger Rabbit?"

"I don't—"

"Well, it's neither here nor there. Unimportant."

Choch sat down on a rock and patted the edge of it, inviting Ashley to sit down as well. Ashley sat. He wasn't sure what else he could do, or if he had a choice. Choch took a cell phone out of his pocket and handed it to Ashley.

"You can give this back to Brady, by the way, when you see him."

The phone was in Ashley's hand, but Ashley wasn't looking at it. His eyes were trained on Choch, his mouth agape. "What is happening?" he breathed.

"Are you asking me, or…" Choch raised his eyebrows, looked up without actually moving his head "…you know. Because, to be truthful, to be absolutely 100 percent honest, most of the time he's just, 'Whatever. Free will. Not my problem.' Like that, sorta. Only he has a bit of a drawl or something. I wouldn't say southern drawl, though. More like—"

"No, I just…what the hell. You literally just turned into a man. You were a…a fricking animal."

"It takes all kinds. You'll get used to it."

Ashley started to rotate Brady's phone in his hand. "How'd you even…"

"Get the phone? Oh, I'm really quite sneaky. You don't know the *half* of it."

Ashley unlocked the phone and scrolled through the last several messages between him and Brady, the plans they had made to meet here, this clearing deep within Blackwood Forest that had become "their place" over the last few weeks. It was beautiful—there always seemed to be a mist hanging over Silk River, like a descended cloud—and private. Now it seemed as though this particular text conversation hadn't been with Brady, but with Choch. But why? Ashley pored over the conversation as though the answers were embedded in Choch's texts and the emoji were syllabics that would divulge secrets. But the emoji didn't give anything away. The bulk of them were obviously meaningless, like the smiling pile of poop Brady responded with when Ashley was too busy to meet because of homework.

Ashley stuffed the phone into his pocket.

"Why'd you bring me out here?"

Choch put his arm around Ashley. "Look around, Ash. Very cool setting, am I wrong? Imagine starting things out in the grocery store, surrounded by overpriced fruits and veggies, not this beauty before us."

"No, why all the *trouble* to bring me out here?"

"It wasn't too much of a bother, really. Don't you go and worry about little old me."

"For what!? And why me?"

"Bingo! There it is. The seven-million-dollar question. I've been totally dying to tell you, but you were far too freaked out. See? You get used to it, right?"

"Just tell me why I'm here, okay? So I can leave."

"Well, you're no fun. *Fine.* I want you to ask Cole Harper to come back home, if you will. Please."

Ashley stood up. "What? No way."

"Yes way."

"If you know anything about Cole and why he doesn't live here anymore, and you clearly *don't*, you'd know asking me to do that is weirder than a…a goddamn talking coyote."

"Weirder than a goddamn talking coyote transforming into a goddamn human being?"

To demonstrate, Choch transformed into a coyote, then back into a man.

"Yeah, kind of."

"Still," Choch said, "I'd like you to *convince*—because *ask* probably isn't the right word, knowing the boy (*and I do know the boy, dear people*)—Mr. Harper to come back home where he belongs. *Pretty please.*"

"Sorry. There's no way Cole is coming home, and I wouldn't ask him to anyway."

Choch made a *tsk-tsk-tsk* sound. "Well, that's really too bad. You're the only person here who talks to the kid."

Ashley shook his head. "Cole's just some messed up guy who's dealt with a lot of shit. Leave him alone. Can I go now?"

"Tell me what you *really* think." Choch slapped his hands against his knees and stood up. "Okay, well, this has been a slice. I feel like we should hug it out."

"Are you serious?"

Choch closed his eyes, extended his arms, and nodded sharply. At this point, Ashley was willing to do anything to get this over with— except ask Cole to come home. He leaned forward and let Choch gather him up into his arms and give him a squeeze around his waist. Choch smelled like he'd shoved about fifty lavender-scented air fresheners into his suit pockets.

They backed away from each other awkwardly.

"There we are," Choch said. "Now, like I said, a *slice*. Nice to meet you. Sorry about all the, you know, deception and whatnot. Had to give it a shot, right?"

"Right," Ashley said, and turned to leave, intent on going directly to Brady's house to tell him all about—

"*Nuh-uh*," Choch said. "Our secret. I insist."

Ashley shrugged and fast-walked out of the clearing, not willing to argue and wondering if it would do any good anyway. Brady believed in this kind of shit, in theory. But would he really buy that a coyote had just tricked his boyfriend into meeting by Silk River? Hell, with each step Ashley took he was questioning whether or not *he'd* actually seen what he had. He must've. He didn't drink, didn't do drugs, and had never hallucinated anything before, let alone a character from the myths and legends he'd learned from Elders growing up.

"You can tell Brady, though, that he needs a better password on his phone!" Choch called out, as though in response to Ashley's internal skepticism. "4-3-2-1, really?! That was literally the first thing I tried!"

NEVER SAY NEVER

ASHLEY: You need to come home. Now.

Joe and Cole were alone on the basketball court, hours before classes began. Cole's sneakers let out a shrill squeak as he pivoted and turned towards Joe. He received the basketball from Joe, cut to the hoop with two quick dribbles, paused, found the ball's ridges with his fingertips, and shot. The ball arched through the air and then clanged off the rim. Sneakers against hardwood and the thud of the basketball being dribbled—even the stubborn sound of a bricked shot—were like music to Cole. He would've rather heard the mesh snap as his ball swished past the rim, but the game, the court, was his calm place. He needed it, especially now.

You need to come home.

Now.

The only basketball-related sound Cole hated was the crowd. He never liked the roars, and never liked so many eyes on him. He always felt like he needed to take his anti-anxiety medication before a game.

The ball trailed away from Joe and Cole in progressively smaller bounces.

"If only you could shoot like you throw a pick," Joe said.

Cole half-smiled. Even though he'd been the team's leading scorer last year, the stuff he did away from the ball—throwing picks, boxing out, guarding the other team's best player—had always been his thing. In fact, his coach had told him to go easy on the picks last year after he'd knocked a player out of a game in the playoffs. Broke the guy's rib. His coach didn't know that Cole was already going easy, and gauging just how easy to take it was often the problem.

Cole jogged after the ball, picked it up, and dribbled back over to Joe. He passed the ball to Joe, and then positioned himself under the hoop as though a defender was behind him.

"I can shoot," Cole said, ready for the rebound.

"Yeah," Joe shrugged and released the ball. The mesh snapped as the ball passed through the metal ring. It dropped into Cole's arms. "But you can really throw a pick."

A few minutes later, the boys were sitting with their open gym bags at the side of the court. Joe didn't waste time. He was already getting his jeans on as soon as they'd sat down. Cole, meanwhile, hadn't even untied a shoelace. He was staring at the gymnasium ceiling, at a birdie stuck in the rafters. The same one had been there since he'd started high school. Ashley's text kept scrolling through Cole's mind.

You need to come home.

Now.

Joe kicked Cole lightly on the arm, bringing him back to the real world.

"Doing anything this weekend, or are you all zoned in for tryouts?"

"I took some shifts at the community centre," Cole said.

Joe chuckled and shook his head. "Dude, you're either playing ball, doing homework, or working at that shithole."

"I have to save money for university, man. My grandma doesn't have money to pay for it."

"What about your aunt? She lives with you too, right?"

"Yeah, but that's the thing, Joe. If my grandma doesn't have the money, it means my auntie doesn't have the money. She supports both of us. Usually works sixteen-hour days just to get us by."

"*Dude,*" Joe intoned. "Dude" could mean a million different things. Here, Cole interpreted it as: "*Holy shit, that's rough.*"

"Anyway, I think by June I'll have enough for my first year's tuition. Mostly."

Joe started buttoning his shirt up. Cole was trying to twirl the basketball on his finger for more than ten seconds straight, still in his sweat-drenched shorts and shirt, still with tied shoelaces.

"So won't your band pay for anything?" Joe asked. "They do that, right?"

Cole shook his head and slapped the basketball to get it spinning harder. It wobbled and fell off his finger. He caught it and started the process over again. "I don't need their help."

"Whatever, dude." Joe stuffed his gym clothes into his bag, then slung it and his backpack over his shoulder.

"Besides," Cole said, "if I work *and* get that scholarship, I'll be fine."

"Yeah," Joe said. "Sure. But then you might want to work on that jump shot." And with a parting, "Later," he left Cole alone in the gym.

"Later," Cole said, but the heavy gym doors had already slammed shut. The gym seemed even quieter now. Cole felt more alone. He didn't mind the feeling. But he did mind the message from Ashley, a message he couldn't ignore anymore. He fished into his gym bag and pulled out his phone. Read the text over again.

ASHLEY: **You need to come home. Now.**

Cole took a deep breath, then responded: **Very funny.**

As soon as Cole had sent the text, he saw the bubbled ellipsis by Ashley's name.

ASHLEY: **I'm not joking, Cole. This is serious. Come home.**

Cole's heart started to pound, fast and hard. His hands were shaking and his head was swimming. He gripped the bench to keep from falling over. He rifled through his gym bag until he found what he was looking for. He fumbled with the cap, managed to get it off, and took an anti-anxiety pill.

The first time he'd had a panic attack Cole's teacher had to call an ambulance. He was eight years old and walking into his fourth-grade class in the city for the first time. All the kids stared in his direction. He remembered Mrs. Benjamin screaming, "Call 9-1-1!" just before he'd blacked out. Next thing he knew he was in Grace Hospital Emergency, eerily calm. Months later, he started to see a therapist.

Now, Cole closed his eyes. He breathed in through his nose, right into his stomach, for five seconds, held it, and then breathed out through his mouth for seven seconds. He repeated this several times until he'd calmed, through the breathing or the pills. Sometimes he couldn't tell which.

COLE: **You're an asshole for even asking that.**

Cole muted his phone and threw it deep into his gym bag. He reached down to his shoes, but instead of undoing the laces he tightened them. He walked back onto the court with the basketball and stood at the foul line. He stared at the rim until its orange metal turned into Ashley's texts. *You need to come home. Now. I'm not joking, Cole. This is serious. Come home.* He bounced the ball once, let out a guttural scream, and charged towards the hoop. He leapt into the air and dunked the basketball with both hands, as hard as he could. He dunked the ball about two million times before class started.

It was a wonder he didn't shatter the backboard.

At 3:41 p.m. Cole stood in front of his opened locker, staring at the gym bag which he had put at the bottom. Throughout the day, he had piled textbooks and binders on to the bag. He had his hands in his pockets. One of those hands was wrapped around his pill bottle, which was always on his person, just in case.

"Dude." Joe walked up and stood beside Cole. They both stared into the locker.

"Hey." Cole didn't look away from the gym bag.

"I thought my shit was messy," Joe said. "Ever seen *Hoarders*?"

"I don't usually—"

"Like, there could be a black hole in there and nobody would know it. Matthew McConaughey could be behind that big stack of textbooks screaming out 'Murph! Don't leave me, Murph!' and, you know, the world would end because there's just—"

"Okay, I get it. I don't keep my locker like this. You know that. I'm trying to—"

"Great movie, though. Every time, I'm like, 'I'm not going to cry,' and then *boom. Crying.*"

"—hide my phone from me."

"Waterworks, you know?"

They fell silent. They kept standing, staring, and the hallways started to empty. Kids rushing for buses. Kids rushing for rides. Kids just rushed. Except Joe and Cole.

"Why do you think my friend from Wounded Sky would ask me to come home?" Cole asked, finally verbalizing a question he'd asked himself all day.

"Dude, I don't even know why you left in the first place. You're just always weird about it," Joe said.

"I could just ignore him, right? I could leave my gym bag right where it is, and come back and get it for tryouts on Monday."

"Your bag would be stinky as shit, dude."

"And by then, if it's such an emergency, maybe Ashley will have given up, you know? We could both pretend like it never happened, go about our lives…"

"Okay, I don't want to play the devil's advocate, but what if *because* it's an emergency, you should, like, go?"

"You were just literally playing devil's advocate there, you know that, right?"

Joe shrugged. "Sorry."

"What could be the emergency? Shit happens there, Joe. Like, last year, there was this flood. That was an emergency. What could I have done? Help sandbag? Ashley didn't text me to come. There was no *come-home-now* crap."

"I've sandbagged before. By the Red River. Last year too. Got free lunch, and we got paid. It was dope, for real. I took you to the Ex with that money, dude. Remember that?"

"Two years ago, they had a flu epidemic. Ashley got sick. I remember how sick he got. I thought he was going to die he got so sick. If he'd have asked me to come out then, maybe, you know? Maybe I would've come."

"*Dude.*"

"But that's the thing, Joe. He wouldn't have asked me, even then. He knows better than to ask me."

Cole kept his eyes trained on the gym bag, crushed as it was underneath the textbooks and binders. He could feel Joe's eyes on him.

"But you should've gone, right? That's your bro, right?"

Holy shit. Joe's comment hit Cole hard. It at once felt like it was overstepping, as though Cole hadn't just invited Joe's opinion, but he was 100 percent right. Absolutely, he should've gone when Ashley was sick. When Cole had graduated from grade eight, and was about to move onto high school, Ashley flew down to the city for the day just to see him graduate. Cole wasn't even sick. Ashley just knew how difficult school had been for Cole, and always would be. Grade eight graduations were so innocuous; near-death sicknesses were not. Cole pried his eyes away from the locker, and swivelled around to face Joe. He said, rushed and angry, "Thanks. *Really* appreciate that, man. I'll see you Monday."

Joe threw his arms up in frustration, turned around and walked away. "Redirect anger much, dude?"

"Whatever." Cole turned back to his locker. He stared at the gym bag for a moment longer, then grumbled, "Screw it," under his breath. He pulled out the gym bag and fished through it, right to the bottom, and pulled out the phone. He had eighteen new text messages. Standing in front of his opened locker, some textbooks spilled onto the floor by his feet. Cole made his way through them.

You're the asshole if you don't come back, Cole, said one text from Ashley, sent immediately after Cole threw the phone into his gym bag this morning.

Seventeen others followed. None of them told Cole why he was needed home, but they all kept asking him to come home anyway— except for the one that read, **Sorry, you're not an asshole, you're just acting like one.**

Cole, when have I ever asked you for anything?

There's a flight that leaves tonight at 10 p.m.

If you're still thinking about it, there's one that leaves tomorrow too. 3 p.m.

Did you turn your phone off? That doesn't make this go away!

Dishonest Cole swore he'd come back if he was needed, now refuses. Sad!

Okay, that was low, but you did say that, years ago. I NEED YOU!

On and on they went. When Cole was done reading through them all, he began to write back to Ashley, but he erased what he had written several times—because he didn't know what to say, because he didn't know what to ask, because his thumbs were shaking so badly that he misspelled almost every word. Finally, he took a deep breath and wrote back, **You need to tell me why, or else this conversation is over, no matter how many times you ask.** Then, as calmly as he could, he slipped the phone into his pocket beside his pills. He got his school bag, placed the books that had fallen onto the floor back into his locker, shut it, and made his way outside.

Usually, he took the bus home. Auntie Joan could only afford a place in a different area of the city, but she insisted he attended schools in a better area; the schools around where they stayed were "too rough" for him. He would've gone to those schools, would've felt comfortable, but arguing with her wasn't much good. After all, it was she, not his grandma, who'd decided that they—herself, Cole, and his grandma—should move away from the community. His grandma had thought they should stay. That's what Cole's parents would've wanted, she'd said to Joan. Moving away wasn't just removing unwanted attention from Cole, it was removing community, culture, language, traditions... *everything*. It was a trade-off, his auntie had argued.

"It'll be too hard for you, you'll see," Auntie Joan told Cole on the night before they left. It had always made Cole feel weak (one of the reasons why Cole needed anti-anxiety medication now, as he and his therapist had figured out over the years). Of course, everything he'd lost in the tragedy, and his role in it, was probably a greater contributing factor. So, they moved. They left almost everything behind and started fresh. Lived in a "rough" neighbourhood, went to a nice school.

Cole started on the hour-long walk home.

He hated the idea of going back to Wounded Sky, but maybe Ashley deserved as much. He couldn't imagine, though, what it would take to make his auntie agree to let him go back. That's who Ashley would really have to convince. Not him, not his grandma.

Cole's phone stayed silent during the walk. Given Ashley's persistence throughout the day, this surprised Cole. As he passed the familiar landmarks he usually saw from city transit he thought about Wounded Sky more than he had over the last ten years. Rather than fight them off, he willingly recalled memories from his childhood. Mostly, the memories centred on the close friends he had. Ashley. Brady. Eva. Mostly Eva. They came in fragments with her, like a remembered dream. Taking off their shoes and splashing around at the banks of Silk River. Cole helping her with math, and she helping him with Cree. How she always smelled like clean laundry. Watching every tear curl down her cheek when she learned he was leaving. Cole was certain he, his grandma, and his auntie moved away almost exactly ten years ago. He wondered if that was why Ashley wanted him to come home. If that were the case, then there was no way he would go.

Grade twelve graduation. He could go for that. A far more important event than an eighth-grade ceremony. That way, he'd have a full year to work up the courage. The thought of some messed up ten-year reunion bothered Cole so much that he texted Ashley again when he got to the front of the apartment complex.

This isn't about a memorial or anything, is it?

By the time he'd climbed up to the third floor of the building, got into his apartment and out of his shoes, he received a simple reply: **Come on, Cole. No.**

"Hey Grandma! Hey Auntie Joan!" Cole called out after positioning his shoes between theirs, against the wall in the entryway, just so. He could hear the television set blaring. Sounded like *CSI*. Somebody was talking about blood splatter. Maybe it was *Dexter*.

His phone buzzed in his hand. **I mean, there is a memorial on Tuesday, but that's not why.**

"Tansi, nósisim!" his grandma called back.

(FYI, dear reader: "nósisim" is a Cree word that means "my grand-child." Fun fact: it can mean either my grandson or my granddaughter. Very forward-thinking. Choch out.)

The television set muted. Cole made his way into the living room as he wrote back, **Right. Knew it**, to Ashley and, his anger returning, shoved the phone into his pocket.

"Sorry I'm late," Cole said to his grandma in a huff. "Needed some air."

"I don't think you got enough, child," his grandma said.

Of course it was a memorial. It couldn't be anything else. Ten years. Cole sat down on the couch aggressively, his arms crossed. His auntie entered from the kitchen with a cup of coffee. There was always a cup of coffee involved when she had a night shift coming up.

"What's up with you?" Auntie Joan asked.

"Nothing." After that, Cole went quiet. He found a spot on the floor, a discoloured area in the hardwood, and stared at it.

"That sort of *nothing* means a whole lot of *something*, Cole," Auntie Joan said.

He was still quiet.

"The quieter you are, the more you have to say."

"I don't want to talk about it."

"Your father was like that," his grandma said. "He'd come into a room with steam coming out of his ears. He'd sit down and look like he was ready to explode. 'I don't want to talk about it,' he'd tell me and your mom. But when he started talking, well…let's just say I put on a pot of coffee."

"I don't drink coffee," Cole grumbled.

"I just had the last cup anyways." Auntie Joan plopped down on the couch beside him. She took a sip of her drink, then placed it on the coffee table. She looked Cole dead in the eyes. "Now, that's enough, Cole. Out with it."

Cole leaned forward and buried his head in his hands. "None of it is going to go away, is it?"

"Not if you don't let it," Auntie Joan said.

"What's troubling you?" his grandmother asked.

Cole came up for air. "Ashley's asking me to come home. I mean, go to Wounded Sky. You know, just when I think I'm over it..." Cole started, but trailed off, as though all of his words got sucked up into the dark spot on the floor.

Auntie Joan was tight-lipped. She looked like she was going to explode, just like her brother used to.

"But you aren't over it, nósisim. You never have been." His grandmother looked decidedly less combustible than his auntie.

"He said it's not because of some memorial they're having, but I bet it is." Cole stood up from the couch and started pacing around the room. "I bet they just want me there to be their poster boy or something, and I'll have to stand up in front of everybody and I'll feel like puking all over them. I will literally puke all over them, I bet. It'll be like *Carrie*, only with puke. You know how I get in front of crowds."

"You're simply not going back there. *Ever*." Auntie Joan's teeth gritted like she might turn them into powder. "It's not even a consideration." She took another, longer sip of her coffee.

"And what if it *is* about a memorial?" his grandma asked.

"Mother!" Auntie Joan hissed and stood up from the couch.

"Well, don't you think it might help Cole to face that, Joan?"

For a moment, Cole may as well have not been in the room. His grandmother and his auntie were in a full-on stare down.

"It'll help if he never goes back there, and you know it," Auntie Joan said to his grandmother. "He is not going back there." She turned to him and said, "You are not going back there," as if he hadn't heard her say it the first time.

"I think we should at least consider—" his grandmother started.

"And who's going to pay for it, huh?" Auntie Joan went into the kitchen and dumped her coffee out, only so she could slam the cup into the kitchen sink. "I work these shifts just to pay for rent and food. Do you know how much it costs to fly there?"

"And how much would you pay for Cole to heal?" his grandmother asked.

"That's not fair," Auntie Joan said.

Cole dropped his arms to his sides, exasperated. "I have my tuition money."

"You just sounded like you didn't want to go!" His auntie returned to the living room, fired up. "Now you want to throw away your future? For what?"

"Maybe it's important!" Cole said.

"University is important. Rehashing tragedy is not."

"Maybe I'll get that scholarship."

"Maybe? Maybe?" That was all Auntie Joan was capable of saying right then. "*Please* side with me here, Mother."

"Look." His grandmother got up and walked over to Cole. She put her hand on his shoulder. "We can't tell you what to do, Cole. You're a man now. We brought you away to protect you. You don't need that protection anymore."

"Protect me from what?" Cole asked.

"From all the—" But that was as far as Auntie Joan got.

"All I am saying," his grandmother interrupted forcefully, "is that maybe you need to think about what's best for *you* long-term. Not us." She shot a look at Auntie Joan there. "*You.*"

"We haven't even prepared him for this." Auntie Joan stepped closer to Cole and his grandmother.

"You're right," his grandmother said. "We've been shielding him for too long, and what good has it done, really?"

"I'm right here, by the way," Cole said, but perhaps his real response was how he began to trace the outline of the medicine bottle protruding from his pants pocket. What good *had* it done, whatever he was being shielded from? He was a bundle of nerves, always. Could going home change that?

"Where do you want your nephew to be ten years from now? Twenty years from now? For him to still be dealing with it like he has been? Like we've been making him deal with it? What will his years be like?"

"His years will be safe," Auntie Joan said. "We've done this all to keep you safe, Cole."

Cole slid his foot over the discoloured patch, and then looked up at them. "I want to go. This is my decision. Let me take out my tuition money. I'll work more. I'll get it back."

"We can make it work," his grandmother said to his auntie. Then, as though conceding the decision to her daughter, she gave Cole a smile, and left the room. She went down the hallway, towards her bedroom.

Cole and his auntie stood there, staring at each other. They said a lot in that silence. Cole did his best to look strong, but felt anything but. Maybe she saw that in him. Maybe that's exactly what she was looking at: if he could take it. "You know I only want what's best for you."

"I know," Cole said, "I do too. And I feel like I have to do this."

"That's the thing, though, Cole. I don't think you *can* do this."

"That's not your decision."

"I'm sorry," his auntie said. "But it is. You're not going. I'm not giving you my money, or your tuition money, to see you torn apart."

Cole shook his head and looked up at the ceiling. A thousand responses went through his mind, but he said none of them. All he could muster was, "Fine!" and then he left the living room on his way to his bedroom. There, he settled into bed, his head propped up on a pillow, with Bon Iver playing through speakers on his desk across the room. The curtains were drawn, he was immersed in complete darkness, he was doing his breathing, but after listening to *22, A Million* three times through, he just felt angry. He knew what was best for his life, not her. He could've handled St. John's High School. He didn't need the shelter of Kelvin. And he could've stayed in Wounded Sky all this time, too, couldn't he? He could've stayed there, stayed with his friends. He wouldn't have felt like Eva hated him now, wouldn't be afraid to even send her a text to say hello.

As an act of defiance, even though going to Wounded Sky wasn't in the cards without his auntie's approval, he sat up in his bed, opened his laptop, and looked up flights from Winnipeg to Wounded Sky First Nation. Ashley had been right about the times. There was a flight tonight at 10:00 p.m., and another tomorrow at 3:00 p.m. He went through the process of booking a flight for 3:00 p.m. tomorrow. He went all the way to the checkout, but ended up slamming the laptop shut.

Breathe in for five seconds. Hold it. Breathe out for seven.

He lay back down, head propped up against the pillow. Music washed over him.

COLE: **Sorry. I can't come.**

Cole was with Eva. They were children again. Seven years old. They were in a field, and it was night. There was nobody, nothing around them. Just the field, stretching for eternity. She was dancing like there was music. She looked like a poem, like the northern lights overhead. "Dance with me," she said. He was standing in place, his body subtly swaying to the unheard rhythm. She spun around, arms high in the air. When she faced him again, she was seventeen. Her dress moved through the air like smoke. There was music. He heard the music. "Dance with me." She reached for him. Beautiful music. He whistled along, and reached for her hand. The lights above came down to them. To her. Ribbons of colour wrapped around her, took her up, danced with her there. "Cole!" He reached for her. She was too high.

"Cole."

"Eva," he said.

"No, nósisim."

Cole opened his eyes. It was light out. Even with the heavy navy curtains drawn, he could tell it was morning. His grandmother was sitting at the edge of his bed, patting his leg.

"You were having a nightmare."

"Sort of." He sat up and leaned against the headboard. "Sort of a dream, sort of a nightmare."

"You're already there, aren't you?"

"Wounded Sky? I don't know where it was. It was about—"

"Sometimes, a place isn't just a town, but the people too. They *are* that place, in a way."

"You're sounding very Elder-y right now, Grandma."

His grandmother gave his leg one more pat, and then she placed an envelope on the bed and slid it over to Cole. He opened it.

"Grandma, you can't do this." There was a stack of money in the envelope. Probably close to $2,000. Cole didn't count it, just flipped through the bills with his thumb.

"I can do whatever I please with my money," she said.

"Where did you get all of this?" Cole asked.

"It doesn't matter." She stood up from the bed. "I want you to use that. Go home, do what you have to do. It really is your decision."

"What about Auntie Joan?"

She looked behind her, like she could see through walls. "Fast asleep. She had a night shift. She'll be sleeping for a while yet."

"She'll kill me."

"You let me worry about my daughter." His grandmother had been clutching something in her left hand. She extended that hand, hesitantly, to Cole, opened it. A tobacco tie was resting in her palm. Cole shook his head, gently closed his grandmother's fingers around the red bundle.

"Nósisim."

"No thanks, Grandma. I don't want—I don't need it."

"Cole. All these years, you've been avoiding part of who you are, our traditions, culture. You won't speak our language. But, nósisim, these are the things that would help you be strong. Isn't that what you want?"

"You're wrong. That...it just makes me hurt more. It just reminds me."

"It should remind you of the good *in* us, not the bad that has happened *to* us."

"I'm sorry, I..." Cole trailed off. Just closed his eyes and sighed.

"If not for you, then for me."

He felt his grandmother's touch. She turned his left hand over, uncurled his fingers, and placed the tobacco in his hand, over a large, ugly scar that stretched from one side of his palm to the other. He closed his hand.

"Lay this for me, at the memorial. Say a prayer, for me. Would you do that for your old kókom?"

"Yeah, sure. I will. For you."

His grandmother looked at her watch carefully, then at Cole. "Now, you slept in, nósisim. It's almost noon and I think your flight leaves at 3 p.m. You have some packing to do, and you should leave quietly. Your auntie isn't the heaviest sleeper."

"How'd you know when the flight leaves?" Cole asked.

"Your computer said so."

"I lock my computer."

"Now, Cole, I might be 'Elder-y,' but even I know that a name isn't the best password. Especially a three-letter one."

2

LITTLE EARTHQUAKES

THE LAST TIME COLE HAD BEEN ON A PLANE was to leave Wounded Sky First Nation. Back then he was nervous to go, nervous about what the city would hold for him. He could still remember the feeling he had, perhaps a harbinger of what was to come. He remembered walking to the plane on the tarmac, his stomach turning, his heart racing, his palms soaked with sweat. He kept rubbing them against his pants. Now he was nervous to return. His body was shaking as though the plane was going through turbulence.

Wounded Sky never did get many visitors, only pilots stopping over when making food deliveries. Nobody really came by car, not over the winter road, not on the old, rusted ferry that could carry one car at a time over Silk River. There was food on the plane Cole was on now. When he was little he would look up at these little twin engine planes, and wonder what was on them. He never thought it was something as benign as groceries. Cole wondered if there was a kid like that now, down there on the ground somewhere, looking up and wondering what the plane was bringing in. What would that kid think if he or she knew it was Cole Harper? What stories had the kid been told by their parents about him, that he was a freak…or a hero?

Cole had been on the plane for two hours now. He'd been look-ing down for the whole flight, watching the city disappear into a kids' model of the urban landscape, watching the highways shrink into grey veins nestled in the green skin of Mother Earth, watching how every-thing seemed so small, even his worries. But when the plane began to descend, and he saw Wounded Sky choked against the horizon by Blackwood Forest and pierced by Silk River, those worries started to feel too big for him.

The sun was just starting to set when the plane landed on the perilously thin landing strip. He hadn't known what to expect when he landed during the plane ride, but he'd imagined a small crowd gathered by the airstrip, waiting to see him come back home, maybe cheering for him. With signs. Cardboard signs with sharpie words: *Welcome home, hero. Thank you, Cole! Cole H. for Hero!* A prodigal-son-returns kind of vibe. He remembered the attention he got back then. All the eyes on him. All the questions. He understood why he'd been taken away from that. But maybe he was ready for it now. Maybe it'd be cathartic. A healing. Then he'd imagined only his best friends from Wounded Sky being there. Eva. Brady. Ashley—the people who used to matter most to him. Who still mattered most to him. Distance hadn't changed that, at least for him. A large crowd might've been cathartic, but those three, that would've been something else entirely. He'd almost prefer a crowd. He wanted to see them, especially Eva, but at the same time, he didn't. At the same time, thinking of seeing them, of seeing her, felt overwhelming. He went over his latest text exchange with Ashley, trying to keep the phone steady, and to dissect whether or not Ashley would've told Brady and Eva that he was coming home.

COLE: **Guess what? See you later today! But you didn't have to lie to me about the memorial. I know that's why you asked me back.**

ASHLEY: **Really? Just like that?**

COLE: **Yeah, just like that.**

ASHLEY: **It wasn't about the memorial though. Just saying.**

COLE: **What was it about then?**

ASHLEY: **Come see me when you're in. When are you coming?**

COLE: **Get in around 6 p.m.**

ASHLEY: **Kk. See you then. Maybe come to see you in.**

COLE: **Anybody else?**

There was no answer to that question, but Cole found that he was disappointed when he stepped off the plane, his bag slung sadly over his shoulder. There was no crowd, no Brady, no Eva. Not even Ashley. Could everything that happened ten years ago mean so little now, that the seven-year-old kid who'd saved some lives didn't deserve any sort of welcome? Maybe this was best. *If I don't like a basketball crowd, a Wounded Sky First Nation welcoming committee would be pretty harsh.* It was never going to be cathartic. And he could understand Brady and Eva not being there. Cole hadn't texted them. He hadn't contacted them in ten years. Even if Ashley had let them know, they might not have shown up. But, Ashley not being there?

COLE: **Here. Where are you?**

Cole waited for a response for several minutes, standing just yards away from the airport, staring not at the beauty the surrounding forest boasted or the vastness of the country sky, but at his phone. Nothing.

"Why'd I bother doing this?" He'd been begged to come. It was *so* urgent. Yet there he was, alone, with nothing but time to welcome him here. The plane was still there. It was going to sit there until it was unloaded and then it was going to leave, back to Winnipeg. If it were leaving anyway, then maybe the pilot would take him. But what would he say to his grandmother? The flight had cost almost $1,000. He could've bought a car for that. No, he couldn't just leave. He owed it to her to stay until the memorial, lay the tobacco she'd given him, get it over with, and go back to the city. Plus, staying meant the added bonus of not having to face his auntie right now. He'd ignored about one thousand of her calls by now. His grandmother was dealing with her, and that was something else he owed her for.

"Fine, okay," he said to himself. "You win."

COLE: **Whatever. I'll come there.**

He pocketed his phone, swallowed his pride, and started on the short walk into the community.

Cole expected everything he saw and everything he came across would stir emotions, jog his memory, but the first thing he actually encountered sent him reeling: the old research facility. The place where his father had worked… and died. It was obviously still abandoned, no doubt since the accident that had taken his father's life. The windows were boarded up, a large chain sealed the front door, and the entire building itself was enclosed by a metal fence that let off a constant humming noise. Cole walked towards the building. He couldn't count how many times he had come here as a child with his mom to see his dad for lunch. He and his mom would pack a sandwich, usually peanut butter and jam, and some kind of fruit. He preferred apples. They mostly brought apples. The picnic table they sat on to eat together was still there. Cole reached out his hand to open the gate—

"Stop!" a voice shouted.

Cole's hand recoiled, and he turned around to see a security guard running up to him from a short way down the perimeter of the fence, handcuffs jingling from his belt.

"Don't touch that!" The security guard stopped inches away from Cole.

Cole didn't know if he recognized the man, his face hidden behind a pair of sunglasses and a black baseball hat pulled down low. The man rested his hand on the grip of his gun. Cole backed away a little.

"Sorry," he said with his hands up in a defensive posture.

"Wait a minute," the guard said. "Are you—"

"Cole Harper."

"—Cole Harper, back from the dead."

"I don't..."

"Sorry, how insensitive of me, considerin' why you left in the first place. Back home, are you? What brings you here, city boy?"

"Can you..." Cole motioned to the man's gun. The man looked down and laughed, then took his hand off the grip.

"Sorry, hero." The guard reached up and took off his sunglasses, and Cole recognized him as Scott Thomas, an older kid from the elementary school back in the day. He was kind of a bully back then. It made sense, him having a gun. "So, what're you doin' here, city boy?"

Cole took a deep breath. "I heard there was a memorial coming up, for the...you know."

"Right, right, right," Scott breathed. "Right. Yeah, Tuesday."

"Tuesday," Cole said.

"Well, good for you, Cole. Leave everybody here to suffer through it all together, save whoever the fuck you wanna, and then come back to soak in the awe and wonder of your return. Right?"

"Save whoever the…no, it's not like that, man."

"Hey." Scott reached forward and slapped Cole on the shoulder. "I'm just screwin' with you, guy. It's all good."

Cole, sensing now that he could change the subject (desperate, in fact, to change the subject) motioned to the fence, and the building. "So what's up with all of this? Are you guarding this place?"

"Yep."

"Why? I mean, what's there to guard?"

Scott took the bill of his cap and moved it up and down a few times, then let out a big breath and shrugged. "Kids are always comin' around here, tryin' to get inside. You know what happened here, city boy."

"Right, sure," Cole said. "I just thought, I don't know, it would've been cleaned up by now."

"Ha! You're funny, guy. You think whoever ran this place gave a shit about cleanin' up their goddamn mess? Far as anybody knows, shit's still messed inside. Hell, your old man's still down there, rottin' away."

"Screw you, Scott."

"*And* that chick. Both of them. Worm food. And kids, y'know, they wanna go check it out, see a dead body. It's like *Stand by Me* or somethin'."

"Shut up!"

"Sorry, that was rude of me. Where are my manners?"

"I'm out of here." Cole turned to leave.

"What's your rush?" Scott grabbed Cole's shoulder.

Cole jerked it away. "What's it to you?"

"I just thought we could spend some quality time together. Everybody else is at the hockey game anyways."

Of course. It was Saturday. How stupid of him. Saturday was hockey night in Wounded Sky, the reason Ashley wasn't there to greet him at the airport, and everybody else. Nobody missed hockey night. Not even, it turned out, Cole.

"Yeah, that's where I'm headed."

A path ambled its way to Wounded Sky from the airport. It forked off twice on the way to the community's perimeter, once towards the old research facility, and the second time towards Cole's former elementary school. Cole took the forked path. He stopped where it stopped. He stood there facing the school a couple of hundred yards away. Only the skeleton of a school remained, a collection of concrete and brick bones, broken and charred. Small sections of the school appeared undamaged by the fire. Bigger sections were completely destroyed, laying in piles on the ground, untouched in ten years and overgrown with grass and weeds. He could see hallways with partial walls, or no walls whatsoever, extend out from the front of the school to the left, where classrooms once were, and to the right, all the way to the gym, with its crumbled walls, ceiling, and metal beams piled on top of each other.

Cole's knees began to shake and weaken. He heard the screams of children. They erupted from the ruins and echoed deep inside Blackwood Forest. Flames roared, thunderous and terrible. He saw everything around him—the grass, the trees, the path to the school—painted in yellow and orange and red. He saw black smoke spiralling into the sky. His heart began to race. He could feel his pulse pound through every vein. Sweat and tears dripped down his face. He felt dizzy and his vision began to blur. He reached out instinctively to steady himself. A hand grasped his wrist.

"Hey, what's up with you?" a girl's voice asked.

"Huh?"

Cole looked to the side, where he saw Alex Captain. Alex had been in grade one when Cole was in grade three. She must've been fifteen or sixteen now. Her father was a teacher at the school, and was in the building when it burned down. He recognized the loss in her eyes, a kind of emptiness that couldn't be filled. He knew that look was in his own eyes, too.

"It looks like there's a tiny earthquake right under your feet. Centralized," Alex said. She was pointing at his feet, at an imaginary earthquake.

"Oh, no. It's more like—"

"Either that or you're drunk," she kept on. "Please don't be drunk. Don't be like those Saturday night hockey idiots. They pour into The Fish after the game, all of them, order the whole menu, and, you know, a third of it ends up in their stomachs, a third of it ends up on the tables or walls or floor, and a third of it gets puked up on the grass outside the building. *Awesome.*"

The Fish was really The Northern Lights Diner. It'd been called that for as long as Cole could remember, probably since time immemorial. Named after the fact that most of its best dishes, most of its dishes *period*, contained jackfish. And there was also a jackfish on the sign, not, as one might think, the northern lights.

"I'm not drunk. It's just tough being here, I guess."

"Waitaminute." Alex leaned in closer and took a good look at him. "Cole?"

"Yep."

"Holy shit!" Alex backed away, slapped her knees, and spun in a complete circle in disbelief. "What the heck're you doing out here?"

"Like here?" Cole pointed to his feet, to the imaginary tiny earthquake.

"No, here, obviously." Alex spread her arms out wide. "Wounded Sky."

Cole shrugged. "Not sure. I could ask you the same thing."

"You mean *here*. Like *here* here. Not here. I live here." Alex was pointing all over the place now, just messing with him.

"Sure." Cole managed a chuckle. "I thought it was mandatory attendance at the arena on Saturday nights."

"*Please.* I defy hockey, Cole. I defy the expectations of hockey worship as a Wounded Sky band member. I'd rather clean up puke out front of The Fish."

"Gross," Cole said.

"I'm walking, I'll have you know. I go for walks. My shift hasn't started yet, so…"

"You work at the diner now?"

"Ever since I could. You know, if a job comes open in Wounded Sky you have to snatch it up. There're only so many of them."

"Right."

They encountered their first silence. It teetered on the edge of awkward, but it was far better than what he had experienced with Scott. Cole felt encouraged. There'd been no welcoming party, but there was this.

"What about you?" Alex asked. "Where are you headed? Here, then over there, then all around everywhere? Trying to find a good door frame for refuge from the earthquake?"

"Actually, I'm one of the sheep," Cole said. "Headed to the arena for the hockey game."

"Oh, fun! I'll walk with you," Alex said, as though she hadn't just trashed the sport and the hockey worship that was evidently still prevalent in the community.

Alex started on her way before Cole had even moved. When he did step forward, back towards the main path, his knees were steady, and he became aware that his entire body was calm. He hadn't even taken a pill. He met up with her as the short trail to the school grounds converged with the main pathway, and they walked together from there.

"Thanks," Cole said.

"Oh," Alex said, "I was heading that way anyway. My kindness is out of convenience."

"Still," Cole said.

"I guess I *did* save you from certain death."

3
HOCKEY NIGHT

THE FISH WAS RIGHT ACROSS FROM THE ARENA. A less imaginative name for Wounded Sky's arena would've been The Barn because it used to be a barn. This was obvious from the shape of it: boxy, with a ceiling that arched upward in large, flat sections. Probably hundreds of hockey arenas across North America had that same moniker. The Barn. In fact, Cole remembered that Winnipeg's old hockey arena was called The Barn. This one was called The X.

Impressively, The X had stood the test of time with little exterior upkeep over the last ten years (none that Cole knew of and none that he could see as he approached). White paint was flaking away in places to reveal a red undercoat, hinting at its history before it was packed with crowds and sticks and pucks and players and ice. And they'd kept the big red doors each with a big white X. The X.

Alex came to a stop beside The Fish. Cole stopped too. The smell of jackfish and fried food wafted over them. Cole took a deep breath in.

"I missed this smell," he said.

"Try working there five days a week," Alex said. "It'll change your opinion. The monsters in my nightmares are deep-fried and breaded."

"Mine are burning," Cole said without thinking. He caught himself too late. "Sorry," was all he could say.

"Wow," Alex mouthed while looking away. She recovered quickly. "Anyway, that's why I hate hockey now too. I associate it with the smell of fish. And puke. Puke too."

"I love it because I was never really allowed to come here. I just always smelled it, and imagined how good everything must taste."

"I remember your school lunches," Alex said. "Apples, salads, all the healthy stuff."

"I swear my folks spent all their money on fruits and vegetables," Cole said.

"Well, when a banana costs five dollars…"

"You have to put a quart of milk on layaway, right?"

Alex laughed. Her laugh was quickly overtaken by a roar from the arena. The whole building shook. Somebody scored.

"Well, this is me," Alex said. "I'll see ya, Cole."

"Yeah, see you," Cole said as Alex ran off inside the diner.

As Cole walked up, he found that he missed the sight of the place, and the sound of it, the ruckus emanating from the arena, a symphony of noise he had heard well before stopping beside The Fish. An entire community packed inside the arena. Sardines, meet can. With the exception of the security guard stationed outside The X, there didn't seem to be anybody around for miles. Cole wanted to enter the arena without incident. He made a move for the door after crossing the road, even gave the guy a polite nod, but the guard took a military step sideways to get in Cole's way.

"Well, I'll be," the guard started. As with Scott, Cole couldn't tell who it was at first, with his black lenses and cap pulled over his forehead. "Cole—"

"—Harper," Cole finished for the guard. "Wherever you guys work, they must provide training on how to welcome me back to Wounded Sky First Nation. It's really nice."

"Oh, you're not welcome here, city," the guard said. "Don't take my…congeniality that way."

"I wasn't, don't worry." Cole tried again to enter the arena. He took a deliberate step towards a white X. The guard shrugged his shoulder in that direction.

"Can I get through?" Cole asked.

"What the hell are you doing back here anyway?" the guard asked.

"None of your business."

"You just thought, 'Hey, it's the memorial on Tuesday. I might as well open old wounds.' Something like that, hero?"

"Would you all stop calling me hero? I never said I was and I never wanted to be. I'll take *city* over hero. It's not original, but at least it's accurate."

"What's *accurate* is that you're a coward, Harper. You do what you did, then you left. High-tailed it to Winnipeg. *Winnipeg*. Who goes there for a better life, anyway?"

"I didn't choose that. I would've stayed."

"You save two kids, your best friends of course, and then what did you leave for the rest of us, hey? The dead, that's what. The dead and the pain that comes with death. I should kick your skinny little ass."

The arena door swung open, nearly hitting the guard on the shoulder. Cole recognized Reynold McCabe immediately. He must've been in his late forties now, but didn't look a day older than when Cole had last seen him. He was a shorter man, but stocky. "Built like a truck," Cole's dad used to say. His black, shiny hair was tied into a tight braid. Cole figured Reynold would be the only person he saw in a suit tonight or any other night in Wounded Sky.

"Now, I've heard just about all I can hear." Reynold McCabe stepped outside into the cool autumn air. He stood in front of Cole and the guard, and gave Cole a hard pat on the shoulder. "I'm not willing to listen to another second of this young man getting chewed out by one of my employees."

"Thanks." Cole shot the guard a smirk. It looked like the guard's face was going to implode it was pulled so tight with anger.

"Boss, I—"

"Cole," Reynold was looking directly at Cole, but talking to the guard, "should be celebrated in Wounded Sky, Mr. Fontaine. *Celebrated*."

Mr. Fontaine. Mark Fontaine? Another guy from Scott's grade (Also an asshole, in Cole's opinion.) Maybe this was a prerequisite for Reynold's employees. Another requirement seemed to be guarding places that didn't need guarding. He understood needing somebody at the facility. Nobody had ever been sure what was actually done there, but everybody knew the accident was bad by how quickly it had been evacuated and shut down afterwards. Maybe it had never been cleaned up *because* it was so bad. But The X? Come on. It was self-policed. Aside from the odd person who'd had too much, and generally people didn't (Alex had been exaggerating), nobody really stepped out of line. They'd have too much to answer for the next day.

"Mr. McCabe, this little bastard…"

"You're fired," Reynold said to Mark. Mark didn't argue, didn't slam a door, didn't storm off, didn't shout. He just shot Cole a quick look, took off his belt—and with it his gun, flashlight, and handcuffs—tossed it and his hat on the ground, then walked away into the night. Reynold picked up the equipment and the hat. He shook his head. "I'm sorry about all that. That's no way to welcome somebody back home."

"It's okay, Mr. McCabe," Cole said. "Thanks again."

"Please, call me Reynold. I insist."

"Sure, Reynold."

"I mean it, son. You're a hero. Don't let anybody tell you otherwise."

"Please," Cole said, "I don't want to offend anybody, but I'm really not. I don't even know why I'm here, to be honest."

"Well, whatever the reason, you're welcome here, you got that?" Reynold put his arm around Cole's shoulder and led him inside the arena, into the lobby, where the flooring, constructed out of adjoining rubber mats, was sprinkled with popcorn, drink lids, and hot dog wrappers. Cole brushed past a guy while entering the lobby. He'd been standing by the door facing away from the entrance. He turned around fast, and had a fist raised almost as fast. "Watch it, kid!"

"Sorry." Cole sidestepped away from the guy just as Reynold pulled him away, too. To Cole it looked like Tristan, only about ten times as big as he used to be, and he was big back then.

"Now, now, Mr. Crowfoot. None of that tonight, understand?"

Tristan glared at Cole, hard. Cole swallowed, also hard. The girl that Tristan had been facing when Cole touched him—only up until then, she was hidden behind Tristan's bulk—pulled Tristan back towards her.

"Come on, Trist." She put her hand behind his neck, went on her tiptoes, and just inhaled him, putting her lips all over his mouth. Just like that, Cole was forgotten. The girl must've been Maggie. That's how he remembered Tristan and Maggie: sucking face.

An unimpressed-looking teenage girl attending the concession stand performed a double take when she saw Cole enter the building. It was probably a quintuple take by now, after the quick incident with Tristan. Cole pretended not to notice all the takes as he moved on from Tristan, relieved. At the same time, he tried to place her name. Pam? She was younger, maybe Alex's age. He gave her a smile. She gave him a shrug.

A few more people were hanging around in the lobby, standing in line for food or just standing around trying to talk over the noise. The hockey game's chorus of sounds was almost deafening in the lobby, even through the two thick, metal doors that led to the playing surface and the stands.

"You need a job, Cole? Turns out I have an opening," Reynold said.

"No thanks," Cole said. "I don't plan on staying for long."

"I see," Reynold said, still with his arm around Cole.

"So you run security then?" Cole asked.

"That's right. Reynold McCabe Security. RMS."

"Yeah, I ran into one of your guys at the research facility there. I've always kind of thought they would've done something about that by now."

"You're thinking about your old man," Reynold said.

"Yeah," Cole said.

Reynold gave Cole a good, comforting squeeze. "You know, your dad's body might be there, but that's not him. You know that, right?"

"I know, it's just, I thought one day he'd be at the cemetery, and it would mean something to visit him there. His gravestone's still just a slab of rock."

"I understand. Well, don't give up hope, son. Never give up hope."

Cole shook it off. "So, that place is safe otherwise? Like, the guards are just there to keep people away?"

"It's preventative, Cole. Merely preventative. Nothing to worry about. We're like an owl on a building ledge, or a scarecrow, see?"

"No crows, no pigeons."

"Exactly."

Reynold scanned the lobby, made an *ahh* sound when he saw Sam Crate among the loiterers, and called him over. "Look who I found wandering outside, Chief!"

"Chief?" Cole whispered to Reynold.

"Not for long," Reynold whispered back through a smile.

Cole knew Sam Crate as the manager at the grocery store when he was younger. Sam used to give all the kids candy for free. Naturally, he was very popular with the kids, but not somebody Cole had ever pegged for Chief. He'd never heard a bad word about Sam, though. Chief Crate excused himself from the people he was talking with and made his way over to Reynold and Cole.

"Cole Harper?" Chief Crate said.

"Yes sir," Cole said.

"In the flesh," Reynold said.

"Are you back for the memorial, or to support your old friend in the election?" Chief Crate asked. "I see my opponent is already trying to butter you up!"

Chief Crate nodded towards Reynold, who nodded back sharply.

"Yeah, I guess," Cole said. "For the memorial, I mean."

"Let's not bore Cole with politics now, Chief Crate. He just got back," Reynold said.

"Of course," Chief Crate said.

"Cole, why don't you go and check out the game?" Reynold said. "The Chief and I have some business to attend to."

"Sure," Cole said, but felt hesitant. He thought about the negative encounters he'd had since getting off the plane—Scott, Mark, Tristan—and extrapolated on those by the few hundred people in the arena. Still, he made his way towards the door to the ice surface.

"And if you *do* need a job, you let me know," Reynold added. "No strings."

Cole overheard Reynold asking Chief Crate to sit down for a moment and have a drink, to discuss etiquette or something to that effect. What a place to have a meeting, Cole thought, at an old card table in the arena's lobby, talking politics over popcorn and soda and the roar of the crowd.

Sounds were more intimate inside the rink: the shred of metal against ice, the snap of wood against rubber, the collision of body against body, then body against board; and finally, the crowd and its fickle crescendo. The noise from the stands died down as people began to notice Cole. More double takes. Triple and quadruple takes. Whispers. Little tremors of curiosity. Cole tried to ignore this all as best he could. He walked towards the ice surface, and settled in to watch the game at the boards right beside the unmanned goal light.

The hockey game was a weekly contest between the young kids in the community and the adults. With all their equipment on it was nearly impossible to tell one player from another, and nobody wore name bars, but Cole thought he recognized Eva's dad, Wayne Kirkness, Wounded Sky's constable. Cole's heart jumped. He realized Eva was somewhere in the crowd, maybe watching him right now. He tried to act cool, putting one hand in his jeans pocket and running the other hand through his hair.

He felt a tap on his shoulder. He turned to find Brady standing at his side, and standing beside Brady was Eva. Seeing Eva made Cole's stomach flip. *Act cool, you idiot.* He ran another hand through his hair. Brady had a genuine smile on his face, though a bit of confusion mixed in with that smile. Eva, though, had her arms crossed, and was doing her best not to make direct eye contact with Cole. Eva and Brady pretty much looked the same as they had in elementary school. Brady's hair was longer. He'd told Cole once that he was never going to cut it. "I'll lose part of my soul. Part of *me*," he'd said. And Eva looked angrier than she had been the last time he'd seen her. He could still hear her. "I promise I'll never forgive you if you leave me," she said to him out front of her house, the morning he'd left Wounded Sky. Cole could still see the tears fall across her round cheeks. She'd kept her promise.

"Howdy stranger," Brady said, and leaned in to give Cole a quick hug.

"Brady, hey." They exchanged pats on the back (a true man-hug), then released each other. "How're you doing?"

"Oh, right as rain, my friend. You?"

"Yeah, good, fine."

"Whoa," Brady said, "convincing much?"

"I know. Look, to be honest, I'm not all that jacked up to be here. I mean, yes, I'm fine, but I can also feel about a hundred eyes on me, and it kind of makes me want to, I don't know, bolt. Just leave, I guess."

"Then why are you here?" Eva asked, and her interjection surprised Cole enough to take his breath away for a moment.

"I don't really know," Cole said. "Ashley told me to come out. He sounded pretty desperate about it. I thought it might be because of the memorial, even though he said it wasn't. I heard it was Tuesday?"

"Bang on. Tuesday," Brady said.

"I'm sure you had that marked on your calendar, right?" Eva said to Cole.

"Eva, I—"

"*Anyway,*" Brady said, "I didn't know he'd asked you." Cole guessed this was actually directed at Ashley—a conversation Ashley and Brady would have later.

"Yeah, when did you even talk to Ashley?" Eva stepped closer to Cole, but kept her arms crossed, like there was something she was holding that she didn't want to drop.

"He was texting me yesterday. Last night. Why?" Cole asked.

"I didn't know you'd been talking to anybody, *ever*," she said.

"We talk, every once in a while," Cole said.

"Good to know," Eva said.

An uncomfortable silence followed. Cole could feel the tension. He thought he could reach out and grab it, it was so thick. Eva's brow was furrowed and she was glaring at him. Brady just looked confused and annoyed. Eva shook her head, looked out over the ice, then back to Cole. Her face softened with a hint of concern. "He didn't show up for the game."

"He's not answering my texts either," Brady said. "He never misses a game, and he never ignores me. He's been acting pretty weird the last two days."

"Did you go by his place?" Cole asked.

Brady shook his head. "Ashley's not into a lot of people knowing about us. He likes meeting in private. I don't like it, but I don't want to push him, you know?"

"Yeah, sure," Cole said.

"He's probably just under the weather, something like that," Eva said. "I wouldn't worry, B."

"Yeah," Brady said, "you're probably right."

"Anyway, I'm going to go cheer on Michael." Eva met eyes with Cole for a moment. There was a lot in that look, anger, maybe, but also a hint of something else—something she was fighting off. Or maybe he was just imagining that. She went back to an open seat in the stands, sat down, and didn't look over at Cole again.

"So, Eva and Michael aren't…" Cole said to Brady.

"Aren't going steady?" Brady said.

"Going out, yeah. That'd be—"

"Weird, right? Sorry, buddy. That's happening."

"No way," Cole said. He had always liked Michael. It was Alex, Michael's sister, who always used to annoy him. He suddenly liked Alex a lot more.

Cole turned to watch the game for a second. He subtly took out his phone and shot a text to Ashley:

Ever going to tell me about Eva and Mike?

Cole and Brady watched the game. Cole kept a particular eye on Michael, as though he might skate over to Eva, take her in his arms, and ride off into the sunset.

Brady nudged him. "It's good to see you again."

Cole looked at Brady and smiled, then canvassed the stands, caught more eyes on him than he could count. He tried to read into their facial expressions. Surprise. Confusion. Resentment. He never would've expected this kind of reception. None of the looks said something as simple as *good to see you, Cole* or *welcome home, Cole.* "You might be one of the few people who actually think that," Cole replied.

"Cole," Brady said, "I know how you feel, 100 percent. I get it, and I mean it. It's good to see you. You dig?"

"I dig," Cole said with a chuckle.

"You get used to unwanted attention," Brady said.

"But most people must be pretty cool with you, right?" Cole asked.

"Yeah, I suppose. Ashley doesn't *have* to sneak around with me. It's never been like that. It's mostly just my parents and their friends. They act like I need an exorcism."

"That's fu—"

There was a commotion near the ice. Chief Crate, who had been sitting in the front row, was on the ground. The game stopped. The crowd turned its attention from the game, from Cole, to the Chief. The players skated over to the glass nearest Chief Crate, chins resting against the butts of their hockey sticks, waiting for when he got up, so they could all clap by knocking their sticks against the ice. A woman Cole recognized as Kate Captain, the doctor in Wounded Sky, as well as Michael and Alex's mom, pushed her way through the crowd that quickly gathered around Chief Crate.

"Back up! Back up!" she shouted.

A clearing formed at the centre of the crowd.

Brady and Cole, along with Eva, who had rejoined the pair, moved towards the crowd, as close as they could get. Cole saw the Chief through a space that had opened up between the heads and shoulders and torsos. He didn't look good. His chest was heaving up and down, he was coughing violently, and his skin was pale. Perspiration dampened his face and darkened his shirt. The man was just in the lobby, looking scrappy and upbeat. Healthy. Now he looked close to death. It hadn't been more than twenty minutes.

"I literally was just talking to him, man," Cole said.

The crowd was throwing around their own guesses.

"It's the flu!"

"Was it something he ate?"

"That can't be food poisoning."

"You never know what's in these hot dogs, eh?"

"Is it a heart attack?"

As the congregation grew, the guessing continued, but the one guess that stuck with Cole was *heart attack*. He remembered the feeling, that first panic attack, when the ambulance had been called for him. When he came to in the emergency room, the doctor spent a long time trying to convince Cole that he hadn't had a heart attack. He went over the symptoms of a panic attack and the symptoms of a heart attack. Cole looked through the crowd and assessed Chief Crate and the work Dr. Captain was doing. That's what this was. He knew what to do.

Cole pushed his way towards Chief Crate, got to the clearing that Dr. Captain had created. He knelt down at Chief Crate's side.

"What are you doing?" Dr. Captain looked up from the Chief. She'd been taking his pulse.

"I can help!" Cole thought back to the television shows he'd watched with his grandmother. He put both his hands on Chief Crate's chest, ready to administer CPR. "He's having a heart attack! Dr. Captain, you do the breathing thing!"

But Dr. Captain didn't do the "breathing thing." She pushed Cole away before he could start chest compressions. "He is absolutely not having a heart attack! You're going to kill him!"

"Harper's going to kill the Chief!" somebody from the crowd called out.

"Good job, city!"

"You dumb shit!"

The eyes returned to him. Countless eyes. "I was just trying to…" He couldn't breathe. His pulse quickened.

"Help McCabe, maybe!"

"Go back home, kid!"

He started to sweat. His legs felt like they were going to give out.

"I...I..."

The room began to spin. Cole got up, stumbled through the crowd and towards the doors.

"Cole!" he heard Brady say.

He pushed through the doors and fell into the lobby, across the spilled popcorn, drink cups, hotdog wrappers, and rubber mats.

He got up and kept moving.

He pushed open the barn doors and ran outside. Fell to his knees, gasping for air.

"Idiot...you...stupid...idiot."

With shaky fingers, he plunged his hand into his pocket and pulled out his pill bottle. He managed to open the lid after a few tries—it felt like "childproof" also meant "anxiety attack proof"—and pills fell all over the ground.

"Shit, no..."

Cole tried to shove some of the pills back into the bottle, but they were all mostly covered in dirt, ruined. Only salvaged a few. He shoved a tablet into his mouth.

Breathe in. Five seconds. Hold it there. Breathe out. Seven seconds.

4

TROUBLE WILL FIND YOU

ATIMA ATCHAKOSUK: THE DOG STARS. KEEWATIN: *The Going Home Star.*
Mista Muskwa: The Big Bear. Ochek: Fisher…

Elder Mariah, Brady's kókom, was always adamant that Wounded Sky kids learned about the Indigenous constellations, not the white ones. "They have their stories. We have ours," she used to say. Despite Cole's best efforts to forget them, they'd stuck in his brain. She'd taught him well, and Cole found them all while he waited for the medication to kick in. As he played connect-the-dots with the stars his breath evened out, and his heart steadied. He dried his palms against his jeans and pushed himself up.

Cole looked back at the barn doors. The big white Xs became a warning: *do not come back in here.* He'd had enough of people staring at him, at least for tonight, and he hadn't done himself any favours either. But regardless of his attempt to out-doctor a doctor, his auntie, his grandma, and Ashley had never mentioned the attitude people had towards him in all the years since he'd left Wounded Sky. Ashley also hadn't told Cole that Eva and Michael were dating. Cole took out his phone again. Ashley still hadn't texted him back. Cole sent another text: **I'm coming over, we have to talk.** After sending the text, Cole called his auntie and grandma back in Winnipeg. He'd ignored enough calls.

"Oh God, you're okay," Auntie Joan said when she picked up the phone. It was better than getting yelled at. That's what Cole was expecting.

"I'm fine," Cole said.

"What the hell were you thinking? Where did you get the money? Your grandmother won't tell me a thing."

"I was saving money when I could, I guess."

"You guess. You saved a thousand dollars?"

"Yeah."

"Cole, that is such a load of—"

"You didn't tell me that everybody hated me."

He could hear his auntie breathing, and then he heard her let out a deep breath. Like a breath that had been held in for ten years.

"We were trying to protect you."

"Is that why we moved away?"

Another pause. "There were a lot of reasons."

"Yeah, well, a heads-up would've been nice."

"I told you not to go!"

"You never said why!"

"Well, this is why, okay? This is why. Just come home, okay? You're not in trouble."

"I'm not coming home. I'm going to deal with it."

"Cole, I'm sorry."

"Yeah, so am I."

Cole hung up, rammed the phone into his pocket. He was worked up, even with the meds in his system. He stared at the pills he'd dropped on the ground, played connect-the-dots with them, too, while he wondered if he'd have ever needed them if people had just been straight with him. Since when did he need protecting? For the love of all things holy, had he not run into a goddamn burning building when he was *seven*? Suddenly, it didn't matter why he'd been asked out here. Ashley had much more to explain.

He passed by the mall and the RCMP detachment on the way to Ashley's house. As he passed by the open field he used to play in as a kid with Eva and Brady, he remembered when Eva had taken her father's gun and she, Cole, and Brady decided that they were going to practice shooting at tree stumps and cans of SpaghettiOs. They'd only just started when Wayne came tearing down the road, running into the field, and snatched that gun back faster than you could imagine. A stern lecture followed that none of them soon forgot, and each of them served one helluva of a grounding.

Near Ashley's trailer, Cole came across the cemetery. He stopped and looked into it from the safety of the gravel road. In the distance, near the back of the cemetery, was a fenced-in area away from the rest of the headstones. He could see it all perfectly, clear as day. In this area, there were five neat rows of headstones, five headstones in each row, all the same size and shape. Most belonged to kids, some belonged to adults. He stood in silence for several minutes, unmoving, then continued on to Ashley's home.

Cole had grown so accustomed to the city's pervasive orange street light. The blackness of a Wounded Sky night was darker than he remembered. Cole could see from a distance that the lights were on in Ashley's trailer. As he got closer, the memories fell thick and hard. The old Ford Mustang was parked in the driveway, weeds growing tall around the tires.

When Ashley's parents were alive, his dad always talked about fixing it up, and he might've too, one day. But his grandpa, who'd raised Ashley up until his death last year, wasn't mechanically inclined. As a result, the car remained where it was, waiting for someone to come around and bring it back to life. Cole remembered playing in it with Ashley, pretending they were cruising around the rez, cooler than shit, the engine revving, windows down, wind whipping their hair. Cole used to hold his hand out the window and pretend he could feel the air rush through his fingers. When they played hide-and-seek, Cole had often hid in the trunk. He stopped at the trunk now, put his hand on the cool metal, and allowed himself to be back in that time.

Cole eased back into reality when he saw shadows moving around within the trailer, pacing back and forth. Ashley was home. He patted the trunk of the Mustang, thanking it for offering some good memories, then moved around it. He walked along the front of the trailer, up the steps, and knocked on the screen door. He'd heard footsteps in the trailer when he was walking up. They paused after the knock, then started again and moved towards the front door. The door swung open as Cole opened the screen door in unison.

"Cole." Ashley looked like he'd just been in an argument.

"Hey, Ashley." Cole had expected something more from his friend—a hug? A smile, maybe, at the very least. But instead, judging from Ashley's voice, and his eyes, he saw agitation, a bit of anger. Cole stepped inside the trailer, and Ashley turned away. Walked across the room and sat down on the futon. Cole followed Ashley there, and sat down beside him.

"What's up with you?" Cole asked.

"It's just…" Ashley was looking down, not at the floor, but at the phone in his hand. His thumbnails, pressing against the screen, were ghost white. "…you shouldn't be here. You shouldn't have come here."

Cole breathed sharply out of his nose. "You *asked* me to come. Remember?"

Ashley shook his head and then looked up at Cole. "No, I didn't."

There wasn't a hint of humour in his face, but Cole didn't believe it. The text had come from Ashley. It was indisputable. Whenever Ashley sent a text, or FaceTimed, or called, his picture, him as a six-year-old boy smiling at the camera with Cole, popped up.

"Are you screwing around with me?" Cole said. "We were *texting* last night. Come on."

"I wasn't texting you, that's the thing." Ashley looked down again. He looked like he wanted to crack the phone in half.

"No, you weren't texting me back *tonight*. You *were* texting me yesterday," Cole said.

"I told you—"

"Speaking of which, why've you been trying to protect me? Why didn't you tell me about Eva and Michael? Why didn't you tell me what people think about me?"

"I'm still trying to protect you, don't you get that? You didn't need to know any of that stuff, and you don't need to be here now," Ashley said. "I didn't text you and you should go home."

Cole looked at the phone, too, and watched as Ashley scrolled through their text conversation from yesterday with violent thumb movements. He scrolled down from the beginning of it, and then scrolled back up, back down, up again. He did this several times, until Cole reached over, put his hand on Ashley's, and stopped the repetition.

"Tell me what's going on, please," Cole said.

Ashley took a deep, deliberate breath. He lifted his head and met eyes with Cole. He half-smiled. "I didn't text you."

"You told me that already. Stop telling me that, Ashley. What's going on?"

"You're not going to believe me."

"Try me."

"The…*guy*…who took my phone, he was trying to get me to ask you to come home, but I said I wouldn't. So he stole it. He brought it back to me just before the game. Said you were here, that you'd come."

"What guy? Everybody knows everybody here."

"He said something was going to happen, some kind of trouble." Ashley looked away from Cole, out the window. "Did you hear that?"

"Hear what? No. Ashley. Trouble, like what kind of trouble?"

"That's why you're here." Ashley started for the window.

"I don't understand."

"Is that—"

In a split second that would stretch into forever in Cole's mind: a *crack* from the window, then a *whizzing*, like a firecracker on its way into the night sky. Ashley's body jerked to the side, and then a mist of red sprayed against the wall and the futon. Ashley collapsed, but Cole managed to stop the fall, catching Ashley around his waist, and then setting him down gently. Cole jumped from the floor towards the window and looked out into the forest. He saw the silhouette of a man disappearing into the thick foliage, but it was too dark to make out any detail.

"Cole…"

Ashley was barely audible. Cole was ready to take after the figure in pursuit, but went to Ashley's side instead. He sat down on the floor, right in a pool of his old friend's blood. He took Ashley's hand.

"I'm here."

"Cole, I…"

"What is it, Ashley? Tell me." Cole leaned in closer, so that his ear was inches away from Ashley's mouth.

"The…trouble…"

"What? What about the trouble? What is it?"

The two words came again, weak and fragile. *The trouble*. Cole could feel Ashley's breath against the side of his cheek.

"Ashley!"

There was choking deep in Ashley's throat. He coughed, and some blood spurted out, across Cole's cheeks. He took a shallow breath in, out, and didn't breathe in again.

5

DEAL OR NO DEAL

COLE STAYED BY ASHLEY'S SIDE FOR A LONG TIME, holding his friend's hand as it slowly drained of warmth and colour. He could have stayed there all night, losing track of time, not willing to leave his friend, to lose somebody else. He shouldn't have come, just like Ashley had said. He should've deleted Ashley's first text, or ignored it and every other text after that. Cole looked at the blood on the floor, all over his clothes, and on his own skin. Would Ashley be alive, too, if he had stayed away? Somehow, had his return led to this? What—

"He would've died anyway, eventually."

Cole looked up to see a coyote standing there, its head tilted sadly to one side. Cole fell backwards, and pushed himself away frantically with his heels and hands, until his back hit the wall.

"It…it's you."

"In the fur."

"Coyote."

"You can call me Choch."

"Choch?"

"What is *with* kids and repeating…okay, listen. I thought of the name and wasn't sold at first, but now I really like it. Fair? Please don't say 'fair.'"

Cole nodded.

Choch moved closer to Cole. Cole, in turn, tried to move farther away, but there was the whole business of the wall.

"I thought I'd imagined you," Cole said.

"Pfft, kids and their imaginations," Choch said. "Did you think you did all of that on your own?"

"I didn't...." Cole's eyes darted back and forth, between Ashley and Choch. It hit him. "*You* texted me."

"Guilty," Choch said, and raised a paw like raising a hand.

"This is my fault," Cole kept his eyes trained on his friend, not the spirit being now walking across the room. "If I hadn't come, if I hadn't texted Ashley back, he'd still be alive."

"Like I said, Coley-Boley, there was no preventing Ashley's death."

"Then why bring me here in the first place?"

"I wish I could tell you that, I really do," Choch said. "But all I can say is that while Ashley's unfortunate demise was inevitable, there are others you can still help."

"Like who?"

Choch moved his paw across his mouth and made a *zip* sound. He said, "But honestly, it's about time you got here. You've got some work to do."

Cole stood up and faced Choch. The shock of seeing a talking animal—a myth come to life—and the disbelief in what had happened ten years ago, was quickly wearing off, giving way to annoyance and frustration. "This is what you meant back then, I guess. If all of that was real. This is the payback?"

Choch laughed. "I mean, I didn't know *what* it would be, but you did owe me one. We had a deal."

"I just wanted to save my friends. If I knew saving my friends would mean losing somebody else, I wish I'd never agreed to it."

They began to walk together towards the front door. On the way, Choch asked, "And then what, my boy? There'd be no Eva, no Brady. Which life is worth more?"

"This isn't a game show. These are my friends." They went outside and stopped at the top of the steps in the cool night air. Cole shook his head. "I don't want to do this. Don't make me do this."

"Look, I've got my hands tied, kid. You've got your boss, I've got mine."

"Who? God?"

Choch shrugged. "You're smart, for a teenage boy. Eighty-seven percent in math last year, right?"

"How did you know that?"

"I keep tabs on all my little projects," Choch said. "Anyway, as I was saying, I may not be able to tell you exactly all the annoying little details, but I can remind you of the abilities you have that'll help you along the way."

"Abilities?"

"Yeah, the ones I gave you…" Choch said, and then added out of the side of his mouth, as though he were keeping a secret from some- body who wasn't even there, "…ack-bay at the chool-say."

"I don't have any…" but Cole trailed off, and thought back on the last ten years. He'd always been—

"Okay, let me stop you right there. Inner-monologue, blah blah blah." Choch rolled his eyes. "I'll save you the thought process: yes, that's why you've always been *stronger* than you should be. Why you can, as kids put it, 'throw it down' on the basketball court."

"We don't say it like that."

"But there's more. It's been dormant, but you can bring it back up like bad Chinese food."

"How?" Cole asked.

"You really want me to…I mean, I gave you the gist."

"Yeah, I really do."

Choch started to dry heave, like he was coughing up a hairball.

"Gross! Stop."

"You wanted to know how."

"I meant how I could bring back the abilities, obviously."

Before Choch could answer, Cole started on his way down the stairs. "You know what? Screw it. I'm not doing this again. I'm not sav- ing people, and I'm not seeing anybody else I care about dead."

"What about everybody you know?" Choch asked, suddenly striking Cole with the uncommon gravity of his words and tone.

Cole stopped beside the hood of the Ford Mustang. He stood silent for an eternity. And then pursed his lips: "I won't do it."

"I thought you might say that. You're a stubborn little thing, aren't you?" Choch tried to whistle towards the forest several times, but couldn't with his coyote mouth. He was visibly annoyed by his failure. He ended up calling out, "Hey! Time for that cool entrance!" Cole looked into the thick trees and underbrush and, bit by bit, the cool air began to warm. A ball of flames approached them from within Blackwood Forest. Finally, the ball of flames moved onto the gravel driveway as though it had just been out for a walk. It turned towards Cole, let out an excited shriek, and ran over to him. At first, Cole recoiled against the Mustang, but then he recognized the little ball of flames. It was Jayne, a girl in his class from Wounded Sky Elementary School. A girl who died in the school fire. Half of her body was in flames, while the other half of her was the perfectly normal little girl he remembered. She'd always been smaller than the other kids. Because of her size, his classmates often excluded her as a "baby," but Cole had always liked her.

"Coley!" she cried out, and put her arms around his waist.

Her flames instantly began to burn Cole, and he politely pushed her away.

"Hey Jayne." He saw she was sad that he'd refused her hug. "Sorry, it's just that I think you're going to have to hug me with the other side there."

Jayne looked at her flaming hand and nodded. "Right." She shuffled over to him and gave him a quick hug with the non-burning side of her body.

"Thanks, Jayney."

"Jayne here has a bit of a predicament," Choch said, moving down the stairs to Cole and Jayne. "See, she's been in the waiting room for ten years."

"The waiting room?" Cole said.

"There's games!" Jayne shouted.

"That's real good, Jayney," Cole said to her. He turned to Choch. "What are you talking about?"

"You know the northern lights?" Choch said. Cole nodded. Choch continued, "Well, that's the waiting room. Sure, there are games, as Jayne says. I'm not cruel. And they dance, of course. But even spirits get bored, once in a while. Especially, you know, when they're stuck there *forever.*"

Cole closed his eyes in submission. "You'll keep her there unless—"

"—you keep your end of the bargain. Right. See? I said you were smart," Choch said. "Eighty-seven percent in math, boy."

"It's okay, Coley! It's fun anyways!" Jayne interjected, jumping in place.

"There's also the whole *everybody-in-the-community-will-die* thing too," Choch said, clearing his throat. "But no pressure." He waved his paw in the air. "You go. Those tryouts next week, the whole scholarship thing. I mean, these are things that would keep me up at night."

"That's enough!" Cole said. "I'll stay."

"Good boy," Choch said. "I knew you'd come around."

The group—spirit being, ghost, and boy—heard the distinctive sound of rubber against gravel approaching, followed by the shadows of trees sliding across Ashley's trailer from the car's headlights, like ghosts marching.

"Good luck!" Choch leapt away from the driveway and into Blackwood Forest.

Jayne remained, her warm, orange light almost overpowering the headlights that were getting closer and closer with each passing moment. Cole gave her a gentle nudge on her non-burning shoulder.

"You better go, too, Jayney."

Jayne shook her head. "Choch says I'm 'vincible!'"

"Invisible," Cole corrected. "You're invisible."

"Yeah that too."

"Go on, though, okay? I'll see you after."

Jayne kicked at a pebble on the ground, and Cole was surprised to see it connect with her toe and skip along the ground. "Okay, fine." She evaporated into a cloud of black smoke.

Even with the headlights glaring into his eyes, Cole could see it was an RCMP vehicle. He stepped out from behind the Ford Mustang with a hand cupped over his eyes so he could see a bit better. He watched Wayne step out of the car. When Wayne saw Cole, he immediately drew his gun and pointed it in Cole's direction. Cole raised his arms.

"Don't move!" Wayne shouted.

"I was just—" Cole started, about to explain how when you had a gun drawn on you, you were generally required to raise your hands above your head.

"What's all over your clothes?!"

Cole took a deep breath, then needed another. Right then, despite sitting beside Ashley's dead body for as long as he had, it all became real. His lips were trembling. "It's Ashley's blood."

Wayne stepped around from the driver's side door of the RCMP car, and walked up to Cole slowly. When he saw definitively that it was Cole, he lowered his gun.

"Cole." Wayne holstered his gun.

"Mr. Kirkness."

"I thought I saw you at the rink."

"Yeah, I was there."

He put his hand on Cole's shoulder. "What happened, son?"

Cole was sobbing as quietly as he could, trying to wipe tears away from both eyes before they fell. He was feeling weak. Not anxiety weak—something else. He felt like falling over, like his legs wouldn't support him anymore. Wayne must've seen all of this happening. He helped Cole sit down on the hood of the Mustang.

"What happened?" he repeated.

"I came to see Ashley, because he…I thought he…asked me to come home. We were talking in the trailer, then, I don't know, somebody shot him, right in front of me, through the window."

"What? Who?"

"I didn't see, I…it was a man, I think. He ran off into the woods," Cole said. "I was going to run after him, but Ashley was…"

"It's okay, Cole." Wayne stepped away from the car, towards the trailer. There was a hole in the window and spiralling cracks leading away from it, towards the edges of the glass. Cole heard Wayne breathe deep, watched as Wayne's whole body sucked in air, then deflated as he pushed the breath out. He ran his hands over the cracks, inspecting them thoroughly, then climbed the steps to the front door. He paused for a moment there. "Hang tight, okay?"

"I'm hanging on."

Cole's arms were tingling. He lifted his hand up, fingers spread, and looked at his own limb, shaking delicately in the wind like it was a leaf in autumn. Wayne walked inside the front door, and Cole looked away from his hand, towards the trailer, to see Wayne keel over, hands against knees.

"Oh, God," Cole heard Wayne say, even though he shouldn't have. Wayne had whispered it. Wayne continued to talk low, and Cole continued to hear the words perfectly, when he made a phone call.

"Kate, it's Wayne…listen, I need you to come out to Ashley's trailer…yeah I know, I was there, I…how many? Three? What spreads that quickly? A flu or…wait, listen…Kate, Ashley's been shot…I don't know. Cole Harper was here, visiting with him. Saw the whole thing…" Wayne looked over at Cole while still on the phone, then turned away from him and continued, "I just need you to be here… right…thanks, Kate."

Wayne hung up the phone and ventured farther into the trailer. Cole could hear light footsteps moving around, like he was trying not to wake Ashley up. *Oh please, wake up, Ash. Please.* He saw Wayne at the window again, looking at the hole, at the cracks. He watched Wayne look all around the trailer methodically for several minutes before getting to Ashley's body. Wayne took off his hat, held it to his chest, and then dipped out of sight as he crouched down.

New headlights approached and Dr. Captain got out of a grey sedan. She walked towards the front door of the trailer first, but stopped when she saw Cole, and rushed over to his side. She looked him over carefully.

Shaking hands, weak knees, dizziness, Cole felt like he'd drunk a hundred cups of coffee. "Hi, Dr. Captain," he said. His voice was shaking as well. "Sorry about earlier."

She had a stethoscope and was listening carefully to his heartbeat. "Well, this isn't a heart attack either, Cole. You're in shock. You saw Ashley…"

"Yeah, I saw it."

She shone a light into each eye. As she did, she said, "That would do it."

"I've seen worse." Cole noticed how dark it was suddenly. Darker than it should have been with Wayne's headlights shining across the driveway and against the trailer, and the trailer's own lights spread out over the area. There were black spots converging in his vision. He wiped at his eyes, and stood up from the car. "I've seen worse. I've seen…"

"I know."

Cole stumbled as he tried to take a step. Dr. Captain grabbed his arm and tried to steady him.

"Hang on, Cole." Her face was covered in black, like a stocking was being pulled over her head. Soon all he could do was hear her, not see her. "Wayne!" she called out.

Cole tried to take another step, but fell to the ground. He could feel Dr. Captain's hand slip away from his forearm. He felt the gravel scratch against his skin as the hard ground collided violently with his body.

6

THE FIRE

COLE WAS SITTING BY THE BANKS OF SILK RIVER. The moon, large and clear overhead, reflected off the water in a beam of white light. He wove blades of sweetgrass into a tiny ring. He heard himself hum a song his mother had taught him. Another light appeared, looming even brighter than the moon, rising up from one side of the river to the other like a new sun.

Cole stood up and put the ring in his pocket. He saw an eruption of flames half a mile away. The school. He ran towards the fire. The closer he got to it, the hotter the air became, the brighter the night grew. *Oh God, no. Please, not my friends.* He could hear screaming now—the voices of people trapped inside the flames. Eva. Brady. His mother. He stopped short of the front doors to the school. The heat was too much to bear. He could feel his forearms, neck, and face burning. There had to be another way. He ran back and forth along the front of the school, looking, but there was nothing. He had only one choice. He rushed up the steps, ignoring the burning of his skin, and clothes. He put his hands around the metal handles. Smoke rose from his burning palms. He screamed in pain. Cole pulled the doors open and ran inside, into the flames, down the hallway. This was what Hell was like.

"No!" Cole woke, drenched in sweat, to find the flames were still there.

"I'm sorry, Coley!" The flames moved away from him, and a little arm was hugging him across his shoulders. "I forgot!"

"Jayney?"

"I shouldn't have made you hot again."

Cole wiped at his face, dug his fingertips across his eyelids, and opened them again. Jayne was at his side, half in flames, half normal, just as she had been last night. It was morning now. Light came in through the living-room windows, casting shadows across the carpet. Jayne was looking at him with a large, apologetic smile. He smiled back at her. "It's okay, kiddo."

"Who are you talking to?"

Brady and Eva were sitting on chairs across the living room. Brady asked the question. They were in Brady's grandmother's living room. He knew the place well, better than most places in Wounded Sky. All of them, including Ashley, and sometimes even Jayne, had spent time here when they were kids. They loved Brady, yes, but Elder Mariah was the coolest Elder they'd ever known. It was comfortable here, and safe. It felt like home for the first time since Cole arrived. He welcomed the feeling until he saw the grief on their faces and remembered what had happened last night.

Ashley was dead.

"You called out Jayne's name," Eva said.

Cole tried to straighten up. He cleared his throat. "I was having a nightmare."

"You were screaming in your sleep," Brady said.

"Sorry," Cole said.

"Do you have those a lot?" Eva asked, "Nightmares?"

The ring of sweetgrass he had made her that night was fastened to a thin leather strap hanging around her neck. She noticed him looking at it and tucked it into her shirt.

"Every once in a while," Cole said.

He reached over with his hand and patted Jayne's arm, and to Eva and Brady it looked like he was scratching his shoulder.

"Can I stay?" Jayne whispered shyly. "I miss them."

Cole nodded as subtly as he could, and Jayne, seeing this, gave him a quick squeeze. He liked having her around. Maybe, he thought, every child who died that night was somewhere, at least somewhere, and in that way, maybe he hadn't failed them all as terribly as he thought.

"I do too," Eva said, responding to Cole's admission about having nightmares.

Brady nodded as well. Looking down, he asked, "Do you ever feel guilty about having nightmares?"

Cole took this to mean that anybody could answer. "What do you mean?"

"I mean, at least we're able to *have* nightmares."

The room grew quiet. Cole spent this time looking over at Jayne, counting carpet fibers, glancing at Eva, and exchanging half-smiles with Brady. When Elder Mariah brought him a cup of hot muskeg tea it was a welcome break in the tension. He loved her tea, always had, and it was good to see her.

"Welcome home, Cole." She handed him the steaming hot liquid. "Drink this."

Elder Mariah never wasted a word. Cole held the cup under his nose, watched the flecks of vegetation dance across and underneath the surface, and took the earthy, bitter aroma in through his nostrils.

"It'll help you relax," she added.

"Thanks." He took a sip.

She left with little fanfare for Cole, acting like he had never left in the first place. Mariah's interruption brought them all out of their doldrums, at least momentarily. Eva said that she was going to meet Michael at the diner. Michael wasn't doing all that well himself.

"We could all go," she suggested.

Cole perked up. "Even me?"

"I think it'll help if we're all together, yeah," she said.

I'll take it, Cole thought. When he finished his tea, they made their way over to the diner. Tagging along behind them (skipping, to be specific) was Jayne.

The Fish was wallpapered with framed photographs. Where Cole, Eva, Brady, and Michael sat there was a group of six pictures: a photo of the northern lights, the Hollywood sign, a pyramid, the Statue of Liberty, Easter Island, and, finally, Niagara Falls. Cole observed the pictures like he was in a museum, thoughtfully, ignoring his friends, and eventually Brady asked, "What the heck are you looking at?"

"It's like these are all places Wounded Sky wished it was, you know?" Cole said.

"I think people who live here appreciate being here," Eva said.

"Here we go…" Brady said.

"All I'm saying," Cole said, "is that I don't think there's a picture of Wounded Sky in some diner in Chile. That's all."

"So we're not commercialized. So what?" Michael said.

"Can you imagine a Northern Lights Diner franchise?" Brady said.

"No," Eva said, "but that's what makes this place so great. It's *ours*."

"Exactly," Michael said.

Their group, along with Tristan and Maggie—who were sitting one booth over and presently involved in an argument about as discreet as their make out sessions—were the only ones in the diner. They had been met almost instantly by an eager waiter with a bright orange t-shirt, purple pants, black dress shoes, and raven-black hair tied back into a braid. His nametag simply read "C." C slid Cole's water over to him, and gave Cole a wink. Cole looked down at C's shoes and shook his head.

"Choch, I'm guessing," Cole said. "Nice shoes."

"They're Hush Puppies, I'll have you know." Choch said to Cole, and then regarded the group. Jayne was sitting comfortably on Cole's knee, the burning side of her hanging safely away from Cole and both her legs swinging back and forth. "Well, aren't you all just a sad lot."

He slid a water past Cole towards Brady, and seemed to intentionally knock over Cole's glass. Cole, though, was quick to catch it without a drop spilled.

"Watch it, will you?" Cole said.

Choch nodded his head with raised eyebrows and his lower lip sticking out animatedly. "Very nice."

"What are you doing?" Cole asked under his breath.

Choch touched the side of his nose with his forefinger.

"Now," Choch said to the table, "what can I get you all? Coffee? Our *special*?"

"What's that?" Brady asked.

"I'm glad you asked, my two-spirited friend," Choch said. "Our special today is the Hungry Man's Breakfast, a succulent dish of bacon, sausage, hash browns, eggs, rye toast, all stacked six inches high. Oh, and there's a little slice of orange on it, too. Garnish. *Very* fancy."

"We don't have a special!" Alex shouted out from behind the counter.

"Yes, we do!" Choch chimed back melodically.

"You're literally making shit up," Alex said.

"Robby, tell dear Alex that we have a special," Choch said.

Robby, the chef and owner of The Fish, appeared from the kitchen. He moved robotically, like he was sleepwalking. He said, "We have a special. It's called The Hungry Man's breakfast," then walked back into the kitchen.

Choch looked back at Cole and mouthed, "Jedi mind trick," and smiled slyly. Cole rolled his eyes. Alex rolled her eyes too. She said, "Whatever," and started to wipe down the counter.

"I'll just have a coffee," Michael said, and after he'd broken the ice, everybody else made their orders. Eva and Brady got coffee as well, and Cole, who realized that he hadn't eaten since yesterday before he'd caught his plane, ordered eggs and toast. He could've finished the special, but thought it'd be weird to the others if he ate a plate so big in light of their friend's death. Nobody else seemed to have an appetite. Choch took their orders and slunk away with his head down—upset, Cole guessed, that nobody had ordered the special after all the work he'd put into presenting it…and making it up.

"Seriously?" Cole said to the group, surprised that the ridiculous name, the ridiculous man, the ridiculous behaviour, hadn't caused anybody else at the table the slightest bit of curiosity.

"That's Choch for you." Michael shrugged it off.

"And *Choch*? What kind of name is that even?"

"Oh my god, Cole, you've been away so long that you don't even remember Choch?" Eva asked.

"He's worked here forever and ever, my friend," Brady said.

"No, yeah, I know. Totally," Cole said. "Forever."

"Forget Choch, forget to text, whatever," Eva said. "No big deal."

When they were alone again, Eva slid her hands across the table and patted Brady's arm. He'd been leaning forward on both forearms, staring blankly at the table.

"You okay, B?" she asked. "Sorry we've been arguing about some stupid pictures and Choch."

"I'm sorry too," Cole said.

"I don't know," Brady said. "It's just, we didn't get any time together. I mean, really together. Now he's gone."

"Sorry, man," Cole said.

"Wait. You and Ash?" Michael asked.

"Ashley didn't want anybody to know," Eva said to Michael. "I was sworn to secrecy," she added, apologetically.

"He was happy," Cole said. "He told me he was happy, if that means anything."

Brady managed a smile. "It does. Of course it does."

Eva fired Cole a look, like she desperately wanted to say something, but she was holding back. What did it mean, that look? That he'd been talking to Ashley about such intimate things, and couldn't as much as text Eva a *hello*? Would she have said something like that? And what would he say in response? That his phone received texts as well?

"I suppose I'm glad he told *somebody* about us," Brady said to Cole. "I don't feel like a dirty little secret."

"You guys were good together," Eva said.

"I just wish I could've told my parents about us, to throw it in their faces," Brady said. "They used to say I'd never be really happy. And that I'd go to Hell."

"How's that?" Michael asked.

"Because I'm gay. They have archaic views about it. They didn't think I could actually have a relationship with anybody that meant anything," Brady said.

"That's the stupidest thing I've ever heard," Eva said.

"They used to talk about sending me away, to the reserves or something. Man me up," Brady said. "That's about when I went to go live with nókom."

"What, because gay men can't be real men?" Cole said. "Does anybody actually think that way anymore?"

"*They* do," Brady said. "They always have, and they always will. And in the end, they kind of won."

"How so?" Cole asked. "You guys were together, right?"

"We were together, sure, but we were going around like we were ashamed or something," Brady said. "But he wasn't ready yet."

"Your parents didn't win, B," Eva said. "You're proud of who you are, and so are we."

This was met with nods of affirmation around the table and a pat on the back from Cole.

"No? You and Cole. That's who knew about Ashley and me," Brady said to Eva. "That smells like victory to me."

"They can know about you now, man," Cole said. "You can tell people. You can tell *them* that you were happy."

"Ashley wouldn't have liked that. He wasn't ready alive; I'm not going to make him ready now that he's dead," Brady said. "Is that stupid?"

Cole and Eva shook their heads. Michael added, "Nah."

"I could give a flying squirrel what my parents think anyway. It doesn't matter," Brady said.

"I think it makes it kind of special, in a way," Cole said. "You and Ashley will always have that, just you and him."

"Sure," Brady said.

"Tell Brady you love him for me." Jayne whispered needlessly. She could've shouted at the top of her lungs and nobody would've heard her. She wasn't as hot right now, or as bright. Cole nodded, and said, "I love you," to Brady, and Jayne put her head on Cole's shoulder.

"I appreciate that, thank you," Brady said, and if he thought it was weird that Cole had said that he didn't let on.

"We all do," Eva said.

"I'm bored. I think I'm gonna go play now," Jayne said.

"Sure," Cole whispered low enough that only she could hear him.

"A tut, tut," Choch said to Jayne, wheeling around the corner from the kitchen. Jayne stopped midway into disappearing into a cloud of black smoke. The smoke was sucked back into her, and she was whole again.

"This coffee's rather cold, you see," Choch said.

He held it out to Jayne. She placed her burning hand around the cup, and within moments steam began to rise from it.

"Thank you, dear," Choch said.

Nobody but Cole seemed to hear what Choch was saying or see what he was doing, holding a cup of coffee out into thin air.

"It's like a dog whistle, sort of," Choch said to Cole with a wink. He told Jayne she was free to go. Jayne, with great pride in her face for being so helpful, burned brighter. She nodded, and then she disappeared.

Choch, now having allowed everybody at the table to see and hear him, gave everybody their orders, including the reheated coffee. He placed Cole's plate in front of him, but then inexplicably, and quite deliberately, poured a few drops of water from the ice water he'd brought Cole (which Cole had *not* ordered) onto the back of Tristan's shirt.

Tristan and Maggie had been bickering since Cole, Brady, Michael, and Eva sat down. They'd all tried to ignore the argument.

Tristan stood up and looked at the cup of water menacingly, which Choch had neatly placed on the table by Cole's eggs and toast. Cole decided now would be a good time to stand up too. He was staring right at Tristan's chest. He craned his neck upward.

"Again, Harper?" Tristan said.

"Wow," Cole said. "I feel like you've grown three feet overnight."

"What's your deal, punk?"

"Nothing. No deal," Cole said quickly.

"You've gone from being a fake-ass hero to a prankster?" Tristan asked.

Cole could see that his fist was clenched. That wasn't good.

"I didn't do that, really," Cole said.

"The hell you didn't," Tristan said.

"He fully did," Choch whispered, secretly pointing at Cole for Tristan's benefit.

Tristan cocked his fist and thrust it towards Cole's face. Cole, before he even realized it, caught Tristan's fist and squeezed. Tristan let out an awful scream. He yanked his hand away from Cole's grip, and nursed it with his other, uninjured hand.

"Whoa…" Alex stopped cleaning to watch the altercation. "*Awesome.*"

"*Alex*," Michael said, as a father might.

"*Michael*," Alex said in a precise imitation of Michael, then returned to her work.

"What the…" Tristan met eyes with Cole, and Cole, unsure of what he'd just done and how he'd done it, smirked. "Let's go, Mag Pie," Tristan said to Maggie, without looking away from Cole.

Moments later, the group settled back down. Cole was trying his best to ignore Choch, who was shooting him these comically proud looks. He didn't know Choch's plan, but Cole wanted nothing more than to leave the diner before Choch decided to do something else, especially if these little interventions were escalating from spilling a cup to dripping water down a giant's back. What was next?

"Cole, what are they feeding you in Winnipeg?" Brady asked.

"That was crazy," Michael said.

Cole shoved a whole egg into his mouth, wiped his lips, then stood up from the table.

"I think I better go."

Eva grabbed his forearm, squeezed it. "Nobody *here* thinks that about you."

"Thinks what?" It felt like a bad time for a breakthrough with Eva.

"That you're some fake," Eva said, "or whatever."

"But you're all looking at me like they look at me," Cole said.

"That's just because you pulled some *Matrix* shit right now," Michael said.

"Come on," Cole said, "*everybody* thinks that about me."

"I might be pissed at you, Cole, but that's just not true," Eva said. "Brady and me, we're both here because of you. I know that."

Brady cleared his throat. "I know it too."

"Guys, *I* don't even believe what happened that night," Cole said. "How could any of you?"

"But I saw you do it," Brady said. "As sure as we're all sitting here."

"You saw me do what?" Cole asked.

"Lift an entire wall to save us."

7

THE TRUTH ABOUT TEXTING

COLE WENT OVER THE EVENTS OF THE SCHOOL FIRE again and again, testing his memory. He had run into the gym only to see the devastation. By that time, most of the kids were dead, crushed by falling beams or walls or parts of the ceiling, or burned alive. Then he saw Eva's leg jutting out from underneath a collapsed wall. He knew her white sneakers and pink laces. Without thinking, he put his hands underneath the edge of the wall and tried to lift it. It didn't move. He pulled at her sneaker, tried to drag her out from underneath the wall. Her shoe came off, and he fell backwards. He got up and tried again. It was useless. He fell to his knees, holding her foot in his hands. He forgot the fire, the heat all around him. He was ready to die in there with her, with all of them. Her toe twitched. "Eva?" It happened again. "Eva!" Cole got up, curled his fingers around the edge of the wall, and was about to try to lift it again.

"You know, I can help you with that."

Coyote was standing next to him, out of nowhere.

"What?"

He pointed his snout towards Eva's foot. "I said I can help you with your little problem here."

"Anything, please! I'll do anything. Just help me save her." Coyote being there, talking to him, didn't register. There was only Eva, and saving her.

"Very well. Only, I'll ask you to agree to help me, down the road, at a time of my choosing. Just say you accept, and that'll be that."

"I accept, yes! I accept! Please."

Coyote nodded his head, like a genie. "Your wish is granted."

Cole lifted the wall with all his strength. He felt it rise from the ground—the whole damn thing. There was Eva, unconscious but alive, and Brady, awake, coughing violently.

Their eyes met.

"Get out of here!" Cole shouted to Brady.

Brady struggled to his feet and rushed out of the gym. With one hand holding the wall up, Cole managed to slide Eva out from underneath. With Eva clear, Cole dropped the wall. He gathered Eva up into his arms and carried her out of the gym. He looked for more survivors after that, darting back and forth across the gym (or what was left of it). He found all of his classmates, all the teachers who had volunteered for the sleepover. Ashley's mom. Michael's dad. Cole found his mom too. He knelt at her body, touched his fingertips against her hot skin, then ran out of the school for the last time.

By late afternoon, Cole had done a whole lot of thinking and not a lot of doing. He was sitting on the porch out front of Elder Mariah's place, watching Brady sit by the firepit in the yard. He had a good fire going. He'd asked Cole to sit with him when he was building the fire, but even though Cole knew his friend was struggling, he'd declined. He'd been straight with Brady. "Sorry, man. I don't like being around fire." Brady had told him it wasn't a big deal, but looking at Brady now, Cole felt he should be there, offering support. He was staring at Brady, wondering what it must be like to lose somebody you loved before you really got to love them, and Brady was staring into the fire, probably thinking about lost love too.

"Hey."

Eva walked up to the porch and sat down a few feet away from Cole.

"Hi," Cole said.

"How is he?" she asked.

"About how you'd imagine," he said.

She was wearing a jean jacket. The sun was dipping and Wounded Sky was getting cold. They could've both used a chair around the fire. She hugged the jacket tighter around her body. She glanced at Cole, then away.

"I just came to walk with you guys to the meeting," she said. "So…"

An emergency meeting had been called earlier in the day. All Wounded Sky residents were to attend the community hall at 7:00 p.m.

"Not a social call," Cole said.

"Not a social call," Eva said.

They both watched Brady for several minutes. Cole worked hard not to look at Eva. Out of the corner of his eye, he saw her playing with the sweetgrass ring. That had to mean something, right?

"You know what I keep thinking about, Cole?" she asked, like she'd been trying to push those words out the entire time.

"Yeah?"

"Even when you knew you were coming back, you still didn't text me, didn't call, nothing," she said.

Cole just sat there. He did look at her. That glance he'd been avoiding. Then he looked away.

"Was I not worth it? Did I mean that little to you? Was it just that we were kids? I've been trying so hard to understand."

"None of that is true."

"It's just, I've thought about that, every day for ten years. Every day."

She shook her head. Cole thought she was scolding herself for thinking of him that much. He wondered if each time she fiddled with the ring, she wanted to rip it off her neck.

"I think every day, in Winnipeg, I had my phone in my hand, had your number typed in, and my thumb was just trying to hit the call button."

"So why didn't you?"

"I thought you'd hang up on me, or not answer at all."

They looked at each other. Neither of them looked away. Her lips kept opening, as if she were about to speak, then closing, changing her mind.

"I might've," she said. *Might've what?* Cole thought. *Might've answered?* "I might've hung up. I might not have answered. I don't know."

"I didn't want you to hate me," he said. "I guess I made you hate me more."

"You never gave me the chance to find out, either way."

"Do you hate me?" he asked.

"Cole, I don't know what you want me to say. You left me, I didn't leave you. And every time you didn't press that stupid call button, you left me all over again. What do you want from me?"

"I don't know, I—"

"You guys ready to go?" Brady had gotten up from the lawn chair by the firepit and made his way over to the porch. "I want to know what they're going to do about Ashley."

"Aren't we super late?" Cole checked his watch. "It's like almost 7:20."

"We'll be fine," Brady said. "We'll be right on time."

"But—"

"Let's just go," Eva said sharply as she looked away from Cole. "We're done here."

People filed into the community hall like drones. Eyes down. Shoulders and spirits slumped. Brady, Eva, Cole, and Michael, who had joined them shortly after getting in line, dutifully stepped in time with the crowd as it inched its way inside. Somebody tapped Cole on the shoulder.

"What?" Cole found Mark walking directly behind him. The people behind Mark looked annoyed, and Cole figured that he'd cut his way in. Without the sunglasses, his face was easy to read: hard and angry, his eyes bloodshot. No doubt it had been an evening of lamenting his job loss. Lamentations and libations. A perfect combination.

"Hey, buddy," Mark said in what was probably intended to be a whisper, but he was too pissed off to actually whisper, and the crowd was so quiet that almost everything sounded like shouting. "I was hoping I'd see you."

"Yeah?" Cole hoped one-word responses might mitigate any further confrontation. *Might.* He wasn't convinced anything would actually help, judging by the vibe Mark was throwing out.

"*Yeah*, I wanted to thank you for messing up my life."

Cole just looked forward, trying to somehow step faster, to get into the hall and leave this behind. Brady nudged Cole. "Don't worry about it."

A hand wrapped around Cole's shoulder and forced him to turn around. No tap this time. The line stopped moving.

"I'm talking to you, city," Mark said.

"Yeah, I know," Cole said, deciding it was time to expand his vocabulary. "I just don't think this is the time or the place."

"I wouldn't mess with this guy," Tristan said, a few rows back in the line.

"Shut up, T," Mark said. "I've got this."

"Maybe you should listen to your friend." Cole wanted to sound tough, and maybe he did, but he desperately wanted to take a pill right now.

"What? Had a bad night last night?" Mark asked.

Cole shrugged. "No worse than yours, I guess."

"You know what I keep thinking, city? You were there, right?"

Cole nodded. "I was there." He tried to fight down the tears, remembering everything, most of all Ashley's blood slapping against the wall, the futon, the floor.

"Right. Well, I keep wishing that the bullet was about six inches off."

"You mean that it missed?"

"No, that it hit *you*, asshole." Mark shoved Cole, one hand to the chest.

Cole didn't budge and didn't push back. "Six inches? Do you think we were making out or something?" Cole estimated six inches with his fingers, right in front of Mark's face. Mark slapped his hand away.

"I wouldn't put it past that fag," Mark said.

"Hey!" Michael stepped forward, between Cole and Mark. "Stop being an ass."

"What are you gonna do about it, Captain?" Mark said.

"Back off, Funky Bunch," Alex said, joining them from back in the line.

(Excuse me. My apologies. Big moment, awkward pause. Won't be but a minute. It occurs to me that the term "Funky Bunch," as it were, may be outdated. A certain narrator may not be listening to his editor. He's stubborn and trying to be hip. So, please, if you are under thirty, use your favourite search engine and look this term up. You won't be disappointed. Hilarity will ensue. But I digress…)

"Why don't you get lost, Mark. It's not happening," Brady said.

Mark looked them all over, one by one, and then he shrugged and stuck a finger against Cole's chest. Cole stood still, wanted to break Mark's finger off, but didn't.

"Well?" he said.

"I'm coming after you, city. Just watch." He pushed his finger into Cole's chest, and then walked forward, cutting through more of the line.

"Okay!" That didn't come out like he'd wanted. It was one of those times where you thought of all the cool things you could've said after the moment had passed. *Okay?* Cole silently berated himself. *You know where to find me. I'll be waiting.* Both would've been kickass things to say. *Okay?* At least his friends had stepped up for him. Unexpected, and welcome. This made him think that not everybody was against him.

"Thanks, guys."

The line started to move again, step by step.

"Wow, you could literally hear a pin drop in this place, no cliché," Choch said, not bothering to whisper, as some might in this situation. "Of course, it is a cliché, but you all know what I'm talking about." He sat down in the row behind Cole, Brady, Eva, and Michael.

Others around gave Choch an annoyed look or two for his insensitivity, but Cole ignored him. He felt a small measure of relief—with a bit of guilt sprinkled in—that nobody was looking and whispering about him. People were more concerned with Ashley's murder. A killer was on the loose, maybe sitting in the crowd right now, and their Chief was gravely ill, along with several other community members.

The number of cases had grown overnight. The hall seemed empty. Cole remembered how the hall could fit just about the entire community—whether for bingo, funerals, career fairs, what have you. There wouldn't be an empty chair available. But tonight, there were a number of empty spaces. He wondered just how many people had gotten sick since the hockey game.

The crowd was older.

It was not just kids from Cole's grade that were missing. Granted, that kind of loss left a gaping hole—a community missing almost all of its seven-year-olds in one fell swoop—but it seemed more than that. Kids from all the grades back then weren't here.

"Have a lot of people left Wounded Sky?" Cole asked.

All his friends kind of shrugged in unison.

"Well, there was that flu," Brady said. "It hit us pretty hard."

"Everybody got sick," Eva said. "Older people, but kids too—"

"And how did the government help?" Brady said. "They sent body bags before anybody actually came to the clinic."

"And we had the flood," Michael said. "A bunch of people had to move. Their homes were destroyed. Just had one of those winters. It melted and boom."

"Mass exodus. A lot of families never came back," Brady said.

"And a lot of kids got sent away because parents were worried another fire might…" Eva stopped. She tried to finish, but couldn't.

"The high school's as old as the elementary school was," Cole said.

"At least," Michael said.

They all took a moment, out of reflection, out of respect, each of them to their own memories.

Eva was the first to talk again. "Some families just wanted better opportunities for their kids, I think. The research facility's never going to open again. Nobody's going to touch that place. What are people going to do for work?"

Brady listed that off for Eva. "Work at the band office, work at the mall, at The Fish, work at the high school, the new elementary school—"

"You mean the trailers," Michael interjected.

"I mean the trailers. They put up mobile trailers instead of building a new school," Brady said.

"Or, you know, people hunt," Eva said. "But people aren't hunting much right now."

"Why?" Cole asked.

"Hunters have been seeing things out there, in the bush," Michael said.

"Mistapew," Brady said.

"*Shadows*," Eva said. "Probably a bear or something."

"It moves like a person," Brady said.

"There's no such thing as Bigfoot," Eva said.

"You'd be surprised what's real and what's not," Cole said.

Eva turned to him. "The reality is, some people wanted more, so there are fewer of us. Who's to blame them? At least they had a good reason to leave."

"Ouch," Choch chuckled behind them. "Shots fired!"

"Shut it," Cole hissed at him, but nobody else seemed to have heard. Cole would have to learn when, and when not, to respond to the spirit being. Of course, Choch probably liked this confusion.

"Anyway, the biggest employer we have now is Reynold." Brady motioned to the stage, where Reynold, speak of the devil, had strode to the microphone, sleek and confident. This was a big moment for him, Cole supposed, with the election coming up. A chance to show he could be "presidential," for lack of a better word.

"Chiefly?" Choch offered.

"Would you stop doing that? Get out of my head." Cole had quickly swivelled around, and now turned back.

"What?" Brady asked.

"Nothing, sorry," Cole said. Even though Cole had decided to learn when, and when not, to respond, it felt like a worthless pursuit.

"Good evening," Reynold said. "With Chief Crate being ill, I am acting Chief, and Dr. Captain *will* get to Chief Crate's condition in a moment. I wanted to start, though, by addressing Ashley Ross's murder." There was a collective gasp from the crowd. "To tell you more about this, I'll call up Constable Wayne Kirkness."

Wayne gave Reynold an unpleasant look on the way to the microphone that not many missed.

"Thank you," Wayne started. "First, let me clarify for our *councillor*, that my office has not yet confirmed this to be a *murder*, so please, let's not panic. We are working right now to process evidence we found at the scene, and are speaking to key people that we believe can shed light on Ashley Ross's death."

People like me, Cole thought. He wondered when Eva's dad was going to want to talk to him. After all, he was there with Ashley's blood on his clothes. And with Wayne, simple questioning felt like an interrogation. Cole had experienced this after the aforementioned gun incident, in the field near Ashley's trailer. And, honestly, that would've been enough, because Cole had been chewed up and spit out. But even worse was the time when Wayne had caught Cole and Eva, curious little kids, kissing in Eva's room. It was the first and only time Cole had kissed anybody, although he would never admit to that as a seventeen-year-old boy.

"We haven't ruled out this being an accident," Wayne continued.

This was met by an angry shout from the crowd: "Somebody *accidentally* shot him inside his trailer, from the outside!?"

Wayne quickly responded. "We need to look at every possibility before we go and say there's a murderer loose. We need all the facts first before jumping to conclusions...." Wayne glanced in Reynold's direction "...and, look, you all know as well as I do that we've had hunting accidents over the years. I want to be certain. If Ashley was murdered, we will put our full effort into finding out who did this, rest assured."

Wayne looked over the crowd once. Cole thought that he and Wayne may have made eye contact, then he nodded at Reynold. The two played musical chairs again as Wayne returned to his seat and Reynold walked up to the microphone.

Cole considered Ashley's death an accident, that a hunter may have been so reckless, that he or she would've taken a shot at a caribou or a moose and missed so badly in the direction of Ashley's trailer. And more than this, that the shot would've not only found its way through the trees, through the window, but to Ashley's body. The forested area around Ashley's trailer was pretty thick, but any hunter from Wounded Sky worth their salt, any experienced hunter at all, would never hunt so close to the community. Of course, it wasn't a coincidence that the day he returned to Wounded Sky—the day he was asked back by Choch—one of his best and oldest friends died. No, Cole decided right then that Ashley had been murdered. He decided, too, that this must've been his purpose for being here: to figure out who had killed Ashley.

As Wayne had said, *rest assured.*

"How is Reynold the biggest employer in the community?" Cole asked as Reynold continued to speak. "How many security jobs could there be in Wounded Sky?"

"The research facility," Eva said bluntly.

"Yep," Michael agreed.

"Kids always want to break into there, check it out," Eva said.

"It's like this unspoken community dare," Brady said.

"But what if it's really not safe to be around there?" Cole asked.

"Kids are idiots," Eva said. "Look at all those stupid stunt videos on social media. Kids doing handstands on the edge of buildings…"

"Selfies near train tracks…"

"Nobody's getting in there anyways," Michael said. "He literally has, I'd say, five people watching it at all times. I mean, a guy at each corner, and one at the front."

"Yeah, I saw Scott there," Cole said. "He hasn't changed."

"And," Brady said, "don't forget the electric fence."

"A lot of people want it converted into housing," Eva said. "That way, a lot of those people who had to move because of the flood might move back."

"And the government, or whoever ran that place, is never coming back to fix their problem, so it's never going to happen," Brady said. "End of story."

"Reynold would never go for that anyways. He probably makes a killing guarding it," Michael said.

"He'd probably sleep on money if he could," Eva said.

"So I take it you guys won't be voting McCabe this election," Cole said.

"Oh god," Eva said. "I've been praying for Chief Crate like you wouldn't believe."

"Nókom's been at Chief Crate's bedside most of the day," Brady said. "I hope he can pull through too."

"He's been nice to *me*," Cole said. "Last night, when I got to the game, Mark was giving me the gears. Reynold came out and fired him. Just like that."

"That explains a lot," Michael said.

"So he can't be that bad," Cole said.

"Anybody as nice as Reynold McCabe has got to be fake nice," Eva said.

"Period," Brady added. "Watch your back, Cole. Guy's like Emperor Palpatine or something."

"But not as cool," Eva added.

"*So* not as cool," Michael agreed.

Eva smiled and gave Michael a kiss on the cheek. Cole felt a bit hot in his cheeks and, against his better judgement, jealous. They probably finished each other's sentences too.

Reynold called Dr. Captain to the microphone. She classified Chief Crate's condition as "grave," and went on to say, "I don't think I've seen a flu, and that's what I believe this is, judging by the symptoms that have presented, that has spread quite so quickly." She advised the gathering that eleven people had now been admitted. "The clinic," she said, "is nearing capacity. We have fifteen beds. If we have to, we'll use what we can. But please, we've seen this before. Not quite this severe,

76 STRANGERS

but we've seen it, and lived through it. I'll remind you all of a few things. Sanitize your hands often, cover your mouth with the inside of your elbow when you cough or sneeze so as to avoid spreading germs, and, where possible, avoid public gatherings."

Cole heard a snicker behind him. Choch was hardly able to contain himself as Dr. Captain continued to give pointers.

"What?" Cole snapped.

"Public gatherings like a community hall meeting perhaps? What do the kids say these days? YOLO."

"Don't say that again. Please."

"Pfft." Choch leaned back in his chair with a dismissive gesture, but not before saying under his breath, "I was simply trying to be colloquial."

That's not colloquial, it's just super lame, Cole thought, assuming Choch would once again invade his thoughts, but he didn't hear from Choch for the remainder of the meeting.

The flu had been down in the city as well. He'd heard the same drill Dr. Captain was going over now at Kelvin High School. In Winnipeg, though, they had better health care. More hospitals, more clinics, more nurses, more doctors. It wasn't that Dr. Captain wasn't capable. In fact, although Cole was no medical expert, he remembered her to be an amazing physician. After all, it was she who pinned his forearm together when he'd snapped it in half during recess in grade one, rather than waiting to have it done in the city. She essentially MacGyvered it and all he had to show for it now was a faint scar. It was more the reality that there was only *one* Dr. Captain in Wounded Sky first Nation and, as Dr. Captain herself had said, a limited number of beds. Cole figured there was a limited number of *everything* at the clinic.

"In light of recent events," Reynold said, back on the microphone, "both Ashley's *death* and the flu, there will be no school, indefinitely." This was met with a smattering of guilty applause. "We've also made the decision to place a curfew on the community. At 10:00 p.m., you're all expected to be home. This is simply—quiet now, quiet please, kids—to keep us all safe. Thank you, that's all."

Cole and Brady were back at the diner, sitting in the same booth they had been earlier. Jayne was wherever spirits went when they weren't skipping along at Cole's side. Eva and Michael, while having been invited to join, thought it best to spend some alone time together. *Probably pecking each other on the cheek for five hours straight,* thought Cole. Choch was back at work, and annoyed (Cole couldn't tell whether comically or actually) that Cole and Brady had ordered only a chamomile tea and black coffee. To his chagrin, they said "no" to his newly made up special (Cole knew he'd made it up, at any rate) of seared jackfish with wild rice, fresh greens, and a side of bannock. "It'll melt in your mouth. My personal guarantee," Choch said about the bannock, but even this selling point wasn't enough.

After Choch left pouting, Cole and Brady went several minutes without saying anything to each other. Cole spoke first, deciding too much was going on inside his head to hold it in (another teaching from his therapy sessions: *share*), and thinking Brady would be the most receptive person to what Cole wanted to say. He decided to dance around the topic until he figured out how to say it.

"Hey, how close were you to actually getting sent away by your parents?"

"I don't know if I was ever *close,*" Brady said, "to getting sent away, physically."

"What do you mean 'physically'? How else can you get sent away?" Cole began to think if his auntie and grandma could've done something similar, if his absence wasn't necessary, and how different that would have made his life.

"It's hard to explain," Brady said.

"I've got all night," Cole said.

"Okay, well…I guess what I mean is that they wanted part of me gone, the part that they didn't like. Like, they wanted to get the gay out of me, on a boat, stranded on an island."

"But…that's who you *are.* They aren't mutually exclusive, man."

"*I* know that. *Nókom* knows that. *You* know that. But they're just not there yet. I don't think they'll ever be."

"Is that hard?" Cole asked.

"Of course it's hard. There's no doubt it's hard. I love them, even now. But at the same time, when they're looking into conversion therapy, that's terrifying."

"Oh god. Crap."

"Right?"

They let that sit a moment, then Cole asked, "But if you had left, what do you think it would've been like coming back? If you had, I guess, a whole community feeling about you like your parents did, or do, what would it have taken to get you back?"

"Okay, so you're 100 percent totally talking about yourself," Brady said.

"That obvious?" Cole began to dip his tea bag, even though it had long since steeped.

"You might as well be at the doctor's office asking about a friend you know that has a rash. Come on. I may have not seen you in ten years, but I know you, Cole."

"I didn't mean to make you feel dumb, if I did."

Brady pretended to brush dust off his shoulder. "Forget it."

"Thanks."

"But let me ask you, then. Only, it really happened. What brought you back?"

Cole took a deep breath. This was it; the dance was over. Still, he chose his words carefully. "I was asked to come back."

"Yeah, you told me Ashley texted you," Brady said. "The memorial then? Is that it? Simple as that? Not *simple*, I know, but it's a pretty straightforward reason."

"No," Cole said. "I mean, the memorial's kind of what convinced me to come, I guess. Facing demons, all that. But it's not why I'm here."

"Sure. I haven't asked you this, but..." Brady paused, then started again, "What else did you and Ashley text about? What did you talk about before—"

"Ashley didn't text me, Brady."

Cole dipped his tea bag more intensely. Some hot water splashed over the side of the cup.

"What? You said—"

"I know what I said, and I thought he was texting me at first. I thought he was, even when I told you at the hockey game. But when I saw Ashley, he told me it wasn't him, that somebody took his phone."

"Somebody took his phone? Why would they do that? Take his phone and pretend to be him just to get you out here? Who would go to all that trouble?" Brady asked, and this was only the start of it. Cole knew it. This was Brady. He could be answering questions for the rest of the night. *Do I tell him the truth?* Cole thought. Was that something he could handle, after the loss of his boyfriend? Brady saw what Cole had done as a boy. He'd handled that. What was the harm, then, in easing the burden that all of this had put on him?

"Brady, look, okay…" Cole dropped his tea bag into the hot water. "The truth is—"

"How *is* everything going?" Choch was right at their side, hands clasped, smile stretching from ear to ear. "Can I get you anything else? Warm you up? The drinks I mean." Choch looked at Brady and said, "Sorry, you're not my type. Not that I have a problem with it. In fact, I—"

"We're fine," Cole said.

"Brady," Choch placed a hand on Cole's shoulder. "Do you mind if your friend and I have a word?"

Judging by his face, Brady desperately wanted to hear the truth. It was the worst time to be interrupted, but he relented. "Whatever. Sure." Cole wondered if Brady was being polite or if Choch had used some of his influence on his friend.

"Thank you." Choch pulled Cole away from the booth and across the empty diner, where they were out of earshot. After the meeting, it appeared as though the community saw fit to hide in their own houses, and with good reason.

"You know what I came up with that's *awesome*?" Choch asked Cole in a half-whisper.

"What?" Cole was trying to shorten their exchange for two reasons. He wanted to get back to Brady, and he couldn't stand being around Choch.

"Obi-Wan Coyote." Choch was delighted.

"That's stupid," Cole said.

"Because of the mind tricks, and—"

"No, I get it. It's just stupid." Cole didn't actually think it was stupid. In any other circumstance, he thought it was rather clever, but would never admit that to—*ha! I knew it!*

"Anyway," Choch said, "it's *awesome*, agreed, but I have to tell you, letting Brady know about me is a no-no. It's an absolute *nu-uh*, as they say."

"Why? What difference does it make?" Cole asked.

"Us *beings*, we positively love being worshipped, but we also like our anonymity. We like the mystery of being the unknown, you see. Now, if you go and tell Brady, good ol' *B*, about me, then I'll seem far less magical, won't I?"

"And if I tell him?"

"Well, I hate to do this, Coley-Boley, but if you insist on telling Brady, the deal is off: do not pass go, do not collect $200."

"What difference does it make? I'm here now. I'm still going to do what I can to figure out what happened to Ashley. I'm not leaving."

Choch shook his head violently. Cole felt some saliva slap across his face. "No no no NO, you don't understand, my young friend. If you tell anybody about me, or our deal, everybody you saved that night, very heroically (but with an assist from yours truly), will be, how shall I say, *un*saved."

"They'll die," Cole stated.

"Yes. I mean, I wouldn't have put it so coldly, but…"

"Okay, fine. I won't tell Brady."

"Or anybody else," Choch said.

"Or anybody else," Cole repeated.

"Good boy. If I'd kept my tail, it'd be wagging with delight right now."

Cole walked away without another word. Choch, though, kept going until Cole had sat back down with Brady. "There's something going on down there, Coley! It feels like twerking or something. Like what the kids are doing!"

"What's his deal?" Brady asked as Cole sat down.

"Great question," Cole said. "Look, what I was saying was, somebody took Ashley's phone, but I don't know who. He didn't know who, and I don't either."

"Do you have any idea? Did you see anything? Do you think that's why—"

"Why he was shot?"

"Yeah," Brady said quietly.

"I don't know." Cole shoved the teacup away, and got up from the booth.

"Where are you going?" Brady asked.

Cole, who had begun to walk away, stopped. He had so much he wanted to say, but it all seemed to be contingent on including the truth, and he knew now that he couldn't spill it. So, with Brady sitting with a half-empty, cold cup of coffee and Cole standing with his hands in his pockets, one of them clenched around his pill bottle, they returned to the silence that they'd started with. Then Cole's eyes widened. Choch put his index finger over his lips sternly. *Careful, boy.*

"I can't tell you everything, Brady, but I can tell you this: I think I'm here to figure out who killed Ashley. I know that won't make sense, and you don't have to even talk to me anymore, but that's what I'm going to do."

Cole walked towards the front door resigned, and expecting, to do it by himself. He heard footsteps almost immediately behind him. He thought it was Choch again, that somehow even saying what he had said was breaking the rules.

But Brady was behind him.

"What are you doing?" Cole asked.

"I'm going to help you," Brady said.

8
COME TOGETHER

"EVA'S ON HER WAY," BRADY SAID TO COLE.

They were near Ashley's trailer, standing by the path to the cemetery. During their walk, they decided to include Eva in the mission. The only point of resistance was Cole who, during the decision making process, said, "She kind of hates me though."

Brady responded, "You're an idiot."

"Wow," Cole said.

"She doesn't hate you," Brady said. "If she hated you, she wouldn't be so mad at you."

It seemed as essential to include her, though, as it did when they were younger. You never got one without the other two. And she was also bringing flashlights, which was going to make their lives a bit easier, especially when they got to Ashley's trailer. They planned to keep the lights off so as not to arouse any suspicion—from Eva's dad in particular. Cole couldn't tell Brady that *his* way was lit very brightly, thanks to Jayne. She kept him warm in the cold air, too, and it was interesting to Cole that Brady seemed to feel some of the warmth. He'd commented before that it seemed a bit warm for an autumn night in Wounded Sky.

The final point in their discussion about including Eva was that she had a set of talents that Brady felt was indispensable.

"Wayne's been hunting with her for ten years, ever since the school fire," Brady explained. "It's like he's getting her ready for the zombie apocalypse."

"What do you mean?" Cole asked.

"Put it this way: if we still played hide and seek in Blackwood Forest, she'd kill us. You said you saw this guy run off into the woods, right?"

"Yeah," Cole said.

"There you go. She can track. I went out with them once. Her and Mr. Kirkness. Watched her follow a moose for like a full day. It was incredible."

"So if she finds a trail…"

"We're golden. And if we get lost, if she has a leaf, rainwater, and a paperclip, she'll get us home."

Eva's presence was announced by a white beam of light in the distance. When she arrived, she handed Brady and Cole a flashlight each. Jayne, seeing that they all had lights now, and that Cole didn't need her help at the moment, announced that she was going to go play with her friends in the cemetery. Three beams of light, then, minus the joyous little burning ghost, continued the short distance to Ashley's place. Eva had run all the way from Michael's house. She pushed some hair away from her forehead that was stuck there with sweat. "Sorry I'm late. We were hanging out with Alex. Dr. Captain's been at the clinic pretty much twenty-four seven, so Alex's been home alone a lot."

"She seems like she's doing okay," Cole said.

"Yeah, she's fine," Eva said. "But checking in with somebody when you know they're *also* going through a hard time? That kind of personal touch goes a long way."

If Choch were there Cole was certain he'd have something to say about that little burn. They stopped at the mouth of Ashley's driveway, feet away from the old Ford Mustang, in front of a line of bright hockey tape Wayne had used because he "probably couldn't find actual police tape," as Eva explained. Cole said, "Eva, I didn't know what else to do after I left. I didn't know what I could say."

"And nothing ever came to you over ten years, not one fucking thing," Eva said. "No ideas."

"Nothing that seemed good enough."

"*Anything* would've been better than nothing, Cole. You know, sometimes I wish that you didn't save me at all. Then I wouldn't have felt like I owed you so much."

"Yeah, and you'd be dead," Brady said.

"I don't know what your life's been like for ten years, B, but I've spent it waiting, hoping, feeling like I'd done something wrong, and then regretting being alive, like I was somehow special to get saved, but not special enough to get a goddamn phone call. Why Cole? Why me? Why us?"

"Because..." but Cole didn't know what to say, again. He fell silent. Again.

"Tell me! Help me understand!"

"Because you and Brady were the only ones alive, Eva! Okay? Everybody else was dead! I saw them all!" Cole walked along the hockey/ crime scene tape, as if needing it for support. He walked away from Eva, to the side of the driveway. "I saw every one of them."

Cole stayed there. He stared into the bush. Took his pill bottle out, opened the lid, and emptied it into his palm, all away from the eyes of his friends. There were only three left. He'd spilled the rest. It was okay right now. He wanted to feel this for some reason. The bottle returned to his pocket. Footsteps approached from behind. He felt a hand on his back.

"I'm sorry. I didn't know." Eva rubbed her hand against his back in tiny circles. His mom used to do that, when he was crying and couldn't stop. It calmed him then, and it calmed him now. "I've been a jerk. I'm trying, you know?"

"I am too," Cole said.

She peeked around so that they could make eye contact. She smiled carefully. "I know this is hard for you too."

Cole shifted his feet and turned around. "You know what keeps me up at night, every night?"

Eva shook her head.

"That if I had a choice, I would've saved you and Brady first anyway. It makes me feel so guilty." What he couldn't say was that he wondered what his prayers had to do with them being alive still, if somehow Choch had ensured their survival, so that one day (now) he could use Cole for something else. He added, "And what'll keep me up now, is that I had a chance to save Ashley, and I couldn't."

"How? Catch a bullet?" Brady moved closer to the pair.

"I didn't do anything, man. I just stood there, and then he was gone," Cole said.

"Well we can do something now," Eva said. "Right?"

Cole collected himself and took a deliberate breath. Then he looked around the grounds, Ashley's trailer, the woods. "I don't know where to start."

"I overheard my dad say that they couldn't find his cell phone. Maybe we could look for that?"

"Good idea," Brady said.

"Why don't you guys look for it inside?" Eva suggested. "Cole, where did you see the guy running?"

Cole pointed to the area of the bush the shooter had run into. "Over there somewhere."

"Okay, I'll go see what I can find."

They agreed and ducked under the hockey tape. On the other side, Cole said, "Lucky that Reynold's staff aren't guarding the place, eh?"

"Oh," Brady said, "I don't think Mr. Kirkness would put a cent into Reynold's pocket."

"I get that impression," Cole said. "Just figured people would be better than stick tape."

"Not *his* people," Eva said.

The group branched off. Brady and Cole went towards the trailer. Eva went to the bush, around the area Cole had pointed out.

"I'll let you guys know when I find something." Eva was already busy inspecting the edge of the woods.

"Us too," Cole said.

"Can I just say something?" Brady asked. They were at the top of the steps, in front of the door. Cole was about to turn the door handle. "Not that I didn't agree to do this. I *want* to know who did it. It's just that, shouldn't we be leaving this up to, you know…" Brady looked directly at Eva "…*your dad*?"

Eva stopped what she was doing. She chuckled softly, "Really? Where is he now?"

"Maybe he's at the clinic dealing with the other stuff, or maybe he's at the office dealing with *this*, you don't know Eva. Either way, we should let him know what we're doing," Brady said.

"What, are you worried we'll find something and it won't be, like, admissible in court or something?" Eva asked.

"Sure, something like that," Brady said.

"How about if we find anything, we won't touch it. We'll call Mr. Kirkness. Deal?" Cole said.

"Sure, okay, deal," Brady said.

"Deal!" Eva continued to shine her flashlight around where Cole had indicated.

Cole had his hand on the door handle. He'd had his hand on it for long enough that the cool metal had grown warm against his skin.

"You ready?" he asked Brady.

Brady nodded, but he was avoiding even looking at the door. Being here must have made losing Ashley certifiably real. Cole hadn't thought about that before—bringing Ashley to the trailer, the effect it would have on him. How would it affect him being *inside* the trailer? Instead of moving to go inside, Brady got down on one knee and pulled out a bundle of tobacco. He opened the bundle and sprinkled sacred medicine just outside the door. He bowed his head and prayed. Cole waited, both eyes on his friend. Brady was trembling. His hand shook when he laid the medicine, and the feeling had spread through his body. Cole thought about his own bundle, but he told himself he had to wait for the memorial. Brady stood up. Cole put his free hand on Brady's shoulder. There was a tear running down Brady's cheek.

"You don't have to do this—"

"—I can't do this." Cole and Brady spoke at the same time.

"Thanks, Cole," Brady said.

"Yeah," Cole said. "It's alright."

Brady descended the stairs, walked across the driveway, and opened the Mustang's door.

"I got this," Cole assured him.

Brady got in the car, sat down, and closed the door.

Cole tried to turn the door handle, but it was locked. He jiggled the knob.

"Come on." He tensed his arm, clenched his hand around the doorknob, and gave it a hard tug to the right. The knob cracked off the door, and the door itself swung open. With the handle still clutched in his hand, Cole looked back at Brady to see how much he'd seen. Brady was staring straight ahead over the steering wheel, his hands around it, as though he were going somewhere, somewhere far from here. Cole opened his hand and saw that the metal handle had been crushed in the shape of his grip.

"What the hell?" he whispered to himself, and tossed the doorknob into the underbrush at the side of the trailer.

He took a long look into the bush where he'd thrown the handle, then stepped inside the trailer. It felt surreal that just last night he'd been in the same place, and Ashley had been there to greet him. Angry. Agitated. Alive. Now there were only remnants of him. A stack of textbooks, a notepad, and a collection of pencils and pens sat on the desk at the corner of the room. Cole thought of the times Ashley had to stop texting him so that he could study. A zipped-up hockey bag was pushed to the side of the room by the front door, with a hockey stick with a candy-cane tape job propped up beside it. The knob was resting against the window and its spidering crack from the bullet. The comic books Ashley had been reading were stacked on the coffee table in front of the futon. A pile of dirty clothes in a white laundry basket sat beside the futon. Finally, there was the blood, splashed against the wall across the room, against the futon, and there was the pool of it on the floor. Cole looked away for a moment, trying to distance himself from the fact that this was Ashley's blood.

Find something, anything.

Cole didn't know what Wayne would've missed. Still, he made his way around the room, looking at everything, in every place, from the ceiling to the floor. He tried not to disturb the scene. He knew that television shows weren't the most accurate in depicting murder investigations (they didn't play rock music while they took blood samples, for example), but he figured it was best not to tamper with much, if he could help it. He did make an exception, though, when he saw that an old framed picture of him, Ashley, Eva, Brady, and Michael had been hit by drops of Ashley's blood. He picked up the picture and carefully scraped away the dried blood before replacing it.

Cole could see why Brady didn't want to come in here. The trailer was flooded with memories of Ashley. From his hockey equipment, to the picture, to the dirty clothes in the laundry basket, ready to be hauled off to the laundromat at the back of the mall. They probably reeked of Ashley, that kind of locker-room, sweat, and stale hockey-equipment scent. There'd be a time when Brady would want to come in here, maybe have to come in here, but it wasn't today.

The last place Cole looked was under the futon. He found a pair of rolled-up dirty socks there, probably because Ashley had missed trying to throw them into the basket. A *Sandman* graphic novel. An empty bag of chips. Ashley had always eaten well, just like Cole. Must've been a cheat snack. A school textbook. And behind all of this, Cole found Ashley's phone. It must've bounced under the futon and settled behind the junk, against the wall, when Ashley had dropped it.

"Always the last place you look." Cole whispered to himself as though he'd just found the TV remote or change in the couch.

He picked it up, surprised that Wayne hadn't found it. It was a good start, because if he were going to solve the murder, it would be hard to do it from jail. Cole knew that the last text exchanges on it were between him and Ashley. If Wayne had found it, added to the fact that Cole was with Ashley when he was shot, that only Cole saw the "shadowy figure" running from the scene, and that Cole had been found covered in Ashley's blood, well, it wasn't rocket science. Wayne probably already held some suspicions. Cole didn't qualify this as something they needed to notify Wayne about.

Cole scrolled through the texts. He reread the ones between him and Ashley, and went on to read others, to see if there were any clues as to who might've killed him. All he found, though, were messages between Ashley and Brady. Apparently, they were supposed to meet two nights ago, the same night "Ashley" was busy trying to convince Cole to come to Wounded Sky. Were these texts to Brady not really from Ashley either? Cole was trying to work out the timeline when—

"Boys!" Eva shouted from outside the trailer.

Cole pocketed the phone and rushed outside. Both he and Brady, doing his own rushing out of the Ford Mustang, met up with Eva on the other side of the car, about ten feet into the woods. She was standing there, pointing a flashlight to an area on the ground.

"Look," she said.

Cole looked, but all he could see was long grass, some twigs, a fallen branch, a bit of dirt. Was he missing something? He inspected the area more carefully.

Cole could see Brady nodding rhythmically in the dark.

"Yeah, I see it." Brady pointed at whatever Eva had found.

Cole squinted his eyes. "Totally."

Eva managed a laugh. "You're such a liar."

"What, did you go and practice hunting and tracking out in, what is that place, Assiniboine Park?" Brady asked.

"You city kids couldn't follow footprints in the snow," Eva said.

"Okay, okay, fine. I have no idea what you guys see," Cole said.

Eva squatted and curled her fingers around some longer grass that was kind of hunched over, some delicate broken blades. "See?" She rubbed her fingertips against the ground, along some disturbed dirt, and pointed at a couple of broken twigs. "It's a trail. Somebody was here, and they left in a hurry."

"Cool," Cole said.

"What are we waiting for?" Eva asked.

"Wait a second. Isn't this where we tell your dad?" Brady asked her. "We kinda found something, right?"

"It's like Cole said, B. If we find something…*else*…we'll let him know. Okay?"

Brady sighed. "Fine."

9

TRACKS

"DID YOU FIND ANYTHING?" BRADY ASKED.

Brady and Cole were lagging behind Eva. They'd been on the trail for about twenty minutes, and it seemed as though the tracks went on and on, deeper into Blackwood Forest. Every once in a while, Eva would swivel towards them with her light and she'd shout, "Come on, boys!" and the two of them picked up the pace.

"Where?" Cole asked.

"In the trailer, obviously."

"Not really, no."

"Oh, dear Lord above, Cole Harper." This was trouble, Brady using Cole's full name like his grandmother would do from time to time. "Eva's not the only person who can tell when you're lying."

"Okay, I found his phone." Cole didn't say anything more about it. He kept walking forward, keeping an eye on Eva's flashlight. He tried to avoid Brady's stare.

"And?" Brady asked, losing patience.

"And nothing. It had the texts between me and Ashley…"

"Cole, please."

"Okay, look. You don't have to feel bad about not going to meet Ashley out in the clearing. I just didn't want to bring it up because of that. I mean, sometimes things just come up. It wouldn't have changed anything." Brady just looked at Cole oddly. Cole felt awkward. "That was it," he added. "There weren't really any clues on it."

Brady stopped. Cole did too. Eva kept going, unaware that the two of them weren't following her anymore.

"Let me see it," Brady said.

Cole reached into his pocket. Brady's face looked even more intense by the way the flashlight was hitting it, like he was about to tell a horror story by a campfire. There was no arguing with him.

"Sure." Cole handed the phone to Brady. Brady grabbed it from him and went through the texts just as Cole had. He often looked up at Cole as he read through the texts that were presumably between Cole and Ashley, probably understanding why Cole had come. Ashley's texts read as urgent for Brady as they had for Cole. There was confusion in Brady's face there. Cole couldn't blame him. He'd been confused, too. He was still confused. Then Brady got to the texts he, Brady, had supposedly exchanged with Ashley. Cole watched Brady go through these texts, leaned forward and peeked as Brady's thumb scrolled up and stopped, scrolled up and stopped. Brady read through the texts a few times, then handed the phone back to Cole.

"Cool?" Cole asked.

Brady shook his head. "No, I don't think it could be more *un*cool if it was the middle of summer."

"I can't even begin to understand how hard it must be for you to read that all over, man. Sorry."

"That's not it," Brady said. "It's that I didn't write any of those texts."

"What are you talking about?" Cole read through the texts between Brady and Ashley and analyzed them. He even checked for matches in Brady's grammar and syntax.

"I didn't write *one* of those texts to Ashley two days ago. Not one. But they're from my phone." Brady pulled out his own phone, opened it, and found the messages from Ashley. "Look." Brady opened the conversation with Ashley. The screen was blank. "There's no history," Brady said. "Somebody took my phone, texted Ashley, erased *everything* they'd written, then returned it without me knowing."

"Crap." Cole breathed, and as the clear, indisputable thought began to form in his head about what had actually happened with

Brady's phone—the same thing that happened to Ashley's—Brady asked, "Who could've done that?"

Cole was frighteningly close to answering Brady, just thinking out loud. Of course it had been Choch. He'd taken Ashley's phone to text Cole, and before that, probably to get *Ashley's* phone, he'd taken Brady's phone to text Ashley. It was a confusing way to go about things, baffling really, but oh what fun he must've had doing it (*as fun as it is to ride a one-horse open sleigh. Carry on, though. PTI – pardon the interruption*). He could've just manifested a text from no phone at all, Cole figured. He could've made the messages look like they were coming from whomever he wanted. It was infuriating. Cole managed to hold his tongue, to follow the rules. In the process, Brady and Eva stayed alive. "I don't know."

"Look at me," Brady said to Cole. Cole did. "Are you telling me that you don't know who took my phone?"

Cole didn't bother lying. It hadn't worked yet. The only option was to tell the truth. And that was, "I know who took your phone, and I know who took Ashley's. Same person."

"And?" Brady prompted.

"I can't tell you. I'm sorry."

"Do you realize that my boyfriend got killed last night? You do, right?" It was the first time Brady had ever shouted at Cole, or, Cole thought, at anybody, for all he could remember. It left him a little stunned.

"Of course I realize that, Brady…"

"I've been trying to hold it together the whole damn day, and you have stuff you know about his death and you're not going to tell me?"

"Hey!" Eva shouted from way up ahead. Her flashlight's glow was dim but loomed large from where she herself had stopped, about a hundred yards away. "What are you guys doing!?"

"I want to tell you, Brady, but I can't. Something bad will happen."

"You mean, something bad like somebody getting killed?"

"Worse." *Like all three of us dying.*

Brady shook his head in frustration. It looked like he wanted to smash his flashlight against a large rock just off the trail.

"I promise you that what I know, it won't help us find Ashley's killer."

"You mean it won't help *you* find his killer. That's your big stupid top-secret mission, right, Cole?"

"I can't find the killer without you," Cole said. "Please."

"Look at what's happened since you got here. What if it's all happening because of that? Because of *you*?"

"Do you want me to go?" Cole asked. "Because I can't do that either. I'm not here because I started all this, I'm here to fix it. I *have* to be." Cole realized that he was trying to convince himself, as much as he was Brady.

"I don't know what I want, I—"

"Brady, you know me," Cole pleaded.

"Boys!" Eva shouted.

"Coming!" Cole shouted back. He said to Brady, "Coming?"

Brady looked all around—at Cole, Eva, back to where they'd come from, like he wanted to go back to a better time. But there was no going back.

"Yeah. Yeah, I'm coming."

They resumed their painstaking pursuit the way they had started, Eva was in the lead, Brady and Cole behind. The boys stayed closer to her now. She kept looking back at them to ensure they'd not fallen back again. Cole was keeping up okay, but Brady was struggling.

"I'm out in the bush all the time," Brady said in heavy breaths. "This is baloney."

"You're doing fine," Cole said.

"You're hardly sweating," Brady said to Cole, then shouted to Eva, "and you're a machine, Eva!"

"Dad and I do this every weekend," she replied. "It's just that we track animals. Small game, big game. Not a killer. Killer's are easier to track, though."

She stopped pushing forward and waited for them to catch up to her.

"You know this isn't a race, though, right?" Brady asked.

"The slower we are, the longer he's got to get away, right?" Eva said.

"Assuming he actually stopped at some point," Cole said.

"Yeah, maybe he just kept going, and that's that," Brady said, but he didn't want it to be this way. Cole could tell by his tone. To reassure Brady that he was all-in on finding Ashley's killer, he replied, "Well, then we'll keep going too, okay?"

"That doesn't make sense anyway," Eva said. "Why would somebody come all the way to Wounded Sky, kill a kid, and then leave? What's the reason? There's always a motive."

"What motive could there possibly be to kill Ashley?" Brady asked. "Nobody but my parents and a few other idiots cared that we're gay. A lot of people don't even know Ashley was."

"He was a model student, a great hockey player, all around nice guy," Eva said.

"Maybe somebody was jealous that he was going places for hockey?" Cole asked.

They were in full-on investigative mode now.

"That doesn't happen here, does it?" Brady asked. "I think people appreciate that we have…that we had…somebody like that living here."

"Plus Michael's just as good," Eva said.

"*Michael's just as good,*" Cole mimicked under his breath, like a child. "None of this makes any sense," he said, this time to everybody. "That's why we have to find this guy. Maybe he'll have some answers."

"And what, now we're interrogators?" Brady said.

"No, I think *that's* when we call Wayne," Cole said. "Right?"

"That's when we call my dad," Eva confirmed.

They continued on together from there, but it wasn't more than a few minutes that Eva held up. She whispered, "We might need to call him sooner than we thought."

She crouched beneath the cover of some thicker underbrush, and Brady and Cole did too. She pointed out a small clearing up ahead, and the corner of a tent that was visible through the maze of foliage and trees.

"I actually see what you mean this time," Cole whispered.

"Kind of more obvious," Eva whispered back, "but good for you."

"What do we do?" Brady asked.

"We check it out," Eva said.

They bear-crawled the rest of the way, kept hidden, tried not to crack a twig and announce their presence. Eva and Brady were predictably great at "stealth mode," as Brady had called it before they set off. Cole, not so much. By the time they were near the clearing's perimeter, he'd been shushed multiple times, and for various, clumsy offences. He'd apologized each time, which garnered a follow-up shush.

It went like this:

A twig cracked. In the woods, in the silence, it sounded like thunderclap.

"Shhhh," from either Eva or Brady.

"Sorry!"

"*Shhhh*," from the other.

Cole's ineptitude didn't cost them anything. At the edge of the clearing it was obvious that nobody was at the camp. They stopped there and huddled around Eva to see how they had got here. She'd been mapping out the route with her phone. The app left a blue trail from here to Ashley's trailer. Surprisingly, where they were now wasn't far off from Wounded Sky, albeit on the other side of the community, closer to the quarry. The blue line zigged and zagged through Blackwood Forest, moving left, jerking right, going north a-ways, doubling back. It's what had taken them so long.

"He was trying to cover his tracks," Eva said.

"You can't hide your tracks from a tracker," Brady rasped, as though he were narrating a movie trailer.

"He's hidden *somewhere*, though," Cole said.

For a camp that had been put up in a forest, where no other camp had been before, it was immaculate and spare: a single person canvas tent and a backpack against a tree. Some smoke was rising from the firepit, meaning the killer hadn't been gone long.

"I don't remember camps being this neat," Cole said as they walked into the clearing.

"They aren't like KOAS," Eva said to Cole.

"Can you imagine an arcade just around the corner, swimming pool, convenience store?" Brady asked.

"Roughing it," Eva said.

"Alright already," Cole said.

"Cole's right, though. Hunting camps usually aren't like this," Brady said. "There's just not enough stuff."

They stopped in the middle of the camp, beside the fire.

"It looks military," Brady said. "Just precise, tidy, you know?"

"So, wait," Eva said. "A soldier killed Ashley?"

"Maybe, like, an ex-soldier who's gone rogue or something," Cole said.

"Don't serial killers keep things all neat like this? Like they're OCD or something?" Brady asked.

"In the movies," Cole said.

"Look at us," Eva said. "Tracking the killer, building a psychological profile."

"Still doesn't explain what Ashley has to do with anything. It *can't* be random like that," Brady said.

Cole crouched by the fire and touched the ashes with his fingers. It was warm, but he couldn't have guessed when the killer had been here last. He picked up a stick and poked around at the white and black logs. He found a can of beans hidden in the remnants of the fire. "I'm glad you guys came. Both of you. I would've been lost."

"I just want to find this asshole," Eva said.

"We can't do anything right now," Cole said.

"You're right. He has a gun, we have our wits," Eva said. "I don't like the odds."

"Do you have reception out here?" Cole said to Brady.

"We can't get reception some places in the rez, Cole." To demonstrate, Brady pulled out his phone, turned it on, and showed Cole the screen without looking at it himself. No service. "Let alone in Blackwood Forest. It's like the Bermuda Triangle of cell service."

"Look," Eva said, "let's go back into Wounded Sky and call my dad. It's time. We can lead him back here."

"He's not going to let you come back here, Eve," Brady said. "He teaches you to do all this stuff, yeah, but at the same time he treats you like—"

"Yeah, well," Eva said, "he can't find his way here without me. And neither could you boys."

"In our defence, I don't think anybody could find their way here even if they were using your app. It's like a bunch of blue lightning bolts," Brady said.

"Shh, shh, shh," Cole said quickly and sharply. He liked shushing somebody for once.

"What?" Brady asked, instinctively whispering.

"Shh," Cole repeated.

There was movement, rustling somewhere in the forest, out of range of their flashlights. They stopped everything. They stopped breathing, it seemed.

A twig broke.

Closer now.

"Somebody's here," Cole whispered.

Suddenly, the faint rustling and twig-breaking exploded into heavy footsteps over the rough terrain, like drumbeats, rhythmic, foreboding.

"Run!" Brady shouted.

All three of them, jolted by Brady's desperate command, took off from the camp as fast as they could go, their flashlights trained in front of them to help navigate the obstacles laid out before them at the speed they were going.

They ran faster.

Cole could hear someone running behind him and his friends, but they didn't gain on them. They bounded through Blackwood Forest, and the footsteps fell behind. Although they were more sure of their safety, they continued to run until they came to the outskirts of Wounded Sky First Nation. Only then did they stop. Brady and Eva bent over in succession, their hands on their knees, trying to catch their breath.

"What…the…hell…just…happened?" Eva asked, panting heavily.

"Beats…me…" Brady panted too.

"I think we found who we were looking for." Cole didn't have to catch his breath, and he didn't feel tired from the run—certainly not like the other two. He hadn't been as tired as Brady during their expedition through Blackwood Forest, either. He wondered if this was included in the abilities that he had been given by Choch, this along with the crushed doorknob. It had to be. He made a quick mental list: endurance, strength.

Should I pretend to be tired? Cole wondered. He didn't want Eva and Brady to ask too many questions if they saw him standing there perfectly fine while they looked like they'd just been through boot camp. What had Brady said? Eva was a machine. Yet there she was, keeled over and trying to catch her breath. Before Eva and Brady looked up, Cole bent over, hands to knees, trying to look like he was breathing hard. While pretending, a slight bit of anxiety reared its head: weak knees, quick pulse, shakiness. Well, if he did have some kind of superhuman abilities, he supposed he needed a weakness. He'd learned as much from comic books. Instead of panting heavily, then, he did his deep breathing. In through the nose, out through the mouth. It looked the same to the untrained eye.

"Now," Brady said, "we have to…worry about him…finding us."

"Check your…phone for reception," Eva was beginning to even out her breath. "We should call my dad now."

"Good idea." Brady reached into his pocket and pulled out his phone. The light from the screen lit his face. His mouth opened slightly and his eyes opened even more, wide in disbelief.

"What?" Cole asked. "What's going on?

Brady didn't answer.

"B!" Eva said, a little more forceful.

Brady's hand dropped against his thigh. The phone fell out of his hand and hit the ground.

"Chief Crate is dead."

10
CITY

"WHEN?"

It was a stupid question and Cole knew it, but he didn't know what else to say. Clearly, it happened between the time they left the trailer to follow the tracks and the time they reentered the community from Blackwood Forest, the time that they were without cell reception. From what Cole had heard since his return to Wounded Sky, Chief Crate had been an amazing leader. Brady and Eva looked devastated, perhaps more today than they would have on any other day.

Another death to process.

Cole felt a sense of loss too. He'd never known Chief Crate as his chief, but there was no severing the connection he had with his home, try as he might. Sam Crate was a part of that connection. And if Cole were straining to feel like he was part of the community again, and discovering how many people thought badly of him, he at least shared something with everybody: loss.

Brady answered obligatorily. "Tonight. Just now."

"What the hell kind of monster flu is this?" Eva asked.

"Never mind swine flu," Brady said. "This thing's like the kraken of flus. He got sick *last night.*"

"How many people are sick now?" Cole asked. "What did Dr. Captain say?"

Brady shrugged. "Lots."

Cole motioned to the forest—to the killer who was now, in all likelihood, hundreds of yards away—then to some nondescript place in the community, weighing two options that he didn't need to articulate. "What do we do?"

"My kókom's probably over at the clinic right now," Brady said, clearly conflicted, following Cole's aimless motion. Did they deal with the man in the woods, or did they put that on hold?

"You should go," Eva said to Brady. "She'll need you."

"I guess I should," Brady said.

"I'll come too," Eva said. "Because you'll need *me*."

"Me too," Cole said. "If we're a team, we're a team, right?"

"Right," Brady said.

As they started walking, Eva said, "Maybe it wasn't even the guy. Maybe it was just some hunter with a neat camp and he was trying to chase off some teenagers."

"You don't have to make me feel better," Brady said. "The tracks lead right there. It wasn't some peeping Tom or something."

"We need to tell your dad," Cole said. "Something else could happen, or he could bolt, even if it looks like he's sticking around. Maybe we scared him off."

"Kids scared him off?" Brady asked. "He just killed one of us; why would he be scared off?"

"I'm just saying, Mr. Kirkness should check it out," Cole said.

"Okay, I'll let him know, give him the directions, whatever," Eva said.

The Wounded Sky Health Clinic wasn't far from where they'd come out of Blackwood Forest. Soon, they were approaching the building. A large crowd was gathered outside the clinic, holding a vigil for Chief Crate. From the back Cole could see that many in the crowd heeded Dr. Captain's advice, too. Wounded Sky residents were holding up candles, lighters, or cell phones, and a good number had masks over their mouths. Younger residents had drawn pictures on their masks: mouths with fangs, clown smiles, zipped lips. The trio held steady at the perimeter of the vigil, and Cole saw that Eva and Brady, taking their cue from the crowd, had lifted their shirt collars up over their mouths. Cole did the same. It would be a shame if he got sick and died before he fulfilled his end of the bargain.

Cole looked at the faces around him. They had been through pain and never had the luxury of being taken somewhere far away. While the pain never really seemed to leave for Cole, even though he was hundreds and hundreds of miles away, there were moments where he'd forget. He'd always cherished those moments. How could anybody forget the pain when they were living in it?

The mourning crowd was quiet like Cole hadn't heard before, like they were all holding their breath, just waiting for the moment to end. Cole could hear the collective flickering of tiny flames, from wicks to butane, like whispers. He also heard the sound of shuffling feet, and he saw people moving away from him. In a strange way, this movement was done almost respectfully, like *sorry, Cole, we don't want to offend you, but we still don't like you all that much*. Or maybe it wasn't that they didn't like him, but rather they were scared of him. He honestly didn't know.

"What the fuck are you doing here?"

Cole craned his neck up. He tried to look over the crowd to see who'd said it.

"You've got a lot of nerve coming to a vigil for a man you killed!"

It was Mark. He saw a black hat bob up and down several feet away. It weaved its way through the crowd, like a shark through water, towards him. Moments later, Mark and Cole were standing face-to-face. Mark got real close. Cole could smell his breath. Beer. Cigarettes. At the same time, Michael appeared from the vigil, drawn by Mark's shouting, and stood beside Cole and Eva and Brady.

"What are you talking about?" Cole backed away, but Mark closed the distance. Cole decided not to go any farther. This was going to happen, whether they were in the forest or here. At least here he'd have his friends.

"I'm not going to buy that it's some coincidence. That the same night you get here, Chief Crate gets sick." Mark scanned the crowd, who were all watching the pair now, and asked, "Do you think *anybody* is going to buy that?"

"Man, do you really think I brought some kind of crazy virus in a little bottle to Wounded Sky, like this was some movie or something? Are you kidding me?"

"Maybe you're sick too!"

"Do I look sick? If I were sick, I'd be dead by now, or at least in the clinic."

"And then Ashley gets shot, and who's there? Cole Harper."

"So you're just going to ignore the fact that I'm not sick? What are you, Donald Trump?"

"His blood was all over you, wasn't it, city?"

"That kind of happens when somebody is shot right in front of you, Mark."

"Do you really believe him!?" Mark asked the crowd. Cole saw some masked faces shaking their heads. He wondered if they still would have if they weren't wearing masks. "We don't have none of this shit happen when he's gone, and then when he comes back, look at what happens!"

"The whole place is going to shit!" somebody shouted.

"Are you guys even listening to Cole?" Brady asked.

"There's nobody to save here, city boy!" another person said.

"Mark is right!"

"He killed Ashley!"

"Ashley was his friend!" Michael shouted.

"So were all the kids he didn't save!" a voice called out.

Somebody threw a candle at Cole. It landed against his chest and fell to the ground. The flame went out before it hit him, but it might as well have burned him. Other candles followed.

"He brought this flu here! It had to be him!"

Brady moved closer to Cole, shoulder-to-shoulder.

"Hell, yeah! The Chief got sick right when Harper came in!"

"Get outta here you coward!"

Eva moved to the other side of Cole and put her hand on him protectively.

"You're city, Harper! We don't need you!"

"We don't *want* you, city!"

"There's nobody here to save, Harper," Mark said. "Why don't you go the hell home?"

"ENOUGH!" Reynold yelled over the shouts of the crowd. The chaos died down gradually, like a volume dial being turned from ten to one. "Please, hear me out," Reynold continued. "Let's be reasonable. I understand what's happening here, and I feel your pain. If I could have Chief Crate back, I would take him. I don't care about this election. Whatever our differences, he was a good leader."

The crowd voiced its approval. Reynold continued.

"We all knew Ashley too. In many ways, he was our hope. He was going to do great things. I could see that in him."

Brady was crying. He'd been staying strong for Cole through the onslaught, but that strength was slipping away. Cole put an arm around him.

"And this all happened when Cole Harper came back to Wounded Sky, yes," Reynold said. "We've lost so much, and now we have lost more. We're angry. We're confused. We want somebody to blame."

The crowd approved of this as well. The wave of anger began to rise, but Reynold quieted them once more. "But this boy," He pointed at Cole. "This boy right here isn't to blame! We should welcome him. We lost him, as we've lost so many others, and now he's home again."

Some heads nodded. But Cole felt too many eyes on him, too many voices against him.

"Let's not forget, either, that this boy is a hero," Reynold said.

"He's a liar! No kid could lift a wall!"

"He was faking it! They would've got out of that fire anyway!"

"He's a hero!"

"He saved them!"

"He saved his friends!"

"Selfish punk!"

"He could've saved everybody, that little bastard!"

"He should've stayed there with the rest of them!"

"Burn, Harper!"

Another candle.

"What makes him so special!?"

"I was just a kid!" Cole shouted. "I never asked for any of this! You people want to know why I got moved away? *I* never knew. I never knew until now, and *this* is why. Imagine hearing this when you're seven. SEVEN!" Cole shook his head. He backed away from Eva and Brady. "Maybe…" his lip began to quiver, tears started to fall "…maybe that makes me a coward." He moved farther and farther away from them all. "But what does that make all of you?"

His thoughts had always focussed on what he'd done, and what he could've done differently when he'd saved his friends, if he would've noticed the school burning earlier, if he could've run there faster. Maybe he could've saved more kids. Maybe he could've saved everybody. Maybe he never should've left the school in the first place. But now he just felt angry, and tired, and lost and, really, that nothing he did back then would've changed anything now. And he wasn't mad at his auntie anymore, or at Ashley, or at his grandmother for keeping this from him, that people felt this way.

Cole stormed away from the clinic, leaving the crowd, now stunned silent, behind. He heard footsteps chasing after him.

"Cole!" Michael followed him.

"Yeah," Cole said.

"Come back, alright? Please?"

"Come back to that? No thanks."

"You were right, what you said."

Cole stopped and turned to face Michael. He hoped that Eva might have chased after him, but it was her boyfriend. Great. And why was Michael being so nice to him? Did he feel guilty for stealing her from him? Was he making amends?

"It doesn't matter if I was right or not. It's not going to change anybody's mind. It's not going to change anything."

"It matters to us. Your friends."

"*Are* we friends?" Cole asked.

"I've been meaning to ask you the same thing," Michael said.

Cole pictured Eva. He pictured Eva and the necklace she wore. Did Michael know that necklace was from him? Did it matter? "I didn't think she was just going to wait around for me, you know. Better you than some asshole."

"So…" Michael laughed a bit awkwardly. "Friends?"

Cole put his hands in his pockets. He shifted the pill bottle back and forth with his fingertip. He wanted to take a pill right now, but there were so few left. It was funny. He hadn't thought about taking a pill after they'd been chased by a killer, but he wanted one now, when he was completely out of danger. "Friends."

Michael put his hand on Cole's shoulder, gently pulled him back in the direction of the clinic. "Come on. You don't have to be anything for anybody."

Cole shook his head. "I'm sorry. I can't be there right now. I just want to clear my head."

"Sure, okay." Michael nodded at Cole, then turned around and jogged back towards the clinic. Cole watched until Michael got to the crowd and stopped beside Eva. They were talking, and Cole could tell it was about him. Michael threw up his arms, like there was no convincing Cole to come back. *That would be accurate*, Cole thought, maybe even if Eva had chased after him, not Michael.

He took a last look at the couple as they and Brady pushed their way through the crowd towards the clinic, where they'd undoubtedly spend the night helping others. Cole thought he should be there, and on another night he would've gone with them and ignored the crowd, but not tonight. He left the clinic and his friends behind with the crowd and their masks and lighters and candles. Cole took out his phone.

"Hello?" His grandma picked up the phone after far too many rings. He'd watched her do this, wait to answer the phone while she was sitting right beside it, testing the will of whoever was calling her, and her own patience for technology. He had convinced her to get a cell phone last year. It spent most of its time untouched, on the coffee table in the living room.

"Hey, Grandma." Cole found it hard to hide the fact that he was crying from her. The tears had stopped after his outburst, but as soon as he dialled her number, they started again.

"What's wrong, my boy?"

Cole paused. He searched for the words. What was wrong? Everything. Was *everything* a valid response? "I want to come home." He cried harder. "Auntie Joan was right." He felt like a child. He felt like the seven-year-old boy that had left Wounded Sky, not the seventeen-year-old that had come back. Not the kid who'd been given this strength. No, he felt weak.

"Oh, Cole. You only just got there."

"I know, but everything's going wrong and everybody hates me."

"That can't really be true."

"It feels like it is." He thought of his home back in the city. He thought about what he'd be doing right now if he were there, probably reading a comic, doing homework, listening to music. The things a kid like him should be dealing with. And then he thought about what would be happening here if he'd have stayed home. How could things have been any worse? And what good was he doing?

"Ashley's dead."

There'd already been a long pause, and this extended it. He could hear his grandma's breath on the other line. He could almost hear her trying to think of what to say.

"That's horrible. I'm so sorry."

"Grandma?"

"Yes, nósisim?"

"I don't know what I'm supposed to do." He barely got those words out and hoped she could understand him through the sobbing. "I don't belong here, I—"

"Do you remember when you first started at your school, when we came to the city?"

"Yes."

"What do you remember?"

"That I was the only First Nations kid in my class and all the other kids were white. I was scared."

"You thought they'd make fun of you, that they'd hate you. Do you remember that?"

"Yes."

"And did it matter if they did? What did I tell you?"

Cole took a deep, calming breath. He wiped at his cheeks. "You said it only mattered if *I* liked me. It didn't matter if anybody else did."

"That's right, grandson. That's exactly what I told you."

"And then I had a panic attack, so what good did that do?"

"It didn't make it not true, and it's still true now. If you can accept yourself for who you are, you belong anywhere. Cole, you belong there, and whatever you have to do, you do it."

"Okay, Grandma." It felt like the conversation was ending, but he didn't want it to. He kept the phone hugged against his cheek like he could hold her there, like she, and his home back in the city, the place that made him "city," was that close. He even missed his auntie, as hard as she could be.

"And, grandson, what else do I always tell you, when you are feeling this way? Troubled?"

"To find my peace."

"Find your peace," his grandma said.

"Thanks, Grandma. I'll talk to you soon."

"I love you, grandson."

11

RIBBONS

"SO, HOW'S IT GOING?"

Choch's voice had a purposefully annoying childish inflection, and since the spirit being was in coyote form, it was just weird.

"What's your deal?" Cole asked.

Choch looked his own body over from top to bottom. "Oh, yes. I'm trying to keep a low profile."

"Yeah, a talking coyote. Good call," Cole said.

"You, on the other hand, are clearly not," Choch said.

"It's going *fine*, since you asked." Cole crossed his arms. He did everything in his body language to make Choch feel unwelcome.

"Cole Harper, are you pouting?" Choch asked. "You just can't let go of your six-year-old self, can you?"

"Seven," Cole said. "I was seven when you messed up my life."

"My apologies. I am awful with birthdays. And you *are* the math whiz."

"Don't you have floors to mop or something?"

"They simply don't understand you, that's all. You can't take it personally," Choch said. "But take it out on me, if it makes you feel better."

"It'll make me feel better when this is over. You can only take so much before you can't take anymore."

"Like I said, Coley-Boley, it's easier for them to call you that than to believe a boy did what you did. *Heavy is the crown*, as it were."

Cole kept wishing Choch would just leave his side, stop walking with him like a dog would. He wondered how long the pest was going to stick around. He'd planned to clear his head after leaving the clinic, walk around for a bit, then go back to Ashley's trailer, alone, and retrace the path to the camp. He might take a more direct route than the map Eva created on her phone. He wasn't sure what more he could find at the camp, and there was very little at the site in the first place, but it was better than being around people—or spirit beings.

"Oh honestly, you're so morose and boring sometimes," Choch said.

"You know, aside from Eva and Brady and Michael, and even they seem to have their own issues with me, the only person who's been nice to me, who's made me feel welcome, is Reynold," Cole said. "I remember him, when he worked with my dad. He always seemed like a jerk, but without him they were going to get out the pitchforks."

"Now that's a bit dramatic, don't you think?"

"You know what I mean," Cole said. "They'd just as soon drive me out of here."

"Of course, they do say keep your friends close and your enemies closer."

"Ha," Cole said. "I'd have to keep half the stupid community closer, if that were true."

"That's easy, just go back to the clinic. And you say I never help."

"I'd rather you left. I'm not in the mood for this tonight. Or *ever*."

"Actually, if you'd get over yourself, boy, you'd realize that I've done nothing but help tonight." Choch raised his snout and closed his eyes, the coyote equivalent of duck lips. "It's completely out of my character too."

"Okay, well, thanks for your help," Cole said. "Now if you wouldn't mind…"

Choch sighed animatedly. "Have it your way, then." He looked like he was going to turn around, but started to look intently at a large stick on the ground. He wagged his tail.

"You're kidding, right?" Cole asked.

"Just this once?" Choch's tail was going so furiously that it looked like it might fall right off his body. "I've always wondered about it. They seem to have so much fun."

"You're not even a dog."

"I'll have you know that a coyote is somewhere in the canine family."

"No you're not, you're like a wolf or something."

"The coyote is a *canid*, Cole, and native to North America."

"What's a canid?"

"I'm so glad you asked. *Canis* means dog in Latin. It's derived from *caninus*, or *of the dog*. Now, canis is a genus of canids, consisting of wolves, dogs, *and* coyotes. We're distinguished by our well-developed skulls, our—"

"Okay, okay. I get it. *God,*" Cole said.

"I was right." Choch whispered to himself, but Cole heard it.

"If I throw the stupid stick, you'll leave?"

"I'll have to, of course, in order to *chase* the stick. But I will add that I'm feeling rather hungry. Trust me, I will leave. There's a special down at the—"

"There is no special!" Cole picked up the stick and threw it. Choch jumped into a full run, impressively fast, and Cole turned around before seeing the creature catch the stick. He continued on the path towards Ashley's trailer.

"That actually sucked!" Cole heard the coyote shout in the distance. "And it tasted bad," Choch added faintly.

Cole stopped, as he seemed to always do now, on the path to the cemetery. He saw an orange glow and knew Jayne was in there. Before giving it a second thought, he entered the cemetery. Going there, where his old classmates and his mother were laid to rest, as well as his father's headstone, wasn't as difficult as Cole thought it would be. What pushed him there was curiosity. Jayne had said that she was going to play with her friends. He figured that's what she was doing now, and he wanted to see what it looked like, if he could see the other children like he could see Jayne, or if it would be just her and her bright flames darting around like an ember shooting from a fire.

When Cole got there, Jayne wasn't darting, jumping around, or spinning in play. She was standing in place, completely still. She wasn't alone, but wasn't with her friends either. On Jayne's unlit side was Alex. Cole could see her clearly in Jayne's light (which was dimmer than normal, in Cole's estimation). Alex was standing, and Jayne with her, at the front of the fenced-in gravestones, her head bowed, maybe in sadness, maybe in prayer.

Jayne was holding Alex's hand. Rather, Jayne's hand was hovering over Alex's hand, because she couldn't actually touch Alex. Cole wondered, though, if Alex could feel something, a presence, a little bit of warmth, a feeling that she wasn't alone. Cole approached Alex with care. He knew that even if Alex could *sense* something, she couldn't see anything clearly in the dark. To Alex, the area was lit only by the moonlight.

"Alex." Cole walked up beside her, the side Jayne wasn't on, and stopped there.

Alex looked up, smiled at Cole, and looked back down. "Harper."

"She's sad, Coley." Jayne met eyes with Cole, and her eyes were sad too.

"What are you doing out here?" Cole asked Alex.

Alex took a while to answer him. Cole looked over the gravestones—the little white, rounded slabs of marble. *Like Mother Earth's teeth*, he thought.

"I come out here a lot," Alex finally said. "My walks usually bring me out here."

"And the ruins," Cole said.

"In circles," Alex said. "I go all around in circles. It's dizzying, sadness."

"It's peaceful here, though, isn't it?"

She nodded. "Yeah. Positively tranquil."

"Hard to find peace right now." Cole thought back to the recent conversation with his grandma. Maybe this was his peace tonight, and thank goodness Choch wasn't around to ruin it as well.

"I don't think it's your fault, you know," Alex said.

"You heard about the clinic already?" Cole asked.

"Oh, Lord, Cole. You've been away *waaaay* too long. I heard almost in real time, dude. I didn't even need Twitter."

"I'm on Twitter?"

"Hashtag shitColedid."

"Come on."

"No, I'm messing with you. It's uncanny though, how rumours travel out here. It's like we're all psychically connected for gossip."

"Anyway," Cole said, trying not to imagine the way people thought about him extending to social media. Fun. "You'd be in the minority if you didn't blame me for something."

"Meh," she said. "Never blended in with the crowd, really." She looked at the gravestones. It was the first time Cole saw her actually look at them. The kids stood together like that for a long time, in the quiet. Then, as though taking the lead from Jayne, Cole reached to his side and took Alex's other hand for a moment, just to give it a little squeeze. "Thanks."

"No worries," she said.

"Sometimes, I feel like there's some truth to what they say. That I could've, I don't know, done more. That I didn't do enough."

"What do you mean? How much is enough? Honestly."

Cole nodded towards the graves in front of them. "All these people. If I'd have been earlier, if I—"

"Shut up. You *saved* Eva and Brady, Cole. There would've been two more graves here, that's the only truth you need to know. Don't let them make you into some whiny bitch. Okay?"

"Wow," Cole said. "That's direct."

"Deal with it, Harper."

"You think that, though? I mean, you believe it?"

"What, that you saved them?" she asked. "Yeah. I always have."

Cole drew in a big breath, and it quivered when he let it out. Hearing somebody believed in him, other than the people who maybe felt obligated to, almost made him cry. He tried not to, though. He didn't want to seem like a "whiny bitch."

"You did all that you could do. I know it," Alex said.

"You can't know that, Alex. Not really."

"Oh I can't? Here's what I know." Alex turned to him, took his hand this time, stared right into his eyes. "One day, at recess, there was this big bully. Remember him? Mark? Marky Mark and the Funky Bunch? From earlier today? Winning personality."

"Sure. I've run into him, once or twice."

They shared a quick chuckle.

"Anyway, he'd shoved me, I don't know what for, probably for nothing, just to show that he could shove somebody. I was walking back into the school, and *you* saw me. You took my hand, and you walked me inside to the nurse because I had this scrape on my knee. You kept holding my hand while she put peroxide on, while she put a bandage on, and then you walked me back to class."

"I remember."

"And you didn't have to do any of that. *That's* how I know."

She turned away from him, and towards the headstones. He saw her head jerk towards him, then stop. He saw her lips open, then close. Finally, she said, "Sometimes I feel like this is all *my* fault. And isn't that screwed up."

"What? Why would you think that?"

"It's stupid." Alex pushed some hair that had fallen across her face behind her ear.

"Stupid is trying to give a guy CPR when he wasn't having a heart attack."

"Heard that, too. That is epic. I mean, R-I-P, Chief Crate. But still. Gold."

"So tell me."

"Alright, Harper. Here goes. I didn't want my dad to go to the school that night. I begged him not to go. I wanted to watch a movie with him. And then…" Her voice began to crack. She took a trembling breath and gathered herself. "When he went, I remember shouting after him that I didn't love him, that I wished he never came back."

"Alex. You were a kid that missed her dad. We've all yelled at our parents. Somebody started that fire, or something went wrong with the electrical, *something*. But it wasn't you."

"Don't you think," she asked, "that people can make things happen sometimes, if they really, really want them to happen?"

Cole thought hard about this. He remembered running into the school. While he was running, he prayed. He prayed harder than he ever had before, all the way from Silk River right to when he got to the gym. *Please let Eva be okay. Please let Brady be okay. Please let Mom be okay.* Then, Choch was there, ready to answer his prayers. Was that the same thing? Was that wanting something to happen so badly that it did? Could it happen in a bad way, too? He shook his head.

"Not like that, no."

"Yeah, well, fuck it," Alex said, remembering she was supposed to be this tough girl. "That's what I got, and it's what we got, eh? Look at us over here. Bubbling little whiny bitches."

"Quite the pair," Cole said.

Cole examined the entire cemetery—not the graves of those that had died in the fire, but others. Somewhere close, his dad was faux-buried, as was the woman that he died with at the research facility. Death all around them. And then he imagined the graves that were yet to come. Ashley's. Chief Crate's. The others that had died from the sickness, the others that would inevitably die tomorrow. Had there ever been a community that had been through more? Cole gave Alex's hand a gentle tug.

"Come on, I'll walk you home."

They made their way out of Wounded Sky cemetery, hand-in-hand. Wounded Sky First Nation was a ghost town. Tonight it seemed that there was only Alex and Cole in the whole community, and it might've been just what Cole needed, to spend time with somebody who'd gone through as much as he had, who had tortured herself for ten years as much as he had, for better or worse. Most of the walk back to Alex's house was spent without words, with them mostly walking in the dark, sometimes past the light of a house, always under the faint, watchful eye of the northern lights.

"Do you ever think about your mom?" Alex asked.

"Most days," Cole said. "Yes."

"What would you say to her, if you had her back for one minute?"

"That I miss her, and that I'm sorry."

She cocked a side of her mouth up. Nodded.

"What about you? What would you say to your dad?"

"I don't know. I mean, I've thought about that every day since he died, but I never know what would be the perfect thing to say. If I said I was sorry that I said what I did, I know what he'd say. Something like, 'Lexy, let it go. You've got to let it go.' He used to say that all the time."

"But you haven't."

"But I haven't," she agreed. "I guess I'd say something like, 'Can you stay a little longer?' Longer than a minute, anyway."

Cole thought about what he might find in the cemetery. Spirits dancing, playing together right there, in a place that cultivated sadness and grief. How could joy like that coexist with sorrow? He wanted to say something to Alex now, as they approached her house. It was dark inside, even darker in the night. He wanted to tell her, at least, that he knew her father was still here, still watching over her. Because he was. He must've been. If Jayne was here for Cole, against her will or not, then surely Alex's dad was watching over his daughter.

Instead, all Cole said was, "I bet he'd like that."

They stopped at the door to Alex's house. Michael and her mother, she said, must still be at the clinic. She said that she would've gone to help, she really would've, but she hated the sight of death, of sickness.

"Stupid, right? I go there all the time." By *there*, Cole took her to mean the cemetery.

"It's different, and I hate it too." Cole wished, silently, that he'd had the choice to avoid it. "Are you going to be okay?"

"Yeah, I have been." She leaned forward and gave Cole a kiss on the cheek. "I will be. Thanks."

"Sure."

"Don't wash that cheek, Harper." She pointed at him mischievously. He touched his cheek. "I won't."

He waited until she was inside the house. He lingered there for a few minutes and watched the lights go out inside. He felt the need to make sure she was okay, with her brother and mother at the clinic. It was something small, doing that, but made him feel a bit like the person some people, a very small minority, thought he was. Heroes didn't just hold up walls, did they?

"Certainly not."

Choch was standing at Cole's side, no longer in coyote form, and not in his diner uniform either. He was wearing a tuxedo and bowtie, of a colour not at all muted by the dark night. Bright orange. His white dress shirt had ruffles on it.

"Chivalry is such a lost art form. It's a shame," Choch said, all whimsical.

"So is good fashion sense." Cole turned away from Alex's house, and started walking. Any intention he'd had of going back to Ashley's trailer, tracking his way to the campsite, had faded. He just wanted to get to Elder Mariah's place. He didn't feel physically tired, but his mind was about finished.

"Yes, unfortunately the abilities I've provided you don't extend to your mind."

"I told you to get out of my head. Holy shit."

"Sorry, old habits. I promise that I will do my very best. What do they say in Cub Scouts?"

"I was never in the Cub Scouts."

"We'll dob dob dob." Choch snapped his fingers triumphantly, remembering the phrase. "Do our best, you see. Dee-Oh-Bee. You do your best, I'll do my best."

"I'm doing the best I can, if that's what you're getting at."

"Oh, I've no doubt, Cole. Not a sliver of doubt."

"So what is it that you wanted?"

"Well, it's just that…" Choch trailed off awkwardly.

"It's just that what?"

"You could be doing *better* is all." Choch gave Cole a toothy, apologetic smile. "Please don't take that the wrong way."

"Is there another way to take it?"

"You see, here it is, and I'm just going to put it out there." Choch picked up a large branch that had fallen from a nearby tree. By now they were walking along the outskirts of Wounded Sky. Choch used the branch as a walking stick. "I gave you certain skills, yes? We can agree on that."

"Yes, I've noticed."

"Great. Now, the thing is, you've got to learn to bring them out. Breaking a doorknob, for example, is just the tip of the iceberg."

"So what, I can break bigger things?"

"You'll learn a whole mess of useful things you can do, boy."

"But you can't help me?" Cole said.

"But I can't help you," Choch said with mock frustration. He even gave himself a harmless little knock on the forehead with the tip of the walking stick.

"Of course," Cole said.

Choch stopped, and put his hand dramatically on Cole's shoulder. "But, if I *were* to help you, I might tell you that while you can throw little sticks for little ol' me to catch, the truth of the matter is, you can throw *really* big sticks." Choch handed Cole the branch he'd been using as a walking stick, winked at him, and walked away.

"Big sticks?" Cole said to himself, holding the branch in his hand.

He rotated the wood in his hand, studying it carefully in the subtle light. Then, he looked to the forest, then over the trees, then towards the sky. He held the branch up like a javelin, ran with it, and threw it as hard as he could with a loud, "UNNNNNGGGH!!!!" To his surprise, the branch flew over the trees, and climbed, climbed, climbed for what felt an eternity before it dipped out of sight. Cole stared for a long time at the path it had taken. Finally, he looked down at his hands, as though they were new to him. But they weren't. They were still the hands he'd always had, complete with the scars on the palms from the night of the fire, when the hot metal handles on the school's front door burned his skin.

Throwing the stick as far as he had didn't add to the list he already made, either. If he could throw a branch that far, however, he did wonder what else he could do. Testing those abilities was for another time. Tonight, it was time for some much-needed rest.

Cole was sitting on a lawn chair in front of an unlit firepit, pretending that it was lit, that he could even remember how to build a fire, that he could just sit there in front of a fire and not think of death, not hear screams. He was staring into it, lost in thought, when Elder Mariah sat down beside him, a shawl draped over her shoulders.

"Cold?" she asked.

"Nah," he said.

"You know, firepits are good for fires, if you are cold."

"It's okay, really."

"I see. Well, I was going to bring you out some tea, but I didn't want to be the Elder who always brought tea."

Cole chuckled. "You do make good tea."

As he sat beside Elder Mariah and continued his staring contest with the black-and-white remnants of wood, the ashes, Cole wondered whether he should add "impervious to Wounded Sky's particular brand of chilliness" to his list of skills. That would be very helpful in the winter, if he were to stay that long. All these skills, and no answers. How helpful were they, then?

"Elder, what do you know about Coyote?"

"Coyote?" Elder Mariah settled into her chair, like she was going to get *into* this. Like it was her wheelhouse. "Why do you ask?"

"Just curious, I guess," Cole said. "It's been in my—"

"Good evening." Cole looked to find Choch walking up to them. "Speaking of wheelhouses, Coyote is my very favourite subject." Choch sat down across from Cole, beside Elder Mariah. He rubbed his hands together in front of the nonexistent fire. Cole rolled his eyes, rubbed his hand against his face like he wanted to pull his skin right off.

"Choch, I didn't know you were interested in Coyote," Elder Mariah said.

"Oh, dear Elder, you have no idea." He patted her knee gamely, turned and winked at Cole, then back to the Elder. "Do you mind?"

"Please," Elder Mariah said.

"Super." Choch stood up. He rolled up his sleeves. "Now, Cole, you were wondering about the *mythological* being known as *Coyote*, which is interesting to me because Coyote isn't really a thing for us Crees. We're more of a Wisakedjak kind of people…

(Here's a fact for you, dear ones: while I have referred to my old friend as Wisakedjak here, the truth is you can spell his name a bajillion different ways. If we had time, we could get into why, but for now, two words: oral culture. I do think it's appropriate, though, him being a shape-shifter and all. Okay, let's jump back in.)

"…but regardless, what we're really talking about here are tricksters. Now, Coyote is more of a Salish Legend thing, and he's kind of boastful, and super, super, super funny. Like, so incredibly funny. And while he can be slightly difficult from time to time, he is actually helpful to humans. For example, he's named a bunch of animals, created mankind out of mud, and so on and so forth. Now, some legends make him out to be foolish, and sure, he's impersonated Creator once or twice, but who hasn't done something they aren't proud of, am I right? The point is, Cole, he's a pretty awesome dude. Anything to add, dear Elder?"

"Well, Cole, there are many legends about—"

(Okay, while Elder Mariah is talking, let me just fill in some blanks for you. As you may have guessed by now, I'm a guy, and while I can maintain some coyote features—you know, keeping your fur in the winter is absolutely divine—I typically prefer being all the way human, when I decide to be human. Of course, I can decide to be anything I want. Like a raven, for example. But you can only eat so many rodents and shit on so many cars before the allure of flying wears off. Likes and dislikes? Like tricking, naturally. Dislike that stories about me often depict my

death. Very hurtful. At any rate, I see that Elder Mariah is wrapping up, so let's carry on, shall we?)

"Sorry, you two, lovely chatting, but I really must be off." Choch walked away without another word, just tipped his hat at the Elder. Elder Mariah nodded politely back at Choch. When they were alone again, Elder Mariah asked if both of their responses about Coyote had been helpful.

"Yours was," Cole said.

"Oh, Choch has his moments too," Elder Mariah said. "There was a time when he was just a troublesome young man. Learning about our stories, our traditions, has really grounded him."

Cole didn't point out that Elder Mariah had just herself seemed surprised that Choch knew about Coyote stories. *Obi-Wan Coyote strikes again,* Cole thought.

"People change," Elder Mariah continued. "Don't you think a lot has changed since you were last here?"

"I don't think much has changed, actually," Cole said.

"How's that?"

"I mean, everything's older. That's different, I guess. The paint's peeling on buildings, there are more broken windows, more sagging rooftops. *People* are older…"

"But?"

"But everything else, I don't know, feels frozen in time."

"That's just small-town life. Time feels like it moves slower out here. There isn't the rush."

Cole picked up a small rock from the ground and tossed it into the firepit. He watched it sit there on a sideways piece of wood. He imagined flames engulfing it, giving it heat. He pictured the sweats Elder Mariah used to hold with the kids. She never used too many grand-fathers *(Dear readers. Choch here again with a quick explanation. When the narrator refers to "grandfathers" in the context of sweats, said narrator is referring to rocks.)* because they were just kids, but they heated the same way. She'd toss them into the fire with a pitchfork, and leave them there until they were white hot.

"I guess when I left, there was so much pain and regret," Cole said. "Now that I'm back, it doesn't seem like any of that has gone away."

"There's been time in between that you've missed though, Cole."

"I always felt like I brought all of it on to the community. All of the pain, all of the regret. Then and now. I didn't know that people felt that way too. I guess *that's* new, out of everything that isn't. It's this secret that was kept from me."

"They don't feel that way," she said. "So many don't feel that way. It's just, sometimes the loudest voices are the ones we choose to hear."

"So why don't people who think differently shout louder for me?"

"Maybe they should."

"I think if I'd have stayed in Winnipeg, Ashley would still be here." Cole sat up. "Maybe I brought this sickness here too."

"Nonsense."

"People are saying that, and who's to say they aren't right?"

The Elder leaned closer to Cole. She smiled, breathed deeply. She pointed up. Above them were the northern lights.

"Do you know why they call this place Wounded Sky, Cole?"

"No. I was never told that."

"A long time ago, an Elder named this place," she said. "He looked up at the sky one night, on a night much like this one, cool and clear. A night that you'd never see in the city, isn't that right?"

"Yes," he agreed. "We never see the sky like this."

"And on that night, when the Elder was looking up, he thought the northern lights looked like scars, like ribbons of scars. Can you see that?"

"I guess so." He looked closer at them. They *were* like ribbons. Purple and green ribbons being held in the wind, moving rhythmically, like rising smoke.

"So, the Elder thought, long ago, before we were here, something must have happened. The sky was cut, and out of that wound came the heavens. Now, that wound had healed, you see, but that past was still there, in the scars that were left behind. It helped shape the beauty that we see now. Above and below."

"That's a legend." He shook his head. "It's nice, but—"

"All legends, Cole, come from some place of truth. Whether they're about Coyote, or a sky that was cut and bled the heavens like tears, or a boy that saved others. Look at your own scars."

Cole turned his hands over, opened them, palms facing the sky. The scars were there, moving from one hand to the other in subtle undulations. Pink. Fluid.

"Okay. Okay, I get it."

"You have brought something here, certainly," she said. "Just not what you think."

12

WHEREABOUTS

COLE STAGGERED OUT OF THE SCHOOL. Cast by the fire behind him, his long shadow spread out over the grass and stretched all the way to Eva's and Brady's bodies. Cole's face was blackened with soot. His skin was singed a deep red from the heat. His clothing, what was left of it, was hanging off his body, torn and burnt. He didn't know why he'd gone back inside. There was no doubt, after what he'd seen, that there were no other survivors. But he went in, because what had happened to him was a miracle, so why couldn't there be other miracles? A child trapped under rubble, somehow shielded from the heat. A mother, somehow breathing, somehow alive, somehow spared so she could raise the only son she had, and not let him grow up alone.

Eva and Brady weren't moving. Brady must've passed out after escaping the gym. Cole walked slowly towards his friends. He'd ripped his shoes off somewhere inside the school. The rubber soles had been melting, burning him. He could feel the cool grass against the bottom of his feet. He slid his feet across the grass, step by step, until he reached Brady. Cole knelt down beside him and placed his hand, palm up, near Brady's nose. He kept it there until he felt Brady's warm breath. He looked over at Eva's body, imagined feeling her breath against his hand as well, then got up and went to her. There was some hair over the side of her face. He brushed it aside, behind her ear. With the same hand, he moved it over her mouth, and waited. There it was—her breath— and he let a breath out in unison.

"You're okay," he whispered to her.

Cole reached into his pocket. He pulled out the sweetgrass ring he'd braided for her by Silk River. He lifted her hand, held it for a second, and then he slipped the ring onto her finger. He could hear shouting in the distance, footsteps approaching through the darkness, towards the autumn-coloured light, towards the heat, towards the hell. Footsteps, like an approaching storm. There was nothing more he could do. He took one last look at it all, at the school, at the flames engulfing it, Brady and, finally, Eva. He ran into the darkness, through the field, into Blackwood Forest. He went as far as he could before he collapsed.

Cole opened his eyes. He found himself back in Brady's living room, on the couch. The dream had been so vivid that he expected to open his eyes and find himself in Blackwood Forest, still seven years old, still ten years of regret to come. He expected to wake up, his side sore from a tree root, and run home to his house. He could still feel the hope that he would find his mother sleeping in her bed. But just like ten years ago, when he found her perfectly made bed empty, reality set in quickly.

A familiar group of people were sitting around the kitchen table. Brady was picking at a plate of scrambled eggs and toast, scraping his fork against the porcelain. Eva was working her way through breakfast, too, and sipping a cup of coffee. Michael was close by her side. He had his own plate of food. Away from the kitchen table, looking over the youths and ready to help in any way she could—with a prayer, with breakfast, with the provision of a hot drink—stood Elder Mariah.

"Good morning," she said.

Cole sat up. He rubbed his eyes, and tried to fix what he knew was an unfixable head of matted hair.

"Morning," he said.

Brady, Eva, and Michael nodded their own salutations. Cole scanned their faces, one by one, and felt instantly guilty that he'd slept as long and as deep as he had. They were exhausted. Cole knew that they'd been at the clinic, probably all night. His eyes were on Eva more than anybody else and, in particular, the necklace and the sweetgrass ring affixed to it. When she noticed, she covered it with her hand and looked away from him. He looked away too.

"Hungry?" Elder Mariah asked.

"Yeah." Cole got up from the couch and went over to the kitchen table. He sat in the only empty chair, between Eva and Brady. Elder Mariah slipped a plate of eggs and toast, still hot, in front of Cole as soon as he sat down. The food tasted magical. Cole was hungrier than he had allowed himself to admit. He shovelled into the food with an unabashed lack of restraint. Between forkfuls, he saw all eyes on him.

"I don't remember the last time I ate," he said defensively.

"Hey, no judgement." Brady himself was almost done his breakfast, although it was unclear how long he'd been working on it. Presumably, though, it had been for more than a minute.

"What happened at the clinic?" Cole asked with a mouthful of eggs, hoping to deflect attention.

It took a long time before Elder Mariah said, "We lost more people."

"Three more," Michael said. "Six total now."

"It's just ripping through us," Eva said.

"I don't even know what good we're doing," Brady said. "It's like an umbrella against a hurricane."

"Sometimes it's just being there near the end for people, so they know they aren't alone," Elder Mariah said. "Sometimes that's all you can do. Sometimes that's enough."

"You went back last night?" Cole asked Elder Mariah.

She just nodded, her eyes closed, like she wanted to keep them closed and sleep, but wouldn't, or couldn't.

"I should've been there," Cole said. "I shouldn't have left like that. Everybody already thinks I'm some kind of coward."

"Nobody blames you, Cole. Talk about umbrellas and hurricanes, that crowd was nuts," Michael said.

"I would've left too," Brady added.

Cole swallowed a bite of food. He put his fork down and shoved the plate away in a symbolic gesture. He really had lost his appetite, but there was almost nothing left on his plate that he could refuse to eat anyway. A bit of yolk-stained toast. A bite of bacon. He grabbed a napkin from the middle of the table. *A Christmas napkin, in autumn.*

He dabbed at his mouth. "Anyway, thanks guys, for sticking up for me last night."

"Where'd you go when you left, anyway?" Eva asked.

"Just walked around," Cole said, which was partially true.

On any other day, Cole wouldn't have thought it was a big deal that he met up with Alex or walked her home because it was dark out. On any other day, he would've thought walking a girl home would score points with the community, even with his friends at the table. But not today. Not after he just finally talked to Michael about his relationship with Eva, not after they just mended fences together. Then, what? "Sorry Mike, but I kissed your sister." It was just on the cheek, and *she'd* kissed *him*, but still…his walk with Alex would have to be between him and Alex, for now. It would have to wait for a time when Michael, along with everybody else, wasn't completely exhausted.

"I thought you might've gone back to the campsite," Eva said.

Cole looked around like, *whoa, that's a secret*, but nobody seemed surprised.

"We told them," Brady said. "Obviously."

"That's nuts, you guys," Michael said. "There was a killer chasing you."

"It was reckless, that's what it was," Elder Mariah said. "We don't need more dead children in this community."

"What else were we going to do, Elder? Ashley was our friend," Eva said.

"I was going to go back, but…" Cole trailed off. He didn't want to lie. *Stick to partial truths*, he thought. Eva and Brady's built-in Cole lie detectors didn't seem to pick up on those. "I was just mentally not there."

"A whole town shouting at you will do that," Michael said.

"My dad checked it out last night, Cole," Eva said.

"Really? What happened?" Cole asked.

"Nothing," Brady said. "She had to beg him to go, and when he did—"

"All he saw was the tent. When he came back he was all like, 'Eva, honey, this could be anybody, just camping out.' Said he couldn't do anything about it."

"Crap," Cole said. "We'll have to go back."

"You're not going anywhere near that place if you think that's where Ashley's killer is," Elder Mariah said.

"It *could* be," Brady said.

"I'll come too," Michael said. "Four is better than three."

Elder Mariah made a disapproving *tsk* sound. "Kids…"

"Elder, we have to find out what happened, and why."

Elder Mariah just stood there. She didn't look happy, but also looked like she knew there was no way to stop them, that maybe she shouldn't try.

Cole stood up. "Right now?"

"No time like the present." Eva stood up.

"Let's do this." Michael stood up fast, looking eager to come along this time around.

"But if we see *anything*…" Brady pushed himself up into a standing position.

"We'll call Mr. Kirkness," "We'll call my dad," Cole and Eva said at the same time.

The youths opened the front door with authority, but when they encountered Wayne on the other side, about to knock, there was a cartoon-style pileup.

"Dad, what're you doing here?" Eva asked, still hanging onto Michael's arm, getting her balance. Wayne hadn't budged, even though he'd very nearly been knocked over. He was standing on the porch, hat in hand, hardly managing to make eye contact with any of them. He was pushing his fingers against the brim of his hat. Cole could see the whites in his fingernails.

"What's wrong?" Eva asked.

"Hey, hon, it's okay," he said to Eva.

"It's clearly not," Eva said.

"Who's dead now?" Cole asked, before he could think about the words. What else could it be, though—a cop coming up to a front door looking like that, hat in hand?

"Mike, can I talk to you outside please?" Wayne asked.

"What's going on?" Michael asked. "Is somebody *really...*"

"Dad?"

"Cole's not right, is he?" Brady asked.

"Just..." Wayne almost snapped. He held out his hand to stop them. Stop them from talking. Stop time from moving forward. Stop all this from happening. He gave up trying to find the right words. "Please. Mike."

"O-okay, Mr. Kirkness."

Wayne stepped to the side and motioned for Michael to walk past him. Michael did. Eva put her hand on his shoulder as he left. Wayne closed the door. Cole, Brady, and Eva watched as Wayne and Michael stopped in the front yard. Wayne had his arm around Michael's shoulders the whole way. Cole could see their breath in the cool autumn morning. Wayne put his hands on his hips.

"What the hell's going on?" Eva whispered.

"No idea," Brady said.

"It's Dr. Captain. It has to be. She's sick or something," Cole said.

"She's been around all those people, ever since Chief Crate got sick," Eva agreed.

"Holy moly," Brady said. "If she gets sick, who's going to take care of people?"

Michael keeled over. He puked Elder Mariah's breakfast onto the ground between his and Wayne's feet. Michael's hands were clutching his knees as tight as they could, like if he let go he would fall into oblivion. Wayne tried to put a hand on Michael's back, but Michael shouted, "NO!" loud enough that the closed door didn't cushion any of the sound. He pushed Wayne back. "Okay, okay," Wayne appeared to say, both hands up, walking slowly back towards Michael.

"What happened!?" Michael shouted, running his hands through his hair, clutching his hair, pulling at it. He bent over again. He stood back up.

Wayne was saying something to him too quiet for the rest of them to hear, and then Michael broke into a full sprint. Wayne chased after him for a few steps, then slowed down and watched Michael run away.

Eva opened the door and all three of them, along with Elder Mariah, walked outside onto the porch. They waited until Wayne turned around.

"What's going on, Dad?" Eva asked.

Wayne was pale and exhausted. He breathed deeply, took his hat off again, and hit it with his free hand. "Alex is dead."

There was a moment that stretched on forever where nobody said anything. The world just stopped.

"No," Eva breathed.

Cole watched as her eyes darted back and forth in confusion, trying to make sense of it, to believe that it could really happen. To Alex. To Ashley. "Michael," she said, and took off running after him.

Wayne tried to catch her. "Eva, wait!"

She pushed through his arms. A flash went through Cole's mind: they were all together by the hill in the field behind the school. A line of older kids from Cole's grade stood on one side of the field, at the foot of the mountain. About fifty yards away, stood another line of the younger kids. Alex. Ashley. Michael. Hands linked together. Ashley was running at them, and when he got to them, he burst through their arms. And then Cole was back, watching Eva run down the path and Wayne give up on stopping her.

"What the hell is going on here!?" Brady shouted, but he didn't wait around for an answer. He stormed into the house and slammed the front door behind him. Seconds after Wayne had broken the news, there was just him, Elder Mariah, and Cole.

Alex. Cole didn't know how to react. He'd just seen her last night, had walked her home to keep her safe, and now she was gone. What did that make him? He touched his cheek, as though the area which she had kissed was still wet from her lips, like it would mean a part of her was still alive.

"Cole, how are you doing over there?" Wayne asked.

"I…" Cole had been picturing Alex's face in the dark, in the doorway to her house, imagining her saying goodbye, thanking him. He wasn't sure what to read into Wayne's question, or if there was anything to read into at all. Was he ready to read hostility into anything anybody said? Should he have run off, shouted, cried, broke something? He felt responsible. But there he was, staring blankly at a face that wasn't there and never would be again.

"He's in shock, Wayne," Elder Mariah said. "Everybody deals with tragedy differently."

"Of course they do. I get that," Wayne said. "Sorry if that came across…"

"It's fine," Cole said.

"I think I ought to go to the clinic," Elder Mariah said, changing the subject. "Kate can't be expected to deal with this sickness right now. I assume she's been…"

Wayne nodded with pursed lips. "Yeah, she knows."

"How is she?" Elder Mariah asked.

"She's working. She's working harder than she was before. Wouldn't let me take her home."

"She can't be working right now," Elder Mariah said.

"If you can pull her away, good on you," Wayne said.

"I need to try at any rate, give her some time to grieve," Elder Mariah said, "at least give her help." She turned to Cole. "Why don't you go check on Brady, Cole. You both shouldn't be alone."

"Okay, yeah." At the same time, Cole and Elder Mariah walked in opposite directions.

"I'll walk you up, Cole," Wayne said, and followed after him.

They stopped at the door. Cole put his hand on the doorknob, imagined crushing it before turning it. Before he could pull it open, though, Wayne gently put his hand flat against the door.

"Is something wrong, Mr. Kirkness?" Cole asked.

"I notice things," Wayne said. "That's my job. It's not rocket science, in this case. I'm sure you've noticed things too."

"Everything's going to shit."

"Everything's going to shit," Wayne agreed. "And maybe it's bad luck, you know, that it all started when you got here. I honestly don't know."

There was a pause. It was the kind of pause that felt like it lasted a year. Wayne let a deep breath out through his nose.

"She got killed the same way as Ashley, Cole."

Cole's heart kicked into high gear. Was he under arrest? Should he ask that? That's what they did in the crime shows in situations exactly like this.

"What are you saying, Sir?" Cole grimaced to himself that he'd called Wayne "sir," reverting to how he'd addressed Wayne when he was a child and was in trouble.

"When Ashley was murdered, you were the last one to see him alive," Wayne said.

Does he know that I was with Alex last night? If he doesn't, should I tell him? That seemed, to Cole, a horrendous idea right now.

"There was also the guy that shot Ashley," Cole said. "He kind of saw Ashley last, too."

"Yeah, there's him, wherever he is," Wayne said.

"We literally showed you where he was camping," Cole said.

"There was nothing there, Cole. I wish I could say that there was," Wayne said.

"Well go back. I'll go back with you," Cole said.

"It was just a campsite," Wayne said.

"Did I act guilty? If you believe this guy exists or not?" Cole asked. "I saw you, and stayed, and told you what happened." Cole was trying to stay calm, but he was feeling around in his pocket for his pills because he wasn't succeeding.

"What about last night?" Wayne asked.

"What—what do you mean?"

"Everybody was at the clinic, or they were at home, trying to stay away from everybody else. What about yo··?" Before Cole could answer, Wayne added, "People said that you shouted at the crowd, then left. Where did you go?"

"I shouted at everybody, but *they* started it, Mr. Kirkness. First Mark and then everybody piled on. They were all looking at me, saying things to me. Calling me names. I was just defending myself."

"Okay, I understand that, Cole. All I want to do is understand a little more."

So do I, Cole thought. Wayne repeated his question. "Where'd you go when you left?"

Cole couldn't tell Wayne he was with Alex, not until he himself understood what it meant that he was with her before she was killed, just like he was with Ashley before he was killed. There had to be a connection. He was pressing the door knob, hard, and felt the metal begin to give way. He loosened his grip.

"I came here," Cole said. "I just walked here, that's all."

"Anybody home?" Wayne asked.

"No, not at first," Cole said. "But Elder Mariah was here pretty soon afterwards."

"How soon?"

"Like, thirty minutes? Forty?" Cole wasn't sure how long it had been, from when he'd left the clinic, walked by the cemetery, found Alex there, walked her home, and walked here himself. It seemed to be something of an honest estimate.

Wayne tapped thoughtfully on the door with his knuckles, in a kind of pattern, like there was a secret knock required for Cole to gain entry.

"Okay," he said. "Okay. That's it for now."

"Thanks, Mr. Kirkness."

Wayne turned away from the door. He walked down the steps to the yard, where he stopped. "Don't go anywhere, though, okay? I need to get this all sorted out."

"Don't worry. I'm not going anywhere."

"Take care, son," Wayne said on his way across the yard and back, Cole presumed, to Alex's house.

When he was gone, Cole took one of the pills. Two left. He checked the door handle to see if there was any cover-up needed there. He wasn't sure how hard he squeezed it. It seemed fine, so he went inside, across the living room, past the kitchen, and down the hallway towards Brady's door.

He knocked on it lightly.

"Yeah," Brady said through the door.

"Hey, can I come in?"

"It's open."

Cole found Brady sitting at the edge of his bed, looking at a photograph. He sat down on the bed beside Brady. It was a school photograph from when they were kids of the entire student body. Cole recognized the field, right out front of the school. It was an aerial shot. All the kids who went to Wounded Sky Elementary ten years ago were looking up, waving.

"Can I see it?" Cole asked.

"Sure." Brady handed the picture to Cole.

Cole looked at it for a long time.

"Somebody climbed up to the roof to take this," Cole said. "That's so funny, right?"

"I'm surprised they didn't find our secret stash," Brady said.

Their secret stash was a backpack filled with comic books, some granola bars, juice boxes, a blanket and two flashlights. Back then, they would sneak up to the roof at night by scaling up the downspout at the side of the school. Brady and Cole would read comics with their flashlights, sitting on the blanket to protect their butts from the rough surface. Sometimes, if they stayed late enough, they'd watch the northern lights. Cole remembered how nervous he was the night of the fire that their backpack would be found. They'd been there for the Northern Lights Sleepover, something grade-three students did at the beginning of every year. They all went to the roof with their sleeping bags and watched the aurora borealis.

The backpack went up in flames with the rest of the school.

"Yeah," Cole said. "I haven't thought about that until now. I remember one of the comics was…"

"*Cosmic Odyssey* and *The Killing Joke*," Brady said.

"And *Elf Quest*."

"Right. *Elf Quest.*"

Cole handed the photograph back to Brady.

"They'd do that with a drone now, a picture up high like that. Weird, eh?" Brady said.

"Some things have changed, I guess," Cole said.

Cole looked around Brady's room. Some things hadn't changed: a stack of comic books by his dresser, some that he and Brady once read together; a *Thundercats* t-shirt sticking out from one of the dresser drawers; a *Star Wars* poster on the wall, right beside a *Batman Begins* poster. Finally, his eyes fell back on the picture. Brady was running his thumb over Alex's face, over Ashley's.

"Half these faces..." Brady started, but couldn't say another word.

Cole put his arm around Brady. Suddenly, as though summoned there by hurt, Jayne was standing in front of them, staring at Brady. Cole mouthed to her that it was okay, and he wanted to make it true. He wanted to tell Brady the kids that were gone were still here, Jayne played with them, that they were gone, but not really.

"I know," was what Cole ended up saying. "They're gone."

"They never found out how the fire started," Brady said. "We deserve at least that, don't we? To know that? To know who killed Ashley and Alex?"

"Yeah, we do."

And it was like those were the only three words Cole had left. He felt like time was running out.

13

THE REASONS

IN THE EARLY AFTERNOON, COLE APPROACHED the Northern Lights Diner. He had some questions for Choch. The sign on the front door was flipped to Closed. It made sense. Other places of business had closed down already, trying to prevent the spread of the flu—the X, the community hall, the mail office, the laundromat. Pretty soon everybody was going to be walking around in dirty clothes. But there was something more to this closure. Not just preventing sickness, but honouring a girl that Cole had really just met. When they were younger, Alex was his friend's annoying little sister. He never paid much attention to her, other than to shoo her away like she was a fly. Now, he just wanted one more walk with her. Like she said: *stay another minute.* Cole pushed at the door, just because, and he was surprised to find that the bell chimed as it opened. He walked inside and instinctively made his way to the same table he had frequented with his friends.

Choch appeared from the back, made a weird gesture—a weird face, for that matter.

"What?" Cole asked.

Choch had one flat hand raised into the air as though he were about to give somebody a high-five. He pointed at his palm over and over again, expectantly. Along with that motion, he was ridiculously scrunching his lips to the right. In fact, his whole face was scrunching to the right. Cole looked at him oddly for more than a few seconds before realizing that Choch was directing Cole's eyes to the back of the diner. Cole looked in that direction to see Eva, the only other person who was in the diner, hidden away from the sight of anyone coming inside. As Cole looked at her—sitting by herself, a cup of coffee in front of her, the sweetgrass ring suspended from her neck and dangling over the black liquid—the questions that he prepared for Choch could wait.

"We open for special customers," Choch said.

He brushed past Choch and walked over to Eva's table.

"Hey," he said to her.

She looked up, forcing a smile. Her eyes were red and puffy from crying all morning. She leaned her cheek against her fist and closed her eyes for a second, like it was okay to fall asleep now.

"Can I sit?" he asked.

She nodded. He sat down across from her.

"What are you doing here?" she asked.

"Same as you, I guess."

Eva turned around, looked towards the counter, beyond it, into the kitchen. "I keep thinking she'll come out, wipe the counter down, something."

"Yeah." They both looked that way for a while, as if they were waiting for Alex to do just that, but they eventually looked away, anywhere around the table but at each other.

"Where's Michael?" Cole eventually asked.

"Sleeping," she said. "How's B?"

"Sleeping too."

"All the energy," she said, "all the life…it's just being sucked right the hell out of here, you know?"

"I know."

"And then what'll be left?"

"Us," he said before he had a chance to think about it, caught up in the fact that she wore his ring as a necklace. Before he could tell her that he'd meant all of them—her, Brady, him, and Michael—she said, "There is no *us*, Cole."

"Yeah, I meant all of us. The group. That's all." He felt like it was too late.

"Tea?" Choch was standing there with a cup of chamomile tea, extending it towards Cole, a pot of coffee in his other hand. For once, Cole was thankful for the interruption. He felt it would allow him to reboot the conversation, as it were.

"Sure, thanks." Cole took the cup of tea. Choch touched his nose and winked.

"Warm you up?" Choch said to Eva. She pushed her cup towards Choch. "Why not?" He filled it to the brim, and then took his leave.

Eva stared into the black coffee like there was something to see in it. Cole squeezed chamomile juice out of his tea bag. He had a chance now to change the subject, but like a stupid teenage boy sitting across from an amazing teenage girl, he went right back there. "Why did you keep the ring?"

He wasn't sure why he asked her. Was it better to think of this than all of the bad things that were happening? Or did he really want to know what it meant, why she'd kept it for so long?

"Cole, I..." Instead of finishing her sentence, she found the ring with her index finger and thumb. "It's not important. Not right now."

"You're right. That was a stupid question."

He took a sip of his tea, then placed the cup down as softly as he could. Eva began to slide her coffee cup from one hand to the other as she dealt with the silence in her own way. He kept expecting her to get up and leave, but something must have kept her here, just like something must have kept her from throwing away the ring. He wondered if she wore it ever since he left. He wondered what she had thought ten years ago when she woke up to find it on her finger. She caught the coffee cup in one hand, and looked up at Cole.

"It's not what you think, or what you thought. Why I still have it, I mean. If you're thinking that there's something—"

"I don't think that." He thought that.

"It reminds me to be strong, like it should, like medicine should. Strong in my mind, my body, my spirit."

"So, it doesn't remind you of a kid you kissed in your bedroom. Got it. You're more in the *hair-from-Mother-Earth* zone."

"That's not fair, Cole."

"I'm sorry, I…" Cole looked out the window. He wished that he could rewind the whole conversation, that he would've just taken the chance to change the subject when he had it, that Choch would come and interrupt them again. Wasn't there another special Choch could dream up?

Eva sighed deeply. "I remember when I found it. I woke up in the field. Dr. Captain was kneeling beside me. She was saying things, but I couldn't hear her. Anyway, I felt it on my finger, lifted my hand, managed to lift my head up…my head was pounding so bad…and I knew you'd given it to me. I didn't know what you'd done…but I knew you'd given it to me."

"We were going to get married." Cole laughed.

They'd been in the gym together, sitting in the corner on the blue mats, stacked up high. They'd climbed up there together, pretending that they were already on the roof and that the gym lighting was the northern lights. "I think we're going to get married one day, Eve," he told her. She looked at him, and her face was red. It probably wasn't as red as his, but still, it was red. She punched him in the arm and said, "Yeah, then what're you waiting for, stupid?" Cole jumped off the mats, all the way from the top, and minutes later he was standing by himself at Silk River, rummaging through the blades of sweetgrass, looking for the perfect one.

"You saved me," she said presently, and leaned forward. She took his hand away from his cup of tea, and kept her hand on his for a moment. "I know that." She squeezed his hand, then let go of it. "But I've been doing okay without you."

"I know you have. Ashley, he used to tell me what was happening out here with everybody, with you. Never mentioned Michael, but…"

"The thing is, Cole. The thing is that the boy who gave me this ring, I knew him so well. I knew him better than anything or anyone."

"I'm still me."

"But that's just it: you aren't. You came back different. You *left* different. But I am too. That fire, it made us all different. And I don't know you anymore, and you don't know me, and that's just the way it is."

"Sometimes I wish that my auntie and my grandma hadn't taken me away. I wonder what things would be like now. Like, even though it wasn't my choice, I still feel guilty."

"I do too," she said. "I feel guilty and special at the same time, that I'm alive. And I shouldn't feel that way either. You know, when people are looking at you, saying things to you…"

"What?"

"Just remember that they've said the same things to me," she said. "They've asked me why I got saved, why their friend didn't, why their kid didn't. And what do I say to them? I've never known what to say but sorry, Cole."

Cole looked away from Eva, out the window, at the ghost town that was Wounded Sky First Nation. "Tell them that some kid you used to know loved you that much."

"Cole," she said. "We didn't know what love was back then." She stood up from the booth. "I should get back to Michael."

"Yeah." Cole stood up too. "Me too. To Brady, I mean. He might be up now."

Eva turned to walk away, then stopped and turned back before leaving. "There's a memorial, I guess, tonight. A memorial *before* the memorial tomorrow. Just for us. The kids, I mean. For Ashley and Alex."

"There's too many of those."

"There are a lot of people to remember. Anyway, you should come, if you can."

"Yeah, okay, I'll come."

After Eva left, Choch was instantly at Cole's side, and they both watched through the window as she walked along the path towards Michael's place.

"Girl trouble?"

Cole shook his head. "No, no trouble."

"I get it, she's cute," Choch said, "and smart and…well…she's just one of my favourite people around these parts. Besides you, of course. You're my special little guy."

"Yeah, well…" Cole began, and his silence said everything without saying anything. Choch knew, though, and Cole knew that.

"And," Choch said, "there are those pesky little deaths happening around here."

"I know that. I haven't forgotten that."

"And yet…" Choch gave Cole a nudge with his elbow, and they both started on their way to the door. "Your mind's full of a *girl. Two* girls."

"That's different, with Alex. And it isn't. My mind. My mind is fine." But Cole knew it was of no use, that no matter how many times he told Choch to get out of his head, he would always be there. *(That's actually true, you know. Part of the job. I'm the boss, need the info.)*

"Not to belabour a point, young one, but you did kind of, sort of, forget the reason why you came here in the first place."

Cole was standing at the door, holding it open, one foot in and one foot out. "You never even told me the reason, asshole." He let the door shut in Choch's face.

Brady was in the kitchen when Cole got back to his place. His hair, usually perfectly braided, was free and dishevelled from the nap. Strands had gone rogue and were stuck up like he'd put his finger in an electrical socket. Brady's Iskwé t-shirt was creased and his cargo pants were wrinkled. His face was a mix of exhaustion and sorrow. Sometimes, Cole thought, the two emotions felt the same. Brady was pouring hot water into a cup, and a waft of earthy aromas instantly filled the house. Brady saw Cole and got another cup out of the cupboard. He filled that one up, too. They both sat down at the kitchen table with their cups. Cole sipped his, and thought it tasted a lot like Elder Mariah's. Brady learned everything from his grandmother.

"It's good." Cole nodded his approval.

"I told Nókom that one day my tea's going to taste better than hers."

"I doubt she'd mind that. I bet she wants that."

Brady looked across the room, distantly, at something that was beyond the walls of the home. "I should be at the clinic with her. She's probably not taking any breaks."

"You're also seventeen," Cole pointed out. "And you've been through a lot."

"And she's an Elder," Brady shot back.

"Touché."

"Sorry, I didn't mean to snap. It's just, I feel helpless, is what it is."

"I think everybody does." Cole included himself in that statement. Him, the guy who was supposed to come save everybody, assuming, of course, that was the deal.

"They're supposed to bring in people to help at the clinic with the flu, but usually when we want help, by the time help actually comes, we don't need it anymore."

"We'll be okay." Cole tried to mean it. "Anyway," he continued, "you *should've* snapped at me. All I meant was, I don't want you to feel worse than you already do."

"Thanks, I appreciate that. But just because I didn't get called back here to do, I don't know, whatever it is *you're* supposed to be doing, doesn't mean I can't feel bad for not doing more."

"Fair enough." Cole took a moment to consider his friend, sitting across from him at the kitchen table. Sometimes, Brady seemed older than him. It was a shame that Brady wasn't given the responsibility that Cole had been given, because Cole was sure that Brady would've handled it better. Brady held knowledge, and he sought it out. He was destined to be an Elder. And right now Brady looked even older, with how the nap had messed up his clothes and hair. Cole wished he could tell Brady everything. "How are you holding up, anyway?"

"Holding up isn't the right way to put it, I don't think." Brady thoughtfully sipped his tea. He tried to flatten some of the stray hairs on his head. "Holding on. That's what I'm doing."

"Maybe that's all anybody can do right now, eh?"

"It helps having friends around. We can kind of hold on together."

"Absolutely." Cole figured now was as good a time as any to bring up the prememorial memorial Eva said was happening tonight. He wasn't sure if Brady would agree to go, but it would sure make going easier. "Speaking of which, did you hear about the…"

"Yeah, I heard about it." Brady took out his phone to display to Cole just how he had, in fact, heard about it. "The Wounded Sky teens have a group text. Everybody's talking about it."

"So…" Cole started, but Brady kept ruminating about it.

"I think most kids just want to go to drink it all away. I don't think it's really about Ashley and Alex. People just want to let loose since it feels like the world's ending."

"Sometimes people need to do that, though. I don't blame 'em. I know that whenever I was feeling mad about everything that had happened back here, I'd, like, dunk a basketball a million times just to blow off steam."

"You can dunk?" Brady looked him over: thin, not impressively tall Cole Harper.

"Hops," was all Cole said.

Brady just shrugged. "Well, that's a little more productive, Cole, than getting hammered."

"Still, we should go," Cole said. "I mean, for us, it would be for the right reasons. For Alex and Ashley." And also, Cole thought, so he could finally make his way back to the campsite and do a more thorough check than what Wayne must've done. That is, providing the murderer wasn't there to chase him off again. Even then, his super strength was meant for *something*.

"We can't go," Brady said.

"What? Why not?"

"I'll keep doing my own grieving for Ashley, and for Alex," Brady said, "but the fact is, Reynold and Wayne have lowered the curfew on the community to 8 p.m.. Nobody's to go out, unless they're going to the clinic to help out there. It's like a damn revolving door over there, Nókom says. More come in, more get sick, more die."

"And what happens if we get caught then? What could happen that's any worse than what's happening now, Brady? They going to ground us or something?"

"I just don't want to go, okay?"

"Look," Cole decided to try a different angle and included Brady in his plans to check out the camp again. "I just thought that if we went to the quarry, it's pretty near that camp, and we could—"

"Wayne's already checked out the camp, like we wanted him to." Brady was having none of it. "It can't have been anything. It was a coincidence, and we need to get over it."

"I don't buy that, and I don't think you do either," Cole said. "Mr. Kirkness, he just went back at the wrong time, man. We need to make sure. What else do we have?"

Brady took a long, slow sip of his tea, and when he placed it down on the table, he took another long, slow breath. He looked at Cole—this time really looked at him. "Okay, I'll think about it."

"That's all I ask."

Brady took his tea over to the sink, and Cole followed him. They placed their empty cups in it and stood there together, looking out the window, where they could see a small section of Wounded Sky and the path that led all the way to the clinic.

"The one good thing about Nókom being away, at the clinic, if there's anything good at all, is that she won't be around tonight when the curfew hits. *If* I decide to go," Brady said.

"Why's that?" Cole asked.

"Because I've tried to sneak out of the house before, late, *without* a curfew. To see Ashley, in whatever weird little nook and cranny he wanted to meet at. She can *see* anything and *hear* anything. She says she has three ears. It's almost impossible to get away."

"Well, if she does," Cole said, "just know that, apart from crime shows, I've watched *Mission: Impossible*, like, fifty times. All we'd need is rubber masks, suspension cables, and blue and pink exploding gum."

14

THE QUARRY

UNSURPRISINGLY, ELDER MARIAH WASN'T HOME by curfew, and Brady and Cole left for the quarry unimpeded. And even though they both agreed that there wasn't much Reynold and Wayne could, or would, do to enforce the curfew ("They've got better things to do," Brady had said), they still took the path through Blackwood Forest. There wouldn't be any adults there to catch them, and it was a shortcut. The woods were quiet. Cole's compulsive pill-bottle touching became more obvious, despite the fact that there were only two pills making a shy, rattling sound.

"What's in your pocket?" Brady tapped the outside of Cole's hand.

"Huh?" Cole tried coolly to move his hand away, shoving it deeper in his pocket.

"You keep touching your pant pocket, like, all the time," Brady said.

"Oh." Cole skipped the ruminations (*Thank God, one can only take so much ruminating, am I right?*) about whether to tell Brady or not, and pulled out the medication. He handed it to Brady.

Brady held it up and tried to read the label. "You're running low, my friend."

"Yeah. Kind of left home in a hurry."

"What is this? Anxiety meds?"

"Good eye." Cole took the bottle back, returning it to his pocket.

"You okay?" Brady gave Cole a quick pat on the back.

"Kind of the product of seeing all your friends burned alive." Cole stared deep into Blackwood Forest as though he was staring at the flames right now.

"I never really considered that you saw all that. Maybe because I didn't *want* to consider it," Brady said.

"It still feels like yesterday," Cole said.

They kept walking. They made their way down the path that had been beaten by young feet making the same journey they were now on.

"My therapist says, since it's kind of out in the open now, she says that having anxiety is like having a cold. That you have to treat it with meds sometimes, like when you're sick," Cole said.

"Makes sense," Brady said.

"But I still feel weak. I feel like I should just be strong," Cole said.

"I mean," Brady said, "you did lift a wall."

"Pre anxiety," Cole pointed out.

"*And* crushed a doorknob," Brady said.

"You saw that?"

"I saw that."

In a way, Cole felt relieved. *One less secret to keep from Brady.* There was no point in keeping anything from him. He was going to figure it out eventually. But (*before Choch interrupts again…*) that didn't mean Cole was actually going to tell Brady about the spirit being. It all just seemed inevitable and, Cole thought, if Brady figured it out on his own, then there would be no rules broken. "You weren't supposed to see that."

"Like you said, I've got a good eye," Brady said.

"Anyway," Cole said, "as much as I hate taking the meds, it's funny because it does give me one good memory. Just taking pills, I guess. So, when I was a kid, every morning, my dad made me breakfast. Eggs, bacon, toast. Like, lard on the toast, straight-up. He made the best breakfasts ever. I think because *he* was making the breakfasts."

"Same. As shitty as my parents were…*are*…I still remember Mom's oatmeal. Brown sugar, milk, slivered almonds. Just the simplest thing, but it tasted so good."

"Right, so I remember that, the breakfast. But what I really remember is that he always gave me vitamins. Every morning. He had them lined up, right beside my orange juice. And he made me eat them all, one by one. I hated them, except the flavoured ones. The *Flintstones* ones. But when I didn't get them anymore, when he died, Mom never knew where they were, or that he was even giving them to me at all. I missed them. Even the gross ones."

"You missed your dad," Brady said. "Not the vitamins."

They could see light in the distance—an orange glow. With the trees in front of them beginning to thin out, it looked like picture frames around a sunset.

"It kills me that I never knew what happened to him over there at the research facility, just that they closed it. That's it. Locked him and that woman in there forever," Cole said. "Mom never gave me details. Nothing. Maybe she never knew anything anyway. And it's right there when I got here, still just like it was. It feels like it's taunting me or something."

"It's like the fire, I think," Brady said. "It'll always be this cloud hanging over us all."

"I think we've got like a thunderstorm hanging over us, never mind."

"The thunderstorm to end all thunderstorms."

When Brady and Cole came out of Blackwood Forest close to the quarry, the gathering had already started. From what Ashley had told Cole, this seemed pretty much like a typical bush party (Ashley used to call them "shakers"). At either side of the gathering, there was the community and Blackwood Forest. In front of the kids there was a lake, if you could call it that. Kids skinny-dipped in it at the shakers, and people used it as a beach during the day—with clothes on. Across the water, maybe a hundred metres away, was a cliff. The cliff was about ten metres high. Very brave (or very stupid) kids had been known to climb the slope in Blackwood Forest and jump off. Ashley's text descriptions of the shakers were of a mountain of teenagers by the water, a huge bonfire, a bunch of booze, music blaring from speakers, the aforementioned skinny-dipping, dancing and, later in the night, kids making out. Tonight, everybody was fully clothed, and it was too early to tell if anybody was going to make out.

"I guess you were right about why kids were going to come tonight," Cole said.

"Yep. A bush party is a bush party."

Cole didn't see Eva or Michael, which was kind of annoying since Eva had told Cole to come. But then again, Michael had lost his sister. Maybe it was too much for him to be there and, well, like it or not, Eva was Michael's girlfriend. She was going to stay with him. She *should* stay with him.

Cole thought he saw a bunch of kids throwing around pieces of burning wood, out of the sheer dumbness of youth mixed with alcohol. But, as he got closer, he saw that it was Jayne dancing around the bonfire, and in and out of the crowd. Funny to see a ghost dancing to Kendrick Lamar. She only stopped when she saw Cole and came running over to him with her arms outstretched. Cole recoiled a bit, covering his torso with his arms. Just before she got to him she screeched sadly to a stop.

"Oh," she said. "Right."

He mouthed "sorry" to her and smiled. The smile was enough for her. She smiled back broadly, and went off to continue dancing. Cole liked to see her dance. He kept his eyes on her throughout the night, the little dancing flame, a special performance just for him.

Soon after he and Brady had arrived, Cole found himself sitting on a rock, out of the way, and a comfortable distance from the fire. Brady had been drawn away, and was having trouble making his way back over to Cole. Brady had become the subject of the teenagers' sympathy.

Both Cole and Brady were surprised to learn some people knew about Brady and Ashley. Brady was surprised, too, that those same kids respected them enough not to make a big deal out of it. They just left Brady and Ashley alone.

"I guess it shouldn't really be a surprise," Brady said when he was able to get close to Cole and shake off the crowd for a moment. "You can't really keep a secret in Wounded Sky."

Except for who caused school fires or lab accidents or killed teenagers, Cole thought. Instead, he nodded, agreeing with Brady.

"Are you okay?" Brady asked.

"Honestly, I kind of like the anonymity right now," Cole said.

"This might be the first time I'm jealous of you," Brady said.

"What, are you saying you'd rather not be a social pariah?" Cole said, dripping with sarcasm.

"No, but a hermit? Well then—"

And just like that, Brady was sucked back into the crowd. Cole returned to watching Jayne and, seeing this, she made a point of dancing around Cole in a circle every few minutes. She smiled at him, and tried to make him smile. Even though he didn't feel like it, he smiled back because he couldn't stand making her sad. She knew others couldn't see her, but she pretended like they could. She danced by them, too, smiled at them, and imagined that they smiled back.

Cole watched the reactions Jayne pretended to get out of people. A teenager laughed at just the same time Jayne danced around her. Jayne was overjoyed, believing the illusion that she had made somebody happy. A girl's long hair swayed slightly when Jayne fingers, moving in dance, came close. The powdery gravel on the ground, like sand, shifted under Jayne's feet. The odd stone or twig moved if she kicked at it with her steps. Cole swore he saw a beer bottle tip to the side when Jayne's dress, mid-twirl, whipped against the glass. Cole remembered when he'd first seen her: she'd kicked at a pebble, and it had skipped along the ground.

Could it be that while nobody can see her, Cole wondered, *she still has some connection with the physical world?*

Interrupting this thought, and quite unexpectedly, Maggie, sans Tristan, sat down in a huff beside Cole. She had a beer in her hand and took a long, angry swig from it before throwing it into the fire. She narrowly missed Tristan's head.

"Whoa, you guys fighting again?" He remembered the bickering he'd heard from them at The Fish, before Tristan had wanted to beat the shit out of Cole a second time.

"You could say that." Maggie reached down and grabbed another bottle by her feet.

"We're either fucking or fighting. It's goddamn true love," Maggie said.

"T-M-I, Maggie," Cole said.

"You kind of brought it up." Another swig, then she cocked the bottle back, ready to throw it. Cole reached across, grabbed her arm, and lowered it as gently as he could.

"What're you doing?" Maggie's words were slurring a bit. Cole kept his hand on hers until her grip loosened and the bottle dropped, then he let go.

"I think we've lost enough people for now, don't you?"

"Oh, he'd just have got concussed is all. He gets concussed like every other month." Maggie shook her head. "God, you're so dramatic."

She slumped down and rested her elbows on her knees. Maggie was older than Cole—*grade six, maybe?*—but still had been in the same school. Grade six was where all the cool people were. Well, to be fair, anybody a grade above was cool to the grade below. Now, two or three grades above? The coolest of the cool. That was Maggie. If Wounded Sky Elementary were a rom-com Hollywood movie, Maggie Green was the popular girl that everybody liked and looked up to and wanted to be around. Tristan had been the luckiest boy in the school because he was her boyfriend. Evidently, that relationship hadn't changed. Only, the girl sitting beside Cole on the rock, slumped over, dejected, wasn't the girl Cole remembered from high school.

"What happened?" Cole asked.

Maggie didn't answer at first, and Cole wasn't going anywhere, so he waited. To cheer Maggie up, Jayne danced around Cole and Maggie's rock. Jayne looked upset when Maggie didn't smile. Cole whispered, "It's okay," to her. Nobody heard him. Jayne stuck both of her thumbs in the air and continued on her way. She did look back at them from time to time, when Maggie raised her head, concerned at how sad she looked.

"Why do you care what happened?" Maggie asked Cole.

Cole shrugged. "Honestly, it's nice to just talk to somebody about something different. I mean, it's not nice you're upset, but…"

"You're going through shit," Maggie said.

"Yeah, but we kind of all are, aren't we?"

"Okay, fine. Here it is, if you really don't mind."

"I don't, for real."

"Alright, you asked for it." Maggie motioned over to Tristan. Her long-time boyfriend was sitting on a rock about twenty feet away from them. He was in front of the fire, and intentionally not looking around for her. In Cole's opinion, Tristan was stewing. "I've been with him for years. Probably since we were in grade four. I remember necking with him under the play structure at recess, when the school was still—" she stopped there for a moment, as though she'd said something taboo. Then she continued, skipping over any mention of the word *school* again "—anyway, or in the closet at the back of our class…do you remember those closets?"

"Yeah, we used to hide from the teacher in there. I never made out with anybody in there, though."

"Never?" Maggie asked.

"I was *seven*."

"Right, yeah. So, those closets…" she said distantly. She looked into the fire, looked at Cole. "He's all I've ever known, know what I mean? And same for him. It's all been me, Maggie all-the-way. Sometimes I think because of that, he thinks he kind of owns me, like I'm his property. I'm tired of him thinking that. And then we fight…" she sounded tired now, as though talking about it was as exhausting as going through the routine that she was describing. "Then he drinks, then he becomes a total asshat. Then we make up, and do it all over again."

"And you're tired of the making-up part of it?"

"Yeah, for sure I'm tired of that, but really I'm tired of all of it," Maggie said. "I think I'm just ready to move on."

"Change is good."

"I mean—" she seemed comfortable to rant about it all now. "Can you imagine being told to do something, when you didn't want to? To feel like you have no choice in the matter? And you think to yourself, 'Why am I even doing this? What's the damn point?' Can you imagine going through that crap?"

"No," Cole said. "Not at all. That would totally suck."

Jayne was dancing close to them. Noticing what she could do when he'd first arrived, and tonight, moving things as though she were physically real, gave Cole an idea.

"Speaking of which, I better get back. He's pretending not to look for me, but he's totally looking for me," Maggie said.

"Sure." Cole subtly tried to wave Jayne over while Maggie was still there. To Maggie, it must've looked like he was shooing away an insect or flecks of ash from the fire.

"You know, you're okay, city," Maggie said.

"Really?"

"Yeah, really." Maggie left, and Cole watched her shimmy through the crowd to stand with Tristan. She put her hand on his shoulder. Tristan turned around briefly, saw her, and nodded an acknowledgement that she was there. A bunch of beer bottles were placed behind him. Some empty, some half empty. Most kids were placing their drinks there when they were done with them. The collection was rather impressive, and the bottles all shone with their own brand of prettiness in the glow of the bonfire.

With Maggie gone, Cole could act as weird as he wanted. Nobody was watching him, anyway. He waved Jayne down more animatedly, even called her name over the noise of the teens and the music. "Jayney!" Finally, Jayne perked up and looked in his direction, then came running over to him.

"Hey, Coley! You're talkin' to me?"

"I'm talking to you," he said. "Listen, do you want to help me do a magic trick? It'll make people really happy."

"Magic!?" Jayne shouted, her flames growing brighter and higher.

"Magic!"

"*Do I!?*" Jayne jumped up and down.

"Okay, here's what we're going to do," he whispered, leaning in and reciting the whole plan quiet enough that only she could hear. When he was done, she had a mischievous smile on her face. She covered her mouth with both hands and snickered.

"Coley!" she said with mock disbelief. "No!"

"Yep. Do you think you can do it?" Cole asked.

She nodded vehemently.

"I don't know," he said. "I bet you *can't.*"

"I *so* can!" She turned away from him, sneaked up to where Maggie and Tristan were, again as though everybody could see and hear her. She looked back to Cole, hands over her mouth.

"Do it."

Jayne took a deep breath, and swatted her arm all the way across the discarded bottles. To Cole's surprise, her arm knocked against all the bottles and they tumbled off the rock, onto Tristan, like bowling pins. Beer and coolers spilled all over Tristan. Cole hadn't been sure if it would work. He'd half-expected her arm to go straight through the bottles, and that would be all. Tristan stood up. His head darted back and forth. Jayne was standing right beside him, of course, laughing and pointing at the dark splotches on Tristan's pants. The only person near Tristan was ·Maggie. He turned to her, and motioned to all the wetness like it wasn't painfully obvious.

"Mags, what the hell!?"

Maggie couldn't help but have a smile on her face. "That wasn't me."

Tristan looked and motioned around to show her that nobody else was near them. "You're so full of crap!"

Maggie's smile vanished. A defiant scowl replaced it. "It wasn't me! You know, Tristan, not everything is *my* fault. Like when *you* forget your phone on my dresser, or *you* forget your wallet on my bed, or *you* forget your jock before the game, like you need that anyway."

The crowd collectively *Oooh*ed at the burn.

Maggie continued the onslaught. "Maybe you're just forgetful, Tristan! Did you ever think of that? And maybe you just knocked over the bottles with your stupid little pancake ass."

"Mag Pie…" Tristan's tone changed in an instant, from angry to pleading. He and everybody else saw what was coming, and nobody could to stop it. Cole, for his part, felt a bit like a real live damn hero for a moment. This was what Maggie had seemed to want anyway, was it not?

"Don't *Mag Pie* me. Don't *Mags* me. Just don't," Maggie said. "We're done."

"What? We can't be done," Tristan cried. "It's us, Mag…Maggie. Please!"

By then, Maggie had brushed past Tristan and was walking away. Without turning around, she said, "If you wouldn't mind forgetting one last thing, try my phone number."

Cole watched from his solitary rock as Maggie walked through the stunned crowd and made her way home through the shortcut that Brady and Cole had used. She walked across the quarry, up the slight embankment towards Blackwood Forest, then into the woods. Moments later, Tristan stormed off. "What the fuck is everybody looking at!?" He went the opposite way from Maggie, towards the community.

"What's going on here?"

Eva was standing behind Cole's rock, Michael at her side.

"Drama." Cole got up and greeted the couple.

"Holy jeez, right?" Brady joined them. "Tristan totally looked like he pissed himself."

"That's the Wounded Sky power couple," Eva said.

"Not anymore," Cole said, a little too proudly.

Michael hadn't said anything. He was just standing there, head down, trying to avoid the kind of attention that Brady had received throughout the night.

"How are you doing, Mike?" Cole asked. "I don't know what to say. I'm so sorry."

"I'm doing," Michael said. "That's all I got right now."

"Yeah, sorry we're late. It was…tough getting out," Eva said.

"You didn't even have to come, you guys," Brady said.

"Break it up, everybody!" Employees of Reynold's security company descended on the crowd of teenagers, surrounding them. It all seemed a bit overdone. The quarry was an enclosed space. There was nowhere to run. There was even a security guard up on the cliff, shining a bright, industrial light down on the teens. To complete the dramatic effect, he also had a megaphone. While other guards were behind the teens on the ground, and within shouting (even talking) distance, it was the security personnel on the cliff overlooking the water who bellowed out: "Attention! You are all in violation of Wounded Sky's curfew, set at 20:00 hours. You are instructed to return to your homes immediately!"

The security team moved into the crowd, hands on clubs and flashlights, to manually disperse the kids. There wasn't much resistance. Cole, Brady, Eva, and Michael exchanged looks.

"Guess we shouldn't have come at all." Eva took Michael's hand, ready to lead him out of the quarry.

"I guess it's camp time?" Brady asked Cole.

"Why don't you go back home?" Cole put a hand on Brady's shoulder.

"You don't want me to…" Brady started.

"Nah. You've got a lot going on. I can do it."

Cole could see the exhaustion in Brady's face. It was the same look on most everybody's face.

"Sure, okay."

Teens started to file out of the area in neat little rows, as directed by security. It was a bit of a pathetic sight, all the kids walking together, step by step, the flashlight still shining down on them, like a scene from a zombie movie. Brady went to join the masses. Eva and Michael left as well. Cole turned to go his own way, towards Blackwood Forest, but he was shoved from behind. He stumbled forward a few steps, and then he turned around.

"City. Fancy seeing you here," Mark said.

"Hello, Mark," Cole groaned.

"You're not going the right way, you know."

Cole looked Mark over. He was dressed in jeans, a black hoodie, and sneakers. *Civilian clothes.* He wasn't part of the security team.

"I'll go where I want. You don't even work for Reynold. You were *fired*, remember? For messing with me."

"You better be careful, kid. There's a killer on the loose," Mark said.

"I'll be fine." Cole tried to leave again. Mark shoved him a second time, but Cole didn't move. "What's your problem, man?"

"You're my problem. See, I may have been fired, but I'm still looking out for *my* community."

Some teens who were heading out had stopped by now and started gathering around Cole and Mark.

"Yeah? How's that?" Cole asked.

"How about we start with you telling your buddy, Michael, where you were last night?" Mark said.

"What?" Cole stepped backwards, like a delayed reaction from the second shove.

"I'm sorry, was I not speaking English?" Mark asked. He went over to Michael and led him to the middle of the ever-growing circle.

"You really need to lay off him, Mark," Michael said.

"Ask Cole where he was last night."

"What's your deal?" Michael tried to walk away. Mark stopped him. He was getting good at stopping kids from leaving. Hands to shoulders, Mark led him back, positioning him right in front of Cole.

"Go on, ask him," Mark prompted.

Michael rolled his eyes, looked at Cole. "Sorry, Cole. Where were you last night?" Michael asked.

Cole didn't say anything. He just stood there, staring at Michael, and picturing Alex.

"Well, go on, city. Tell your friend where you were!" Mark said.

"Cole?" Michael said.

"I..."

"What's going on, Cole?" Eva asked from the front of the crowd.

"Cat got your tongue?" Mark started to pace around the perimeter of the crowd. "You know, ever since I got fired, thanks to city boy here, I have a lot of time on my hands. I walk around a lot. All around Wounded Sky. It's amazing what you see, walking all around Wounded Sky."

"Enough!" Cole said.

"What the hell is he talking about, Cole?" Michael asked.

"I was with—"

"—Alex last night," Mark finished for Cole. "Bingo! He walked her home, kissed her goodnight."

"You didn't..." Michael stepped up even closer to Cole.

"It was dark out. I just wanted her to be safe, I..." Cole said.

"So city boy here," Mark stood right beside Cole and Michael, "was there when Ashley got killed, and was there when Alex got killed. Who, by the way, also got shot through her bedroom window. Same M.O."

"Did you kill her?" Michael whispered to Cole.

"Mike, how could you ask that?" Cole asked.

"Where there's smoke there's fire, Michael," Mark said.

"You said we were friends," Michael said. "I asked if we were..."

"We are!" Cole said. "That's why you can't believe this."

"Cole," Brady said, stepping in. "Tell me this isn't why you didn't want me to come tonight. You didn't do this, right?"

"Brady, come on. You can't think I did any of this," Cole said.

"You sure have a lot of secrets, Cole. I just...I don't know what to think anymore," Brady said. "Just tell me you didn't. Tell me you couldn't have."

"But he was there, Brady. He admitted it," Mark said. "Ashley's blood was all over him, wasn't it?"

"Ashley was your boyfriend, Brady," Michael said. "Alex was my sister."

"We wouldn't even be here without him," Eva said, but it didn't sound like she was really defending him. It sounded like she was trying to convince herself.

"But Alex *would* be here!" Michael charged at Cole and pushed him as hard as he could, both hands against Cole's chest. Cole didn't budge. Instead, Michael fell backwards as though he'd been pushed. He slammed his head against the ground.

"Michael!" Eva ran to him. He was out cold. She knelt at his side and propped his head up. She looked up at Cole. "Who *are* you!?"

"He came at me," Cole said.

Mark stepped in front of Cole, getting right up in his face. Their noses were almost touching.

"What?" Mark said, "You gonna kill him too, Harper?"

"I didn't kill anybody!" Cole said.

"Why else would you be here?" Mark asked. "The moment you came back, people started dying." Mark surveyed the crowd. "Come on, people, do the math! This asshole let how many of us die ten years ago, and now he's doing it all over again!"

"I came back to save people, not kill them!" Before Cole even knew what he was doing, he thrust forward with one fist and connected with Mark's stomach. Mark flew through the air and skidded along the ground, knocking a few teenagers over in the process. The teens gasped. Mark tried to get up, but stumbled back to the ground holding his stomach.

"Is this part of the saving?" Mark asked. "Kicking everybody's ass?"

Cole looked at Michael and Eva on the ground. Eva wouldn't even look at Cole. Michael was still unconscious. Then, Cole locked eyes with Brady, tried to see something in there—that Brady didn't really think Cole had killed anybody, but all he saw was confusion, and that was enough.

"I'm sorry," he said. To Brady. To Eva. To Michael. To everybody.

He turned to leave.

"We're not done," Mark said. "Not by a long shot."

"You may not be, but I am."

15

33-29-8-45

"WAIT UP!" JAYNE SHOUTED.

Cole hadn't gone very far into the woods when the bouncing ball of flames approached from the distance. He was glad to see Jayne. Once again, he had planned poorly and hadn't brought a flashlight, and the deeper into Blackwood Forest he went, the thicker the forest became overhead. No help from the heavens. Jayne, bounding down the trail with reckless abandon (and having no reason to bound down the trail any other way), caught up quickly. She took Cole's hand without breaking stride and they continued towards the camp.

"Thanks, Jayney." Now, Cole could see the entire forest, bright and clear as midday. Jayne was happy. With his affirmation, her flames grew brighter and bigger.

Cole wondered if somebody could ever make Jayne so sad that her flames would go out entirely. It was a quick thought, and a theory that he'd never wish to test. Her presence renewed his determination. If he succeeded, then she got to go to the Hunting Grounds. Looking at her and thinking of what she'd been through, but seeing a joy that couldn't be extinguished, told Cole that it was exactly where she deserved to be.

"Where are we goin', Coley? Are we goin' on an adventure?" she asked.

She was swinging his arm back and forth, humming a song.

"Something like that. We're going to a camp," Cole said.

"Who woulda put a camp all the way out here?" Jayne scrunched up her face, deep in thought.

"That's what we're going to find out."

Cole wasn't sure where the camp was, exactly. Eva would've been helpful right about now. All he could do was find his way back to where he figured that he, Brady, and Eva had been running. Jayne's presence made the task far easier. When he found that place, he'd just walk deeper into Blackwood Forest until he found the camp. Jayne liked the game, as she called it.

"It's like hide-and-seek!"

"You're right, Jayne, it's just like that. Only in this game, the *camp* is hiding, not a person. We have to find it."

"Well if it's not even moving, that'll be easy!"

"Yeah, you'd think."

Jayne promised to keep a sharp eye out for the camp. From time to time, she let go of Cole's hand. She would run up ahead, skip to either side, and light a bit more of the forest. During one of Jayne's brief excursions, Cole—very proudly, it should be added—saw what he thought were broken branches on the ground and bent grass blades around that same area. Someone had walked right here. Maybe it had been him or one of his friends. Maybe it had been the killer.

"Not bad for a city boy." Cole said this out loud, but he was really talking to an absent Eva. Granted, she might have found this path much sooner than he did, but he still found it. Maybe she would've been proud. That is, if she wasn't wondering now whether or not *he* was the killer.

"Eat your heart out," Cole whispered to himself.

"Gross!" Jayne ran over to where Cole was crouching.

"Huh?" Cole was looking along the ground, away from them, trying to make out which direction they should follow.

"Why would anybody want to eat hearts?!" Jayne stuck her tongue out like she'd eaten something disgusting.

"It's a figure of speech, Jayney."

Cole found the right direction, he thought, and together they followed the trail of bent grass, footprints, and broken twigs. The path was more obvious this time; it had been broken in by three or maybe four people. Before long, the clearing the camp was set up in was visible up ahead. They approached it slowly and quietly.

"Don't be scared if we see somebody," Cole whispered to Jayne the closer they got. "Or if I have to run."

"I'm not scared," Jayne said with her chin raised defiantly. "I'd protect you, you know."

"I know that," Cole said.

Nothing much changed since Cole had last seen the camp, only that the firepit was cold this time, which set him at ease. Nobody had been here recently. He poked around the firepit with a stick, but he only uncovered a few cans of food. The only thing left to inspect was the tent, which was still set up. With Jayne by him, he crawled inside. In the tent was the backpack he saw last time.

Jayne watched Cole go through the backpack like he was opening a Christmas present. Each time Cole pulled out an item she gasped or *ooh*ed or *aah*ed, and said the exact same thing: "I love surprises!" He laid the contents on the ground as he went through them. He pulled out a first-aid kit (Jayne loved the assortment of stuff in the kit, from the antibiotic cream to the latex gloves); a few pairs of socks, expertly rolled; a survival knife which, Cole admitted to himself, looked pretty badass; and an MP3 player (he filtered through the music quickly, and thought, *okay, this makes sense,* when he saw an array of '80s rock music). Then he pulled out magazines of ammunition. That sealed it for him. Cole didn't need the gun or a ballistics match. *Terminology from crime shows, thank you very much.* Of course, Wayne *would* need these things, but right now, that was neither here nor there.

This was the killer.

Cole was so excited at this revelation, so caught up in making plans on what to do next—namely, contact Wayne, at which point the whole ballistics thing would happen—that he almost missed the last item in the backpack. Stuffed in with the socks, the first aid kit, and everything else, was a file folder. Cole pulled it out of the backpack, and held it up to Jayne's light.

"What is that?" Jayne asked.

"Probably nothing," Cole said.

The unassuming brown folder was thickish, but not *War & Peace* thick. Cole opened it to a file on a classmate of his who'd died in the fire. Derek John Folster. His friends called him DJ. There was a picture of DJ beside information that included his age, height, weight, mother and father. Under his picture was a word in block letters: EXPERIMEN-TAL 715. Underneath the picture and the personal information was a biographical review of DJ's family background, his reaction to some kind of drug testing, and then his date of death. Ten years ago tomorrow. UNSUCCESSFUL was stamped in big red letters over the bio.

"Awww, did DJ fail a test?" Jayne asked.

"I'm not sure," Cole said.

He flipped to the next file, another classmate of his who died in the fire. Tasha Evans. The layout of the file was the same, only under Tasha's name the block letters read: PLACEBO. Cole flipped through file after file, and each one revealed another dead classmate, and the words PLACEBO or EXPERIMENTAL followed by a three-digit number. Each file that read EXPERIMENTAL also had the big red letters: UNSUCCESSFUL. Jayne Flett was the last school fire victim. EXPERIMENTAL. UNSUCCESS-FUL. Cole quickly tried to flip past it as soon as he saw Jayne's picture.

"Hey, I saw that!" Jayne shouted.

"You don't need to see it," Cole said.

"No fair, Coley, come on," Jayne said.

Cole turned back to Jayne's file. She read with her index finger, moving it across each line like she'd been reading Braille until she'd ran it over the date of her death.

"I didn't do good?" she asked when she was done.

"No, Jayney, you did good. You did just fine," Cole said.

"What did I do wrong?" she asked.

"Nothing," Cole said. "This is just some, like, medical trial or something. I think they were trying to give kids a drug or something. Maybe they were trying to cure a disease, or a sickness, something like that."

"What kind of disease?" she asked.

"Maybe we'll find out." There weren't many files left. Cole turned to the next one. It was Ashley's. EXPERIMENTAL. UNSUCCESSFUL. No date of death. Of course, he wasn't in the school fire. But what was different about Ashley's file was that his picture, Ashley at six years old, had a red X drawn crudely over it.

"This is so messed up, Jayney," Cole whispered. He had another word for it, rather than "messed," but he felt like even though Jayne was a ghost, she was still just a little girl.

The next file was Alex's. Alex Captain. PLACEBO. Her picture also had a red X drawn over it. Cole ran his thumb across her picture. He remembered the time they'd spent together, just a day earlier.

"They both got shot," Jayne said.

"I know," Cole said. "Look at this." There was a tab attached to the next file. It read: "The Reckoner." Cole took a last look at Alex's picture, and turned the page to find a file on himself. Cole Harper. There was a picture of him, too, from when he was eight. Under that picture read: EXPERIMENTAL 354. Paper-clipped to the file was a photograph of Cole leaving Kelvin High School, backpack over his shoulder, basketball under his arm.

"What the…"

"That's you, Coley," Jayne pointed out.

"Yeah, I know."

The file had the same logistical information on Cole: his height (6'0"), weight (179 lbs), age (17), place of birth (Wounded Sky First Nation), current residence (Winnipeg), and so on. But his file also had a schedule. It listed Cole's typical day, from start to finish. What he did, where he went. This was from Sunday to Saturday. From what Cole read, it was pretty accurate. "7:05 a.m. was breakfast. Bus came at 7:28 a.m. Route 19. Subject arrives at school at 7:58 a.m. Practices basketball from 8:00 a.m. until 8:45 a.m."

There was a biography on Cole, too, starting right from his birth, but the bulk of it concentrated on his youth, when his father was alive. In particular, it mentioned his father's work on a biological agent called God Flare (or Agent 33-29-8-45). He read through a lot of medical and scientific terminology that he could hardly understand, but saw that the symptoms listed for the biological agent matched what he'd seen in Chief Crate the night he came to Wounded Sky.

"I'm going to have to run this by Dr. Captain," Cole said.

"It's like another language," Jayne said.

"It kind of is," Cole said. "It's like a language for doctors. But what if that's what people have now, here?"

"Like when they're coughing and stuff?" Jayne asked.

"Yeah," Cole said.

"Like when you were trying to push Chief's chest in?"

"Oh my god."

Information on the accident that killed his father and his lab assistant had been redacted. That mystery would continue to live on. Cole, the child, came into the picture via speculation in the file that his father had attempted to run a different experiment on his son. They called it an "Unauthorized Parallel Design Trial." Cole wasn't sure what any of it meant, only that instead of a big red stamp on his file, there was a big green stamp that read: SUCCESSFUL.

"Holy shit," Cole said.

"Coley, you said a bad word!" Jayne gasped.

"Sorry, Jayney."

He read the part over again about the Parallel Design Trial. As he did, his mind wandered back to his father, the time they spent together. Breakfast.

"The vitamins," Cole stated.

"I like those!" Jayne said. "One time, I ate too many of 'em, and Dr. Captain had to pump my stomach. That's what they called it, pumping my stomach."

"Gross," Cole said absently.

"Well, nobody was eating hearts!"

There was one file left. Cole pried himself away from his own file and turned to find a file for Eva Kirkness. PLACEBO. The only thing that was missing from Eva's file, and Cole's for that matter, was the red X that had been drawn over Ashley's and Alex's faces.

"Why do they each have an X over their pictures, and we don't?" Cole thought out loud. "I don't—"

"Because they're dead and you guys aren't," Jayne said. The light that Jayne had been providing on the files went dim. He could hardly make out the words anymore, could hardly see Eva's picture. Eva at seven. Eva, sitting on top of the blue mats. Eva, Waiting for Cole to come back.

"Jayne, you're right," Cole said.

"I don't wanna win this game." Jayne's voice was shaking. A hot tear landed on Eva's file, and a small puff of steam exploded from where it had landed.

"Somebody's killing us off, one by one. Everybody in this file is…"

Pop!

Cole stood up and frantically looked around. He couldn't hear anybody approaching. He could only tell about where the gunshot had come from.

"Eva," he whispered to himself.

Every night, one of his friends had died. First Ashley, in the file. Then Alex, in the file. The last people alive were Eva and himself.

He crouched down in front of Jayne.

"Can you stay here?" Cole asked.

"But I wanna come with you, Coley! I said I'd protect you!"

"I know, but I need you to stay here and watch over this stuff." Cole started to stuff it back into the backpack as neatly as he could with his hands shaking the way they were. "Can you do that?"

Jayne hesitated. She looked at him, she looked at the backpack, and she looked off into the woods, to wherever the shot had originated.

"Jayne!" Cole placed the backpack into the tent, just where he'd found it.

"Okay, I guess." Jayne had her hands on her hips, pouting.

"This is an important job, Jayney. Tell me if anybody comes here, okay?"

She nodded.

Cole ran out of the camp and through the woods.

He had never run so fast. The trees were whizzing by him in a blur, like grass at the side of the highway. He couldn't tell whether this was another ability or if it was just the adrenaline. The agility seemed to be something new. He managed to navigate over roots, branches, underbrush, rocks, and all with precision. Within minutes, he came to a stop in front of the body of a girl. She was face down, arms stretched-out in front of her. There was a wound in the back of her head. The hair around the wound was matted with blood that looked like tar in the dark. The ground beneath her, too, was thickened and black. It looked like her hair. It could've been her hair.

"No, please. Not her." He kept praying as he approached her quietly. Begging for Choch to come back, give him another deal, and bring her back to life.

He approached as though Eva was only sleeping, and he was careful not to wake her. He placed his hands under her body and turned her over. He pictured her face, now, and the seven-year-old school picture that had been in her file.

"Oh no," he whispered when he saw Maggie's face. He felt relief and then guilt immediately after, that he was happy it wasn't Eva, that he would've traded anybody for Eva.

Cole brushed some hair away from her face. His mind went into overdrive. Could this have been Tristan, getting revenge on her after their very public fight? He instantly banished the theory. Tristan was an asshole, but he wasn't capable of doing something like this. Could she have done it herself? So upset about the break-up from her long-time boyfriend? No. *You'd talked to her about this*, Cole thought. She seemed to want the relationship over, and that's what she got. It had to be the same killer. There weren't two people going around shooting kids around Wounded Sky.

"But this doesn't make sense," Cole said, as though she could hear him. "You weren't in the folder."

He fished around the ground with his fingers. His fingertips connected with something hard and cool. He wrapped his hands around the handle of a pistol. Could she have? He looked at her wound more carefully. Oh, but if Jayne were here, he could've seen it so much more easily. Still, it didn't take an abundance of light, or medical expertise, to tell that the wound was created at the back of the head, not the front.

"Who did this to you?" Cole asked, but the answer seemed painfully obvious. It was the third time he had failed. All he could do now was figure out why he, Ashley, Alex, and Eva were on the list, why he and Eva were still alive, and why Maggie had been killed when she wasn't in the folder.

Cole looked for any evidence, something that might lead him to the killer, because the murderer certainly wasn't at the camp. *God,* Cole thought, *while I was rummaging through stuff in his backpack, he was here, killing Maggie.* The thought gave him a chill.

He heard a sound behind him. Cole's body tensed. His heart raced. No time for a pill. Surprisingly, he didn't even think to take one. In fact, he was about to turn around and face the killer, rather than run. Before he could turn, though, he heard a familiar voice order, "Don't move!"

"I didn't do this, Mr. McCabe. I found Maggie like this, I swear."

"And the gun?" Reynold asked.

Cole looked down at his hand where, yes, he was holding the gun. "*Shit.*" Was it not the number one thing you should *not* do at a crime scene—touch *anything,* especially the murder weapon? And not only had he picked up the gun, but he'd also turned over Maggie's body, got down on his knees right beside her. He looked away from his hand to the rest of his body, and sure enough, her blood was everywhere, on his knees, his hands, his clothes. Had he not learned anything from Ashley's murder scene?

"It was here on the ground," Cole said of the gun, knowing that the explanation was never going to fly. "I picked it up, I..."

"Drop it!"

The gun fell to the ground and landed with a hollow thump.

"She was on her stomach when I found her. I turned her over to see who it was..." Cole stopped recounting his own stupidity. He realized how this all looked.

He heard Reynold's footsteps come closer and then kick the gun further away.

"Put your hands behind your back," Reynold ordered.

Reynold put cuffs around Cole's wrists. Was this it, the end of his journey already, the path behind him lined with his own failings? What would that mean for the ones he'd saved ten years earlier? Eva. Brady. Would they now cease to exist? Would he? Or did that even matter? Would Eva be next, with Cole locked up, helpless to save her?

"I'm disappointed." Cole heard Reynold take two steps back. "Here I was, *defending* you, in front of everyone. Now look at what you've done. Ashley, Alex, Maggie. How can I defend you now? Help me understand, Cole."

"I didn't do any of this. Think about it, Mr. McCabe. Where was the gun at Ashley's trailer if I'd killed him? Mr. Kirkness was right there with me. What's at Alex's house that's tied to me? Why would I leave there, but stay here with Maggie if I killed her?" Cole was scrambling, and he knew it, but Reynold had believed in Cole before, so why not now?

"I might have believed some of that, if you weren't standing over Maggie's body, blood all over your clothes, and a gun in your hand."

Cole had nothing to say to that. He considered telling Reynold the truth, that he was at the camp and heard the gunshot, and came running. As quickly as he considered it, however, he decided against it. For the first time, and not only because Reynold had him at gunpoint, Cole could see why others were wary of him.

"Mr. McCabe, how'd you get here so fast?" Cole asked.

"Excuse me?" Reynold said.

"I was close when I heard the gunshot. Ran here faster than I'd ever run. But you got here almost as fast," Cole said. "No offence, Mr. McCabe, but you don't look that fast."

"I was looking for kids out here, making sure they got home from the bonfire. It's not safe, Cole. They could've run into *you*."

"But everybody was leaving through Wounded Sky. Why would you be—"

In the middle of his sentence, Cole heard Reynold take two quick, heavy steps towards him, and then he felt something strike the back of his head. Wounded Sky's dark night got a whole lot darker.

16

JAY BIRD

THE NIGHT WAS ETERNAL. There were no stars, no northern lights, no moon. The feeling in Cole's body—the weak knees, the racing heart, the shakiness—had all ceased. In this numbness and darkness, Cole considered that it wasn't the butt of a gun he had felt against the back of his head, but a bullet. How would he know the difference anyway? He felt the impact, and then nothing. He wondered if, when he opened his eyes, he'd be in the "waiting room," hovering majestically over Wounded Sky First Nation. Jayne would be beside him. More than that, there'd be Brady, and Eva, if that's what his failure meant. They would be together, and this decade of grief and sadness would be over for all of them. They would dance across the sky in those ribbons of light, those healed scars, and they would be a part of that healing. And, when it was time, they would move on to the Hunting Grounds.

And all of this here on Earth, would be mercifully forgotten after an eternity there.

An almost unbearable pain flooded into Cole's head and resonated through his entire body. He groaned, and reached to the back of his head, where he felt an enormous goose egg. His head was resting on a thin pillow, and his wound had been positioned over an ice pack that had long since gone warm. He opened his eyes to find that he was lying on a flat bed protruding from the wall inside a holding cell at the RCMP detachment. He remembered what had happened last night. He felt pain, then panic. If he was in here, how was he going to protect Eva? Even if Maggie was an anomaly, Ashley and Alex were still murdered, and if Eva was in the file, it meant she was in danger.

"Relax," Choch said before Cole even tried to get up, to find a way to break out of here. Choch was sitting at the edge of the bed, his back straight and his legs crossed, occupying himself with a traveller's crossword puzzle book.

"Relax!?" The officers in the building—a younger woman Cole recognized but couldn't quite name, Wayne, and Jerry, who, along with Wayne, had been a constable when Cole was a kid—looked at him. He kept his voice low. "Are you kidding me? Do you realize what's going on right now?"

Choch had a pencil between his lips. "Mmmm-hmmmm." He took the pencil and erased a word on the puzzle he was working on. Once the word was erased (or rather, smudged), he asked, "You wouldn't know a seven-letter word for "opposite of success," would you?"

"I…" Cole finally sat up, and a rush of pain hit him in the middle of his forehead. He bowed his head. "I don't know." He realized that he needed to whisper so as not to attract attention, but to also spare his pounding head.

"Ahh," Choch gave Cole a triumphant nudge on the shoulder that felt like a sledgehammer. "*Failure*. That's it."

"Nice," Cole whispered.

"I'm kidding, of course. Pay no mind," Choch said. "But this is quite the pickle you've got yourself in, isn't it?"

"That's just what I was thinking, exactly. I was thinking that I'd got myself into a 'pickle.' Now, I need to get out of the pickle. Can you at least help with that?"

"No need to rush, Coley-Boley. Have you heard of any killings happening during the day?" Choch asked.

"No, but—"

"Then don't get yourself all in a tizzy. We have time."

"Do you swear? If anything happens to Eva…"

"Cross my heart." Choch crossed his heart.

"Hey," Wayne said with a thunderous tap on the prison bars, standing outside the holding cell. He had a glass of water in one hand and two aspirins in the other. "Looks like you could use this."

Cole reached forward and Wayne handed him both items.

"Thanks," Cole said.

"I'll come back in a bit." Wayne was completely ignoring Choch sitting at Cole's side. He hadn't looked once in his direction. *How was that even possible?* The man was wearing another outrageous outfit, fit to attend the Mad Hatter's tea party.

"Mr. Kirkness, can't you…"

"Hang on, now." Choch snapped his fingers, and Wayne, along with the other two constables in the office froze. Literally. "I'll have you know that, *A*, this is my favourite suit, hands down. I've gotten a lot of compliments on it, as a matter of fact."

"Yeah? From who?"

"From *people*, and *B*, Wayne and his constables can't exactly see me right now."

"Oh great, so if I'm talking to you, they'll think I'm talking to myself."

"Well, just keep talking quietly," Choch said. "You'll be fine." With that, he snapped his fingers again, and the constables continued on as though nothing had happened.

"Can't I what, Cole?" Wayne asked.

"Nothing, it was nothing."

Wayne looked at Cole suspiciously, which Cole figured was the way he would get looked at a lot now. "Alright. Sit tight. You have a lot of explaining to do, son."

Cole just nodded.

Wayne went back to his desk, sat down, and buried his head in a pile of papers and photographs—the desk of a constable who was dealing with murders and sickness and mystery. Although now, Wayne must've figured that the mystery was over. Cole was the murderer. And everybody in Wounded Sky probably thought the same thing. Michael already wanted to kill him. So did Mark and Tristan. What about Eva and Brady? They'd for sure think he'd done it now. Eva had probably ripped that ring off her neck for good.

"Oh, would you stop with the ruminations, Cole?" Choch said.

"What else am I supposed to do, huh?" Cole asked.

Choch straightened out the crossword puzzle on his lap, and ran the pencil along the "down" clues. He stopped at one. He said, "Well, you could help me figure out 'foe' for one. It's, ummm, ten letters, my boy. That's a toughie."

"I'm not helping you with your stupid crossword puzzle," Cole said. It was hard to keep whispering.

"Third letter is a 'T' and the second last letter is an 'S.' This is something you should really be thinking about, kiddo."

"If this guy's going to kill at night, what am I supposed to do? Wait until night to try and get out of here? By then it might be too late," Cole hissed. He stood up, ignored the jackhammering in his head, and started to bang on the prison bars. "Mr. Kirkness, you have to let me out of here! Please!"

The officers didn't budge. They didn't turn their heads, and they didn't get up.

"They can't hear you," Choch sung.

"Why would you do that? I could convince them! I could—"

"All in good time," Choch said. "Now, please, sit."

Cole, lost for anything to do or say, and feeling like it wouldn't have mattered right now regardless, did as he was told. He sat down, took the aspirin, and chugged the water. Then he lay down on the hard prison bed, propping his head up on the pillow.

"Good," Choch said. "I'm so pleased about this. When was the last time we were able to spend some quality time together, hmm?"

"Yesterday?"

"Well it feels like forever," Choch said. "Honestly, what with the—" Choch imitated the javelin throw Cole had made with the branch "— and all that."

"That was two days ago," Cole corrected. "And a lot of good that'll do me now."

"Quite right, quite right. Time flies, you know?" Cole could see Choch writing the ten-letter word into the section that he'd asked Cole about. ANTAGONIST. When he was finished writing, he looked over at Cole and winked. "But you just never know, am I right? What good something will do for you?"

"Maybe if the killer was, like, running away from me, really far away, and I had to throw something at him to knock him down before he got away," Cole said. "But then again, this isn't a stupid cartoon show." Choch ignored Cole's sarcasm. He stood up, walked closer to Cole, and sat down there. There was no chair. Choch was sitting on air, leaning back with one leg crossed over the other, perfectly relaxed.

Cole craned his neck to the right. "Is there, like, a chair there for *you*? Do you see a chair and I don't?"

Choch shook his head. "Look, let's not get into all that psycho-babble garbage. Nobody wants to hear it." Choch looked at the wall behind Cole, or somewhere beyond the wall, then he uncrossed his legs and leaned even closer to him. He said, like a friend Cole hadn't seen for a long time. "So, how's it going with you?"

"How do you think?" Cole asked.

"Sorry, how insensitive of me." Choch slapped his knee and sat straight up, alert. "Well, since we've got all this time, why don't you work through some of those thoughts with me, hey? See what we can figure out together."

"Why don't you just, you know, read my mind?"

"There's a time and a place for that, Coley. But I've found, in my experience, that it helps to simply talk out loud. You'll see. I'm a good listener. I won't say a thing if you'd rather me not."

"You're full of shit," Cole said.

"I assure you, I am full of gumdrops and rainbows."

Cole took a moment to consider this, but he felt that Choch wasn't going anywhere anyway (*True!*) so what would be the harm? He pushed himself up into a sitting position. "I don't know where to start."

"What's that?" the female officer asked from her desk. "What'd you say?"

Cole shook his head. "Nothing." They stared at each other uncomfortably for what seemed like forever, until she looked away. "Could you tell me when people can hear me, and when they can't? Is that too much to ask?" Cole said to Choch.

"That would be decidedly less amusing for me. Now, you were about to work out some of your thoughts with me. So, whatever comes to your mind. Go on, now. I'll *zip* it."

"Fine," Cole whispered, darting his eyes back and forth from Choch to the officer. "I actually thought I was finally onto something. I went back to the camp, and found these, like, files in a folder. There were files on my friends from elementary school, on Eva, Alex, Ashley, and even on me."

Choch nodded and placed a finger against his chin, trying to seem as interested as possible.

"We were all getting experimented on somehow, but my file said my dad was doing something else with me that he wasn't supposed to do."

All of a sudden Choch had a bag of popcorn and was eating out of it, staring at Cole, like he was watching an intense movie.

"It was about some, like, biological agent called God Flare," Cole said.

Choch put up his hand.

"Yes?" Cole asked.

He pointed to his mouth, full of popcorn, asking to say something.

"Fine, go ahead."

"Cool name," Choch said. "Somebody must've tried really hard to think up *that* name. For the sake of wordiness, you could call it a virus, you know. 'Biological agent' is just—"

"Okay, you can keep your mouth shut now."

Choch nodded.

"I think that it's the same *virus* that people are getting here. Like, all the symptoms match." Cole paused, waiting for Choch to say something, but Choch behaved, and kept nodding, rubbing his finger against his chin, quiet as can be. "I'm starting to think that this is all related. Like, the virus, me, the murders. But I still don't know what to do about it all, and now I'm stuck in here and the only people left alive in those files are me and Eva."

Choch shrugged and leaned *away* from Cole, like Cole smelled or something. Cole remembered last night, right before he was knocked out. He rubbed the goose egg at the back of his head. "I think Reynold's involved too."

Choch raised his eyebrows at this. Encouraged, Cole continued. "I ran *so* fast to get to Maggie's body, and Reynold was there *right* after me. I don't think he could've got there that fast no matter where he was running from, unless he was already there. Weird, right?"

Choch returned to nodding. He tapped his finger against his chin.

"Fine, you can talk," Cole said.

Choch let out a huge, exaggerated breath. "Those are *very* intriguing theories, Cole Harper. Or should I say, Cole *Holmes*."

"I'm not going to call you Watson, if that's what you want."

"Of course, you've the teensy problem of being behind bars, even though we've established that Eva is probably safe until—" Choch then mouthed: *tonight*.

"I can't…" Cole started, but instead motioned to the prison bars to make his point.

Wayne was walking back towards the prison cell.

Choch put his two fists together and pulled them apart from each other, grimacing as though exerting great force.

"What? What are you doing?"

Choch did it again.

"You look constipated. I don't get it."

He did it again, grimacing even harder.

"Stop that."

Choch rolled his eyes. "You are absolutely impossible. Have you not used your strength to get out of sticky situations before?"

"What do you want me to do? *Bend* the bars? Is that what you were doing? Are you crazy?" Cole asked in a loud whisper.

"Crazy like a fox, errr…you know." Choch casually walked through the bars and out of the RCMP detachment.

"Who are you talking to?" Wayne dragged a chair up to the bars and sat down.

"Nobody," Cole said. "Just talking to myself."

"About?"

"About how stupid it is that I'm in here," Cole said. "How stupid I am for being here."

"For getting caught?" Wayne asked.

"For putting myself in that position, more like," Cole said.

"You're not thinking about breaking out of here, are you?"

Cole reached forward and grasped one of the bars firmly, tried to shake it as though to display the impossibility of a jailbreak. "Come on."

Wayne leaned forward and looked Cole square in the eyes. "If what people say about you is true, you could lift an entire wall as a little kid. Why not break out of prison as an adult?"

"I was lucky to make it out of the school myself, Mr. Kirkness. You shouldn't believe everything you hear."

"I shouldn't believe one of your best friends?"

"Brady?"

"He swears up and down you did it, when it comes up. You know, when people around here are talking about you."

How it must've looked to Brady, to see Cole, at seven, lifting an entire gym wall. Cole had never thought of it from Brady's perspective. Maybe he *could* bend the bars. Or maybe there was another way. "I shouldn't be in here."

Wayne took off his hat, played with it in his hands. "None of this looks good for you. Mark says he saw you with Alex before she was killed. You were with Ashley, you were with Maggie…"

"Mark has it out for me," Cole said.

"Were you with Alex, or not?"

"Yeah, but…" Cole sighed. What could he say? Wayne was right on all counts. "You know me, Mr. Kirkness," Cole said, a bit more desperately.

"I do," Wayne said, "that's right, I do. I thought I did, anyway. But Cole…" Wayne leaned back so that he could fish into his pocket. He pulled out Ashley's phone. Cole's heart sank. That other way out that he was working towards was quickly disappearing. "Things just keep adding up. Last night, I find his phone in your pocket, and the last texts on there are between you and him. Aside from everything else, assuming you're really just that unlucky to be around three people on the nights each one of them gets killed, Maggie's blood was all over you, Ashley's blood was all over you. That's a lot of blood, Cole."

"Don't you think this is all too neat and tidy?" Cole asked. "Like, having everything you need to pin on me just laid out right in front of you?"

"Maybe," Wayne said. "Or maybe you're just some dumb kid, and you didn't even think to cover your tracks."

"Why would I kill my best friend? Alex? Maggie?"

"I don't know. Maybe you got sick of everybody talking about you the way they do, looking at you the way they do. Maybe you got mad, just like at the clinic."

"Yeah, that was Mark too. I told you that."

"Stop blaming Mark. Even if he's trying to get back at you, you were still doing what he said you were doing, or am I wrong?"

"No."

"Maybe *you* know what you did at the school, that you saved kids, saved my daughter, and you're mad nobody believes what really happened."

"Do you believe it?" Cole asked. "Do you believe that I saved Brady? That I saved Eva?"

Wayne and Cole looked at each other for a long time. Wayne's eyes burrowed deep into Cole's soul. Then he nodded, reluctantly. "Yeah, Cole, I believe it."

"Then how can you believe I did this?"

Wayne shook his head. "That's my job, son. I have to look at all the facts, not the feelings. And all the facts, well…"

"Reynold," Cole stated, as though Wayne knew everything that Cole did.

"What about him?

"I was at the camp Eva told you about…"

"I checked out that camp, Cole."

"Once, Mr. Kirkness. You said you looked at the facts, right? There were tracks leading all the way from Ashley's trailer to that camp."

"I know, Eva showed me."

"I went back there last night and I heard a gunshot. I ran there as fast as I could. I found Maggie, but Reynold was there too. Right when I was."

"Maybe he ran, too, Cole. That doesn't prove anything."

"Yeah but, I ran *really, really* fast. And he's, you know, *old*."

"Still, he's the one who caught you, Cole. Are you saying, that he, what, framed you?"

"I don't know what I'm saying. All I know is that there's more going on here. You have to see that."

"Do you have any *proof*? Anything at all to give me?"

"The folder!" Cole said. "I found a folder at the camp last night. It had all these files in it about me, and lots of other kids, including Eva. That's why you have to let me out of here!"

"Wait, what about Eva?" Cole had Wayne's attention now. He couldn't be more on the edge of his seat. The back legs of his chair were off the floor.

"Every single person in that folder, Mr. Kirkness, every single person except me and Eva are dead. They either died in the fire, or they've been murdered the last three days."

Wayne shook his head. "What are you saying—that Eva is in trouble?"

"Yes that's exactly what I'm saying! You have to let me out of here. I can…I'll save her again."

"Why should I believe you?" Wayne asked.

"What have you got to lose? Find the file, it's at the camp. Let me come; I can show you. Handcuff me, whatever."

"You know I can't do that." Wayne got up. He went to the door, opened it. "If you're lying…"

"If I'm lying then I'll still be here when you get back. Just find it, then you'll believe me. And don't let Eva out of your sight."

Wayne hesitated only a second more, then he was outside, and already dialling a number into his cell phone.

"Yeah, Brady? It's Wayne. Would you mind…" Cole could hear Wayne say before the door shut behind him.

The next two hours were excruciating. Cole tried calculating how long it might take Wayne to find the camp, if he was walking. He considered the distance between the RCMP detachment and the camp. In addition, Wayne needed time to look over the camp, search through it, and read through the files *if* he found the folder. Cole thought his calculations were pretty precise—as precise as possible. As Choch said: 87 percent in math. Given that precision, two hours seemed the maximum time Wayne needed to do all this and return to the detachment. Had something happened to him? Had he encountered the killer? Was the tent gone, and the files with it? Jayne was supposed to be watching over the stuff Cole had found, but maybe she'd grown bored and had gone to play.

"Hey," Cole called over to the officer, who was sitting closest to his cell. "Do you want to call Wayne and see where he is? If he found anything?"

"If Wayne found anything, he'd call me," she said. "I can't believe he bought enough of your crap story that he went in the first place."

"Why would I make up anything while I'm in here?" Cole thought his question was reasonable. "What would be the benefit for me?"

"Maybe to avoid his grilling your ass."

"I've had my ass grilled by Wayne lots of times. I can take it. There's a killer on the loose—that's what I'm worried about."

"The killer is right here."

"Just text him! How hard is that?"

Her jaw was clenched. He could see the little muscle protruding at the side of her face. She whipped out her phone and rattled off a text.

"There, happy?"

"Thanks," Cole said.

She went back to her paperwork, and she was pulverizing it. Cole could see her white knuckles grasping the pen. He was surprised the pen didn't break in half. Her hand movements were aggressive. He looked over her desk as she worked: A pad of paper off to the side next to some neatly stacked sticky notes. A wooden pen holder was full of highlighters, pens, pencils, and a pair of scissors. Her hat was placed just above the pad she was demolishing. Her name bar was at one corner of the desk—Lauren Flett. A framed picture faced her from the other corner. A school picture with a misty blue background. Jayne looked deliberately and uncomfortably posed. The same picture he had seen in her file, in the folder back at the camp. He hadn't looked at it carefully then, had worried too much about reading the contents. He looked at it now, and her smile took his breath away. It was a genuine smile, from a girl who seemed to always be smiling, even when half in flames. She was beautiful. School photographs were like passport photos, Cole had always thought, but not Jayne's. Uncomfortably posed, but full of pure, unabashed joy.

"No!" Lauren slammed Jayne's picture onto the desk, face down. "You don't get to look at her!"

Cole was trying to summon Jayne through his thoughts—*Jayney! Come here, please! Jayney! Can you hear me?*—while he said, "Lauren Flett," out loud.

"Don't change the subject, you little prick."

"Jayne," Cole said, half calling her, half working his way up to convincing Lauren of something he wasn't sure was breaking the rules or not. "Jayne's your sister."

"That's right." Lauren got up from her desk and walked to the prison cell. "And you let her die."

Cole shook his head. He pictured Jayne's body in flames and remembered how he wished he could've saved her. "She was already dead."

Lauren punched the cell bar closest to Cole's face and she didn't flinch when her flesh met metal. She punched it hard enough that Cole thought she may have broken her knuckles. The metal vibrated. It filled the short silence.

"You're lying!" Lauren said.

Cole shook his head again, slowly. "I saw her. She'd been crushed, burned…"

"You wanted to save your friends. You could've saved *anybody*." Lauren, though, sounded less assertive to Cole, and more desperate, like she was trying to hold on to the anger. Maybe that was all she had now, just like so often in the city he felt like all he had was regret.

"I would've saved her. I don't know why Brady and Eva were the only ones left alive. I'll never know that, and I'll always live with it. I saw Jayne. I saw everybody."

Lauren stared at Cole. He didn't know what it meant, but he tried to understand. He was pleading that he could go back somehow, even now, and find her, save her. He wanted that too. This was something they shared. Finally, she sunk into the chair that Wayne had left behind. Cole stayed where he was, standing there, watching her. She put her head in her hands, and slowly shook it back and forth. She was clutching strands of hair between her fingers.

Cole felt warmth beside him. He turned to see Jayne standing with him, looking at Lauren. She reached to the side, without looking away, and Cole took her hand.

"Why's she sad?"

"She misses you," he whispered.

Lauren raised her head. There were tears flooding her cheeks. She sat up straight and tried to fix her hair, wipe the tears away, as though she'd just realized that she was vulnerable. But she gave up. She put her hands in her lap and kind of grabbed and released her pants several times.

"What happened?" Lauren asked.

"I can't..." Cole started to say, but he saw in Lauren's face that "I can't" wasn't an answer he should give. He couldn't tell her that it was too hard to relive the memory. And using Jayne to help him get out of the cell was no longer an option. Jayne meant more than that, and so did Lauren's grief.

"Eva. We were talking about how we were going to get married one day. Just kids, you know. We were best friends, and so of course we were going to get married. I snuck out, went through the field, over to Silk River. I found some sweetgrass around the banks." Cole sat down on the bed against the wall. Jayne did, too. He started to mime braiding the sweetgrass, as he went back to the past for the millionth time.

"I braided it into a ring. And then I saw the fire in the distance. I ran back as fast as I could, faster than I'd ever run before. When I got there, I went inside, and managed to get to the gym. I saw almost everybody there, dead. They were burning, they…" Cole felt tears falling down from his cheek. Jayne tried to wipe them away with her burning hand. The tears evaporated into steam, and when a little welt formed on his cheek from her heat, she stopped. He wiped away the rest of the tears, but more came, and like Lauren, he gave up trying.

"I saw a foot, Eva's foot, underneath a wall that had fallen. It was kind of, at an angle. There was some space underneath it. I wasn't thinking, you know. I wasn't thinking that it was a wall, and I was a kid, and I shouldn't be able to pick it up. I put my hands underneath the side of it and lifted, just lifted. I tried as hard as I could, harder than I ever had before…and then it was up, away from the ground, over my head. Eva was there, Brady…and Jayne. She…" Cole couldn't say anymore. He squeezed Jayne's hand as hard as he could, and his forehead dropped into his free hand. He sobbed. He cried so hard that he felt like he couldn't breathe. He was gasping for air.

"I would've saved her. I would've saved her. Jayney, I would've saved you."

"Hey." Lauren knocked against the bars lightly. "Hey, it's okay. It's okay, Cole."

"I know you would've, Coley," Jayne whispered. "I know that, of course, silly."

"That's enough," Lauren said.

Cole thanked Jayne with a forced smile, and that was enough for her. He couldn't imagine how he looked to Lauren. His cheeks, like hers, were soaked with tears. His eyes were red. He took a deep, shaky breath. But he felt calm somehow.

"I'm sorry," he said.

"Me too," she said. "I've spent all this time hating, just blindly hating you…"

"I've been hating myself too. Not blindly, either."

He wished that Jayne and Lauren could talk to each other, that Lauren could know that Jayne was here now, beside him, with them. He wondered how many nights Jayne had spent with Lauren, without Lauren knowing Jayne was there, but just maybe noticing that it was a bit warmer in the house. Did Lauren feel it then, and know that Jayne was there? Of course, he couldn't say that to her, not only because he didn't want to use Jayne, or traumatize Lauren, but really, how would Lauren ever believe him? What was he going to do? Try to get Jayne to lift a penny for Lauren, like they were in some melodramatic Hollywood movie?

There was something, though.

"What would you say to Jayne, now, if she were here?" Cole asked.

Lauren smiled, just imagining Jayne there. She shrugged. "I talk to her every night," she said. Jayne nodded to Cole, happily confirming that she visited her sister.

"I guess," Lauren continued, "I would tell her that I miss her, that I love her."

"Why don't you tell her, like she's here, right now?" Cole said.

"O-okay," Lauren said, a bit awkwardly.

Cole tugged Jayne's hand so that she would stand in front of him, so that Lauren would be looking right at her, and only her. Lauren cleared her throat, feeling silly about it. But then, that feeling seemed to go away. Maybe Lauren felt Jayne's warmth. Maybe she felt that Jayne *was* there, and it didn't matter if Cole told her the truth or not.

"I love you, Jay Bird. I miss you."

Jayne reached through the bars, right through them, and put her hand against Lauren's cheek. Cole saw the metal start to glow red. Lauren gasped and reached up to touch her cheek in the same area.

A tear fell. Jayne disappeared in a puff of black smoke.

Lauren looked up, and as though emerging from a trance. She shook her head awake. "Uhhh..." Finally, Lauren looked at the clock. "I should go, sorry. I should get ready. The memorial."

Lauren stood up.

Cole thought for a moment, would Lauren let him out anyway, without him asking? Could he go with her, and save the community, like he was supposed to? But she said, "Sorry, Cole, I know you should be there. But all of this—"

"Don't worry about it."

"All of *this*, you know? Sorry."

After Lauren left, Cole just stood at the bars, looking at the clock. A staring contest. Him against time. *The memorial.* He'd almost forgotten about it. That's where Eva would be, 7:00 p.m. at the ruins. She'd be there, and so would the killer.

17

BEND, DON'T BREAK

6:46 P.M.

The memorial was fourteen minutes away. Cole hoped that Wayne would come back with news that he'd found the folder at the camp, and the backpack and ammunition, and all of it together would be enough to exonerate Cole. Then he could get to the memorial, just in case something was to happen. But Wayne's returning to the detachment seemed less and less likely with each passing second. It was stupid of him not to ask Jayne about the folder while she was here, but where was the opportunity? *Excuse me, Lauren, I know you're having a moment, but I just have to ask ghost-Jayne about something.* Jayne was gone before Cole had time to talk to her alone. She was probably off to the memorial too. He could picture her skipping around with Lauren while her big sister got ready, and then walking with her there, pretending to hold her hand all the way to the ruins.

6:48 p.m.

Everybody would be there but Cole. Even a ghost would be there and not Cole. Well, he and Jerry, Cole supposed. Jerry was sleeping soundly. In the time since Cole had woken up after getting hit on the back of the head, Jerry had gotten up exactly once—to go to the bathroom. After he'd returned to his desk, he lowered his cap over his eyes, and was out cold. If Cole had any plausible way to get out of his jail cell, he bet that Jerry wouldn't even stir. He could see the keys to the cell hanging off Jerry's belt, but Jerry was napping all the way across the room. There'd be no tension-filled escape with Cole using some kind of hook to get the keys and Jerry dramatically stirring, none of Cole freeing himself while Jerry woke up, followed by a chase.

He couldn't warn anybody either, about what he feared could happen to Eva. Of course, it was possible that nothing would happen, that the memorial would pass by without incident. The one thing Cole knew was that if something did happen and Choch were there—and Cole was sure that he would be—that he wouldn't lift a finger. Maybe he couldn't. Maybe Choch had his own rules. But it was still maddening.

What were the truths in what Choch told Cole before? Had there been truths, really? Maybe. After all, he had thrown a branch about *forever* long, Cole estimated. He bet that the branch was still flying through the air.

"Oh, dear Creator above, please do shut off this child's mind for one second!" Choch was standing beside him.

"I'm figuring things out!" Cole said.

"Everybody, and I mean *everybody*, wants you to try and bend the gosh-darn bars, Coley-Boley. I wasn't giving you some unsolvable riddle, was I? I literally mimed bar bending. Just get on with it already."

And like that, Choch was gone.

Was that really possible? Throwing a branch was one thing, but bending metal bars seemed something else entirely. Cole turned his attention away from the clock (it was now 6:52 p.m.), and focused on the bars. He took a deep breath, glanced over to a might-as-well-be-dead Jerry, then gripped his hands around the bars, one for each hand. He began to pull with all his strength. He grunted loudly. He could feel the muscles tear in his arms and chest. He could feel beads of sweat start to drip down his forehead. He could feel himself start to faint from the exertion. He could feel all of this, but he could not feel the bars move. Not by a fraction. He took his hands away from the metal and turned away from the bars, disgusted.

"Liar!" Cole shouted to an absent Choch.

He took another deep breath and returned to the bars like a fighter after round one. He gripped the metal again, and this time he moved to the side, trying to gain leverage by pushing on the bars with his feet. Any advantage he could get. He pulled at them even harder. He let out a guttural scream. This time Jerry did stir, but didn't wake. "Come on!" Cole called out, as though the bars would comply. He pulled harder, harder, and then released the bars in defeat. The sudden removal of force threw him against the concrete wall, and he slid to the ground, panting and heaving, drenched with sweat.

"You're letting her die!" he shouted to himself, to Choch, to anybody that would listen.

Cole was there again, running through the field towards the burning school, screaming the names of his friends, and hearing their screams in return. He was inside the school, looking over the bodies. They'd been trying to make it out alive. Bodies near the doors. Bodies trapped under debris. A body on the stack of blue mats, someone trying to get away from the flames. He hadn't run fast enough. And then he was in front of Ashley, watching his body jerk to the right, watching his blood splash across the trailer. He was kneeling beside Ashley's body. He was holding Alex's hand as they walked through the night. She was kissing him on the cheek. He was sitting with Maggie on a rock. He was running to the sound of a gunshot. He was standing over her body—

No. Not again. Cole stood up. He walked over to the bars and wrapped his fingers around them. He pictured each of the people he couldn't save. He saw their faces and pushed them deep down inside his chest, and then he pulled. His body shook. His muscles burned as though they were on fire, as though he were there, lifeless, on the gym floor with his friends, with his mother. He pulled. He was a seven-year-old boy, lifting a wall. Doing the impossible. He pulled, and he felt the thick, round metal bars begin to give. He pulled harder, and the bars began to spread apart from each other, further and further. He let out one last scream, and everything came out of him, everything he had been holding in for ten years, all the tears, all the pain, all the faces of the kids that had passed away. The bars burst apart like pieces of tin foil. He let go. Cole stood there, looking in disbelief at the large space he'd made between the prison bars. He hesitated for only a moment, then stepped outside of the cell. He walked up to the front door and checked the clock.

6:57 p.m.

He would make it. Before leaving, he looked across the room to where Jerry was snoring loudly.

"Really?"

18

MEMORIAL

COLE RAN FASTER THAN WHEN HE'D HEARD the gunshot in Blackwood Forest. Out of desperation, and knowing that if Choch had brought up something happening tonight, Cole needed to be there. He felt like he was moving at warp speed. Everything blurred as he sprinted by—the cemetery, The X, The Fish, the clinic, the path that led to the airport, where he'd arrived what seemed like an eternity ago. When Cole came to the perimeter of the old school, where it now lay in untouched ruins, he skidded to a stop and found cover in the woods. It would suck if Mr. Kirkness saw him and took him back to jail before he was able to save Eva. Never mind having to explain the bent prison bars. It was 6:59 p.m., one minute until the memorial started. Only a few people were gathering in front of the ruins, a much smaller crowd than Cole had expected, even given the murders and the sickness.

Returning here, staring at the ruins, panic came over him again. He checked his pocket instinctively, but remembered that the pill bottle had been taken away. It was probably stashed in Wayne's desk, in an evidence bag along with Ashley's phone and the tobacco his grandmother had given him to offer here and now. That wasn't going to happen, and the panic wasn't going to go away so easily. Knowing he didn't have his pills increased his panic. Whether he took them or not, when his anxiety reared its head he always had them to fall back on. His knees were buckling, his legs shaking, his heart racing, and sweat pouring out of every pore. He felt like he was going to faint at any moment.

7:00 p.m.

A couple of people walked past Cole on their way to the ruins. He ducked down, concealing himself. They didn't see him, even while he tried to moderate his panic with deep breaths—*in through the nose, out through the mouth.* They continued on to the memorial. Cole didn't rise out of the underbrush until they'd joined the others already there. And when he did stand up he wasn't sure that he'd make it all the way, wasn't sure that he could stay up. His legs felt brittle, about to crumble beneath him any given moment. Cole counted community members, curious about how many were there, and also to distract himself from the anxiety. It didn't take long. Seven. *Really?* That's what the school fire meant to people? Or was it just too hard to be there? He looked around the area, over the field, at the path leading up to the school, back towards the community, trying to will somebody else there, to give a shit.

7:03 p.m.

In through the nose, out through the mouth, right from the belly. Five seconds in, seven seconds out. Cole did this over and over, but it didn't get better. He closed his eyes and pictured himself on a boat on a lake, and he imagined calm, housed within a ball of light, floating around him. He reached out and grabbed the ball, shoved it deep inside his chest. He felt burning in his chest, and then flames burst out of his body. He opened his eyes with a gasp for air, patting at his chest as though he were on fire.

"What kind of hero am I?" he whispered.

7:07 p.m.

Twelve people now. No killer. No Eva, Brady, Michael, or Mr. Kirkness either. No news was good news. It was a bit more encouraging that the crowd had almost doubled—but still, *come on.* Cole was leaning against a tree, steadying himself due to his wobbly knees. He'd picked a twig from the same tree and was methodically pulling out leaf buds, as though playing "she loves me, she loves me not." He'd become quite adept at quickly crouching down when he heard footsteps approaching. And though each time he was sure he wouldn't be able to stand back up, so far he had accomplished what felt like a monumental feat. It felt a bit easier, too, with each success-ful attempt.

7:16 p.m.

"I ran *why?*" Cole whispered to himself as he continued his very slow squat workout, crouching down, standing up, crouching down, standing up. There were thirty-seven people now, but he was a bit too bored at this point to be encouraged by the turnout. The anxiety was beginning to subside, though, probably out of boredom. *Should've tried that strategy with my therapist,* he thought. *Boredom. Just sit in the bush, and do nothing, for a long time. Anxiety cured.* The memorial hadn't started yet. Reynold was there now. He'd come from the other direction, from the clinic. Cole was glad that Reynold hadn't walked past him, because he wasn't sure what that would've done to his anx-iety, or if he would've been able to keep hiding. He had a question or two for the presumptive Chief. There was still no Eva, nor her dad, and no gang yet either. Cole couldn't imagine the memorial starting with-out the two survivors.

7:22 p.m.

Cole's anxiety returned when Eva walked past the bush, flanked by Brady, Michael, and Mr. Kirkness. The boys looked like some kind of security detail. Mr. Kirkness had obviously heeded Cole's warning, even if he didn't quite believe him. Better safe than sorry. Of course, Mr. Kirkness wasn't about to hire Reynold for the job.

It was either increased anxiety when Cole saw Eva, or some foolish schoolboy feelings that were returning at the worst possible time. She looked beautiful, as always. Beautiful and tough. He wanted to jump out of the bush and say, "I'll take it from here, boys." It seemed more likely that he was there to do that, rather than hide in the woods. At least it would've been *something* to do. Wayne might've shot him, but this was getting ridiculous. The memorial was now twenty-four min-utes late, but there were sixty-two people there, including Eva and her detail.

7:31 p.m.

Cole was peeing against the tree that he had steadied himself with earlier when he heard the drum thud to life. He gasped for a breath, quickly stopped what he was doing, getting a bit of pee on his pant leg. He zipped up and assessed the wet spot, patting at it as though this action would instantly dry it. Then, even though he was hidden well, and everybody was across the field, he looked around like somebody might've seen him and the wet circle on his pants. But he was still alone, and thankfully spared the embarrassment.

Thump.

A heartbeat. He felt it in the ground, through his body, in his chest. A memory came to him as the drum continued to beat...

Thump. Thump.

He was holding his mother's hand. His dad's. They were at the school, in the gym. The grade six kids were graduating. The Grand Entry was winding its way to the front of the crowd, Elders, chief and council, the principal, teachers.

Thump. Thump. Thump.

The drum was part of his spirit, coursing through his veins. He let go of his parents' hands, put his cheek against the hardwood floor, listened to the drum, felt the drum. It was life.

Thump. Thump. Thump. Thump.

He felt it now, like he did then.

The honour song began. Cole stood up straight, clasped his hands, and bowed his head. He listened to the beat, the rhythmic singing. Even though he was hiding in the woods, waiting for a killer that he hoped wouldn't show up, it was something he felt a part of. It sounded like all eighty-three people were joining in on the song. Cole started singing, too. The words came to him, in his language, as though he had sung them every day for the last ten years, like he hadn't neglected them. He sang through tears, and—

"It's like riding a bike, isn't it?"

"I think there's a better term for it." Cole quickly wiped his tears away, as if he could hide anything from Choch. But it wasn't the tears Choch was looking at. He was staring at the wet spot on Cole's pants, snorting, trying not to laugh.

"Dude," Choch said.

"Shut up," Cole said.

"Do you know what's great about being me?" Choch didn't wait for Cole to answer. He transformed into a coyote, lifted a leg, and peed against a tree. "See?" he said while the pee trail died off. He farted, then turned human again and rubbed his hands together. A job well done. "No fuss, no muss. Or should I say mess?"

"You're literally the worst," Cole said.

"Of course, I don't really ever *have* to pee, but I find it soothing." Choch checked his watch. Cole checked it, too. 7:42 p.m. "Have you been standing in the bush here for forty-two minutes?"

"Yeah," Cole said, "they started, like, half an hour late."

"Gosh, that is *so* annoying. And you sprinted over here with a head full of steam, didn't you? Wanted to get here right on time, I'd imagine."

"Well, Eva possibly getting killed kind of motivated me," Cole said.

"How inconsiderate! And after you'd run *so* fast," Choch said.

"Right?"

"It's almost as if *you're* from the city, where everybody is a slave to time, and *they're* from a place where there are things far more important than a clock," Choch said.

"Right," Cole said. "I get it."

"If you can remember a song, Coley-Boley, you've got to remember that, too."

"Well, thanks for reminding me. I knew you were good for something. But if you could stop calling me Coley-Boley, that'd be awesome."

"It's a nickname, a term of endearment, like Choch."

"You gave yourself that name. That doesn't count."

"It's just short for something," Choch said, sounding a little offended.

"Short for what?"

"Chochinov."

"What? Why would you call yourself something like that? Who's named that up here?"

"Anyway," Choch stepped out of the bush and into the field. He started walking towards the memorial and didn't look back. "Time waits for no man."

"You just said—"

"Keep your eyes peeled, Coley. Like an overripe banana."

7:59 p.m.

Cole scanned the crowd for the millionth time. Lauren was there, with Jayne's dim fire beside her. Jayne's little arm was raised into the air, pretending to hold Lauren's hand. Wayne, Michael, and Brady were all standing next to Eva. Reynold was at the front of the crowd, speaking to them. Dr. Captain wasn't there. This didn't come as a surprise. She was most certainly back at the clinic, helping others, as futile as that seemed, and working through the pain of losing Alex. Elder Mariah wasn't there either, and this surprised Cole. She was the community Elder, and would've been important at a gathering like this. He had no way to find out where she was, either. His phone was confiscated, and he wasn't sure Brady would've answered him, regardless. Brady's body language wasn't an indication. He looked sad, of course. It was a gathering for all their dead friends. A pall hung over the memorial, over Brady and everybody else. Cole could feel it as clearly as he could a panic attack. The only beauty Cole could see were the northern lights overhead, the community's namesake. They were lively tonight, moving in waves. Cole imagined, Cole *knew*, the spirits of those that had passed on were dancing for the ones that were left behind, left in mourning.

8:29 p.m.

Another Elder from Wounded Sky, Elder Bear, closed the memorial in prayer. The crowd bowed their heads. People removed their hats and their glasses. Cole bowed his head too. He couldn't quite hear what was being said. It didn't matter. He whispered his own prayer to God. He used to pray for different things as a young child than as a teenager. He used to pray for all of it to be taken away, all the pain, all the death. He used to pray for the night to start again with him and Eva on the blue mats, and he wouldn't leave, and the fire would never happen. As he grew older, he just prayed for healing—for the community that he'd left behind, and for himself. He did that now, but he prayed that there'd be no more suffering. *Please, God, no more.*

When he finished, when he opened his eyes, he saw that the memorial had ended. People were walking away from the school ruins. He crouched down to hide once more from the crowd that walked past. Some people lingered behind for a minute, approached the ruins, to touch a stone or a brick that had been destroyed, as though they could make it whole again, as though they, too, were hoping for the same thing that Cole used to hope for. For everything to be as it was, for none of this to have happened.

Before long, the only people left at the memorial were Brady, Eva, and Wayne. Michael had left, reluctantly. Cole had observed Michael and Eva discussing something—maybe how Michael wanted to stay, but Eva convinced him to be with his mother. Or it could've been the other way around, Cole supposed, but Eva was strong like that. Eva didn't need anybody sticking around to support her. She never did. It's why being saved ten years ago had been so hard on her, feeling indebted in that way. And she probably was none too pleased with a wall of men around her. Or maybe it was neither. Maybe they were just saying goodbye to each other for now, and Michael had gone off to the clinic.

Watching the memorial and taking part in it, even though he was hiding in the woods, had been healing for him, in a way. And it was fitting, too, in that he was separated from everybody else, as he always had been. But now the memorial was done, and he'd been in the woods for an hour-and-a-half. It hit him that he'd broken out of jail. What was Wayne going to say when he went back to the RCMP detachment to find Cole gone, and the prison bars bent like they were pipe cleaners? What would *Cole* say? What *could* he say? He began to pace around the little area of Blackwood Forest that he'd claimed for himself. *Get used to it here,* he thought. How could he ever leave, or show his face in the community? He was a fugitive. How—

Eva screamed. Cole returned from his thoughts. He looked across the field to see a man with a gun emerging from the woods. He was dressed in black from head to toe, with a balaclava over his face. He had his gun pointed directly at Eva as he slowly drew closer and closer to her. In response, Wayne and Brady stepped in front of Eva. Wayne went for his own gun.

"Don't try it!" the gunman shouted. "Get your hands up, now!"

Wayne and Brady complied. Cole stepped forward. This was it. This was why he broke out of jail.

He was a foot closer to them, a foot closer to the ruins. He felt the panic return.

"Not now." Cole took another step, but almost fell over. His whole body was shaking, like he was naked in the winter.

The gunman was no more than five feet away from them now.

Cole took another step. Each step was getting harder to take. He was having a heart attack. He swore it was a heart attack. He could hear Mrs. Benjamin crying out for somebody to call 9-1-1. He looked at his t-shirt, saw it vibrating from his heartbeat, fast and hard. He went through the techniques his therapist taught him. He took another step, almost out of the woods now.

"Show us your face, coward!" Eva said.

"Eva!" Wayne backed up closer to her.

Deep breathing. Visualization. Mindfulness. None of it worked now. Cole fell onto his hands. He couldn't walk anymore. He clawed his way forward. "Please. Help me."

"Don't move!" The gunman cocked the hammer on the gun.

"I'm weak," Cole had said to his therapist.

"You're not weak, Cole. You're sick," she'd said. She'd told him that when the anxiety was at its worst, it was fight or flight, just stuck there. It was like adrenaline. "You know what you should do?" she'd said. "Run, lift weights, do something. Use the energy. It's there. Use it. Don't let it stop you."

"What do you want!?" Brady said.

"Eva," the gunman said. "I'm here for Eva."

"Eva," Cole said, down on all fours. He lifted his knees up, pushed his knuckles into the ground like he was starting a race. *Use it. Use the energy. Don't let it stop you.* "Eva!" He exploded into a run. Wind rushed against his face. Grass whipped against his shins. "EVA!"

They all looked in Cole's direction. Eva. Wayne. Brady. And by the time the gunman looked in Cole's direction, Cole had already catapulted himself through the air, towards him. Wayne saw the opportunity. He drew his gun. The gunman let off a desperate shot. Cole's shoulder connected with the killer's torso, and the gunman flew through the air, skidding along the ground. He came to a stop twenty feet away. Cole landed on the ground, and rolled almost forever himself, just from the momentum. He leapt to his feet, ready to charge at the gunman again, who was just pulling himself back up.

"Cole!" Brady shouted.

Wayne was on his back, his head on Eva's lap. Eva's pants and shirt—her hands—were covered in Wayne's blood. Cole could see a gunshot wound in Wayne's stomach. His light blue dress shirt was almost deep red now.

The gunman was running towards Blackwood Forest.

Cole looked back and forth.

"He needs to get to Dr. Captain!" Brady said.

Eva was trying to put pressure on the wound, but all Cole could see was blood rushing through her fingers, over her hands.

Wayne was going to die.

The gunman was almost at the woods. Cole could catch him. "I can get him!"

"No!" Eva cried. Tears were falling across her cheeks. Tears were mixing with the blood that had splashed against her skin.

The killer was gone.

Cole rushed over to Eva and Wayne. He lifted Wayne up into his arms, and ran towards the clinic.

19

THE GUNMAN

FIVE HUNDRED NINETY-THREE DOTS in the ceiling tiles. That's what Cole had counted while Eva paced back and forth down the hallway of the clinic. They hadn't said much to each other, but they had spoken in glances. At least she hadn't looked at him like he was a killer. It was just after 11:00 p.m. Cole had spent the last two hours counting the dots (after he'd counted all the ceiling tiles) and praying to God that Dr. Captain would be successful and Mr. Kirkness would be okay. Dr. Captain had come out of the room when she could, giving Eva updates. The updates had become more hopeful, from "grave" to "critical-but-stable." Hopeful was better than what they'd experienced lately. Hopeful had to be enough.

Cole, all the while, counting this, counting that, hearing bad news, hearing encouraging news, chastised himself for once again being too late or too incompetent to prevent more violence. He had his head rested back on the top of the chair, staring up. Good for counting dots, and praying.

Dr. Captain came into the room again. She called Eva over. Eva was over by the ancient coffee machine, trying to get it to work. She was hitting it, but not getting anything out of it. That might've been a blessing. Clinic coffee tasted like hot soap. Eva ran over to Dr. Captain, who took her into her father's room.

Six hundred thirty-seven dots in the ceiling tiles. Cole counted up that high before Eva came out of the room. She sat down beside him. Cole looked away from the ceiling, to Eva. He tried to rub the soreness out of his neck.

"How is he?" Cole asked.

"He'll make it," Eva said.

"Thank God."

"Thank Dr. Captain," Eva corrected.

They fell silent. Wayne's heart monitor filled the silence. After fourteen hypnotic beeps, Eva said, "You should save Creator for Elder Mariah."

That was another prayer Cole had offered up. When they first arrived, Cole had carried Wayne through the hallways, following Dr. Captain to one of the only open beds After Dr. Captain and Wayne were inside and the door closed, Eva started pacing the hallway. When it was just Brady and Cole, Cole had heard the news. While Cole was incarcerated at the RCMP detachment, Elder Mariah had fallen ill. If she followed the same trajectory as every other Wounded Sky band member who had gotten sick, then she'd be dead sometime tomorrow. Presently, Brady was holding vigil at his grandmother's side, giving her medicines, the ones that he had learned from her. He sent up his own prayers, maybe counting ceiling tiles, waiting for the inevitable while hoping against it.

"I've been talking to God about it all," Cole said. "I'm not sure if He's listening." Cole wasn't even sure if Choch was listening, for that matter. Since spending some time with him in the bush, the spirit being had been conspicuously absent. Maybe he was just as frustrated with Cole's ineptitude as Cole was.

"Sometimes I think He's forgotten all about Wounded Sky," Eva said.

"I want to think He's got some plan for us," Cole said, and according to Choch this was, in fact, the case. Cole was the plan. *Shitty plan, though. Maybe back to the drawing board on that one. Super strength, super speed, and still...*

"How'd you get out anyway?" Eva asked. "We could've used a miracle somewhere else. No offence."

"None taken." Cole had been thinking since the incident that if he hadn't charged across the field like some idiot, the gunman wouldn't have been distracted, Wayne wouldn't have tried to shoot the gunman, and Wayne might be okay right now. Maybe he, or Eva, or Brady, could've talked the shooter out of it. It was all cause-and-effect. Too late now. Always too late.

"So?" Eva prompted, wanting an answer to her question. "The jail? You were kind of in there for suspicion of murder. They wouldn't just let you out. Even Jerry wouldn't have let you out."

Truth? Cole couldn't decide how to respond in these brief moments. Wait too long and it would seem like a lie anyway, even if it wasn't. A half-truth, then. She couldn't know what he did now, but eventually she would, and so he was careful not to say anything that would be called a lie later. "I got out on my own?" *Totally, 100 percent true.*

"Obviously, Cole. Did you steal keys, did you—"

Cole tried a distraction technique, then. "I knew you were in trouble, so I had to get out. Didn't your dad say anything? I told him that."

"Yeah, he said I might be in trouble, but that was about it. I could tell he was worried. I think he was trying not to worry me, but, you know, that worried me." Eva shook her head. "How did you know?"

Cole told her about his subsequent trip to the camp, and about the folder and the files. He told her about hearing the shot, and how he thought it was her.

"Shit," Eva said.

"Shit is right," Cole said. "And he's just going to keep coming and coming…"

Eva stood up. She pulled Wayne's gun out from the back of her jeans.

"Whoa!" Cole said. "Eva, what the heck?"

"If he's going to come for us, then I'm just going to go to him. At least then I'll have some kind of an advantage, right?"

"No," Cole pleaded. "We should call Lauren or Jerry. You can't just face off with this guy. You saw what happened to your dad."

"Jerry? Really?"

"Okay Lauren. Let's call Lauren."

"No," Eva said. "I have to do this."

No, Cole thought, *I have to. And do it right, for a change.* It wasn't her mission, it was his. There he was, trying to pawn it off on Lauren. He needed to find a way to convince Eva not to go, and go on his own, like it was supposed to be. But, looking at her, right into her eyes, he knew that she couldn't be convinced. He knew her well enough to know that. So, there was only one alternative. "*We* have to do this. Not you. I'm coming." Cole stood up.

Eva nodded, like *okay, let's do this*. Maybe she saw the same thing in Cole, that there was no way he wasn't coming. "It'll be just like old times. We even have my dad's gun again."

"This isn't shooting cans, Eva. This is a person, with his own gun, too," Cole said. "And he wants to kill us."

"Well, we won't be hard to find." It was the perfect, most kick-ass thing to say.

"Just, let's not go to the camp like Rambo, okay?"

"Please," Eva said. "He won't even see me coming. This is my thing. I'm more worried about you, city boy."

"I'll be okay," Cole said. "I've been practicing."

They started on their way down the hall, to the front door, through the field, towards Blackwood Forest.

It wasn't a long walk, now that they knew where to go. It was Cole's third trip there, and Eva's second, but she didn't even need the app she'd used to track the path. Eva probably knew the woods as well as she knew the community. She was holding the gun the whole time, turning blind corners with it like she was in a cop show. Cole wasn't sure if she'd learned how to do *that* from her dad.

The gunman was waiting for them, gun drawn, balaclava over his face. There was no need to sneak up on the camp, in case he was ready to ambush them. He was standing at one side, Cole and Eva entered at the other.

"Oh good. Two birds with one stone." The killer pointed his gun, waved it back and forth, from Cole to Eva. "Which of you wants to go first?"

"Why are you doing this?" Cole asked. "Who wants us dead?"

"That's classified," the gunman said. "I'm just tryin' to do my job."

"How honourable of you," Eva said.

The gunman stepped forward. Once, twice. "Who said anythin' about honour? I'm not crazy. This pays. Cash."

"You're really just doing this for money? Killing kids? Do you know what we've been through?" Cole asked.

"I'm doin' it for a *lotta* money, if that matters," the gunman said. "Plus, you know, my day job doesn't pay that well…" The gunman reached up with his free hand, and slipped off the balaclava. "But if you know Mr. McCabe, that's not a surprise, I guess."

"Scott?" Cole said.

"You could say that, in a way, this is kinda your fault, city boy," Scott said. "You had to show your red-apple ass back here. You made more people hurt than me just by comin' back, Harper."

"You killed Ashley, Alex…" Eva started.

"Maggie…and you shot Mr. Kirkness," Cole finished. "How do you think this is going to end for you?"

"First of all, I never killed Maggie. Second of all, they're gonna take care of me."

Eva raised her gun. "I'll take care of you first, shithead."

"What do you mean you didn't kill Maggie? Who's going to take care of you?" Cole asked.

"Oh my God, shut up," Scott said. "Let's just get this over with." He cocked the hammer of his gun. Eva did the same.

Cole watched as her index finger tensed over the trigger.

"I can help, Coley!" Jayne appeared in front of Scott, who was oblivious to her. She'd never looked so bright, and never felt so hot. She looked at Cole, pleading for him to say "yes." She couldn't be hurt.

Cole nodded.

Jayne walked forward calmly, put her burning hand on the nozzle of the gun.

"Sorry, Scott," Cole said. "I have a job to do too."

The gun turned red. Scott screamed in pain. He dropped the weapon. Before the gun hit the ground, Cole rushed forward and jumped at Scott. They flew through the air, and then they tumbled across the ground, between the path and the forest. They came to a stop with Scott on top of Cole, his hands pressing down on Cole's throat.

"I've been waitin' for this," Scott said.

Cole's vision began to go black. He wasn't unfamiliar with this sensation. He'd felt it each time he thought he was going to faint. Scott was pressing down on Cole's carotid artery. Soon, he'd be out cold. That meant Eva would die.

"Get off him!" Eva shot her gun into the air.

Cole grasped at Scott's wrists, which were covered in black sleeves and black gloves. Flashes from the prison break pulsed in Cole's brain. Scott was human. Cole's strength wasn't. He pulled hard on Scott's wrists. They flew apart. He fell towards Cole. Cole kicked him off. Scott grunted and landed on the ground ten feet away, tumbling even further along the ground and over the tent. He got up instantly—just in time to find Cole charging at him again. Cole punched him in the chest with both fists.

Scott didn't get up so quickly this time. Blood dripped from his mouth. He was gasping for air. Cole approached him.

"Come…on…" Scott said. "City…boy."

Cole obliged. The two men hit the ground. Cole was on top this time. He straddled Scott, sent blow after blow across his face. Cole screamed. He kept punching, punching, punching. Scott's face grew bloodier with each hit, until he went limp. Cole felt a hand on his shoulder. He turned around with a raised fist, his eyes wild with rage.

"Cole!" Eva said. "Stop! This isn't you."

"Eva?"

She reached forward and put her hand over his fist. She lowered his hand.

"Stop," she said.

Cole looked back at Scott, unconscious and almost unrecognizable, then at Eva. For a moment, he felt like they were back in the gym, sitting up on the mats, away from the world.

"I wish I would've stayed that night," he said.

Eva let out a sharp breath from her nose. She smiled. "And then where would we be?"

Cole shrugged. "Together."

"Dead together." She pulled his hand towards her. "Come on, we have to go."

"Is it over?"

"Yeah, it's over."

With Eva's help, Cole started to get up from his knees, but was pulled backwards. His head hit a rock. This sent him into a haze. Scott rolled over on top of Cole.

"Sorry," Scott whispered. Maybe that's all Scott could do was whisper. He looked almost dead. Blood dripped from his mouth onto Cole's shirt and skin. "I don't have a choice…"

Cole felt cold steel pierce his chest.

"No!" Eva screamed.

Cole's vision began to cloud, and he could feel blood rush from his limbs. He saw a blurry Eva lift the gun and aim it at Scott. Scott was digging the knife deeper and deeper into Cole. Fire burst from the gun's nozzle. *Pop.* Scott's body jerked, and then he collapsed on top of Cole, which plunged the knife deeper into Cole's body.

Eva dropped the gun. She ran over and struggled to roll Scott off Cole. She knelt down at his side. He could hardly see her. He was slipping away. He could see the handle of the knife sticking from his chest, blood painting his shirt red. She reached for it, deciding if she should take it out or not. The sweetgrass ring was hanging from her neck. He tried to touch it, but his arm wouldn't listen. She grabbed his hand.

"Cole!" she cried.

She sounded so far away.

"Don't leave me," she said.

He let go of her hand and jumped off the stack of blue mats. He looked at her. She'd inched up to the side of the mats.

"Don't leave me."

"I'll come back."

Cole walked across the gymnasium floor. He walked to the back door and pushed it open. He went outside and was hit by the cool air. It was nighttime. Dark outside. The black. Cole ventured into the black, and was covered with it. There was the moon, soft and white in the distance. He stared at it, begging for any light. It drew closer—bigger, brighter—until there was only a soft, white light.

20

ONCE MORE, WITH FEELING

IT WAS ALMOST MIDNIGHT. That's how late it felt, anyway. Cole didn't dare peek his head out from under the comfort of the blanket. His mother could come in at any point, and then he'd be busted. The flashlight wasn't visible from outside the blanket. He knew: he'd tested it. The blanket, handmade by Elder Mariah, was thick. What he hadn't planned for was how it might look for his mother to enter his bedroom and see a large, upright lump underneath the blanket.

When he heard the bedroom door open, he stopped turning the pages of his comic. He stopped breathing too. The door shut. He heard footsteps moving across the bedroom floor. They stopped at the side of his bed. He felt the blanket compress over his right shoulder, a gentle touch. He heard his mother say, "Cole," almost apologetically. This didn't feel right. When he'd previously been caught reading comics in the night his mother had never sounded sorry about it. *Oh, sorry, honey, I didn't mean to interrupt your reading; please, stay up all night,* was something he absolutely never heard, and never expected to hear.

He pulled the blanket off his body and turned towards his mother, shining the light directly in her face. She smiled and turned it off. It was just them, sitting there in the glow of the northern lights, so close that they looked like mist hanging over the grass in the morning.

"Cole." She sat down at the side of his bed.

He put the comic down. Her eyes were red. She'd been crying.

"What is it, Mommy?"

"Come here." She gathered him into her arms. She squeezed him tight. "Your father, Cole. He died today."

He tried to pull away from her, as though it was her fault, as though if he ran away from her as far as he could it would make what she said not true. He started to cry, then sob, and it made his mother's shirt wet. She just held him tighter and tighter, and they sat there well into the night. She rocked him back and forth in her arms. He cried into her shirt, she cried into his. Finally, sometime in the morning, when the northern lights had given way to the warm hues of the rising sun, he asked, "Are you going to die, Mommy?"

"One day I'll die," she said. "But not for a long time."

"Promise?"

"Promise."

"I like that memory best," Choch said.

Cole opened his eyes to white as his vision came into focus. There wasn't pain, not at first. There was only the white light at the end of the tunnel, the pathway to the sky above, with the spirits dancing, waiting for him. After everything he'd been through, he would've been happy there. But Choch's intrusion meant that Cole was alive. If that weren't enough, a dull ache in his chest closely followed. He held the wound, bandaged now and coated in dried blood.

"But she lied," Cole said.

"She was wrong." Choch sat forward and handed Cole a small cup of water. Cole took it, sipped it, and handed it back. "There's a difference."

"Maybe I'm the liar," Cole said with a grunt. He grunted after everything, every word, every movement.

"How so?" Choch asked.

"I wanted to save her as much as I did Brady and Eva. I wanted to save all of them, and I didn't," Cole said.

"Now, Cole, you really need to get over it. Honestly, it's been ten years of beating yourself up, and look what it's done to your poor nerves."

Cole didn't respond to that. He was listening, but didn't have anything to say. In fact, he agreed with Choch, and was surprised that he did. It surprised him as much as Choch saying something without a hint of humour or sarcasm.

"Mr. Kirkness," Cole said.

Choch rolled his eyes, and nodded like, *okay, okay, okay,* as though Cole were a child in a store having asked for a toy one thousand times. "To avoid any unnecessary exposition, because Creator knows how boring that all is, especially to *readers,* and because nobody wants to see you go from bedside to bedside, here's what you need to know: as Dr. Captain indicated, Wayne will pull through. He was brought here just in time, thanks to *you.* Eva's been playing musical chairs between you and her father. It's rather cute, actually…"

"She sat here?"

"Yes, yes, yes, she sat right *here.*" Choch got up from the chair and briefly motioned to the red cushion before sitting back down again—farting at the same time, it must be said, as embarrassing as it might be (but not for Choch, of course). "Wetting your lips with a damp Q-tip, and playing with that ring you made her like it was some charm, I suppose."

Cole managed a smile at this. She hadn't thrown it away.

"Where was I?" Choch asked. "Oh yes. Scott, whom yes, everybody now recognizes as the one who killed your friends, also survived. He's here in the clinic, near death I should add, due to being pulverized by yourself and shot by your lovely friend. You won't be able to see him, so don't bother trying. Move things along, you know. And—"

"Elder Mariah…"

"I was just about to…" Choch started, flabbergasted. "*Honestly.* I say I'll summarize, and then—"

"Sorry."

"I suppose you did just almost die, so I can forgive your rudeness."

"Thank you," Cole said, but Choch didn't start right away. *Always the showman.* "Elder Mariah?" Cole prompted after growing impatient.

"Quite ill, I'm afraid," Choch said. "Quite ill." At this, Choch sounded unequivocally upset. He looked away from Cole, to the floor, lost in thought. *Imagine that,* Cole wondered, *a spirit being like him, lost in thought.* Choch snapped out of it, and said, in a rush to finish, "And Jayne is probably off playing with her friends at the cemetery. I'm sure she'll be by to check on you as well. You are, after all, the man of the hour."

Cole thought of Elder Mariah. He wondered how bad she really was, how close to death. Frantically, as frantic as he could allow himself to be, he checked the clock on the wall. It read 3:57 p.m. But—what day?

"Relax," Choch said. "It's just the next day. There's time."

"Time for what?"

"Time to get your strength back up before you go trying to save another life. You are, after all, The Reckoner, are you not?" Choch got up, straightened out his pants, his hat, and got himself looking perfectly fine.

"Choch, you didn't just—"

"Now, now. No need to get all *weepy.* I'd best get back to the diner." He made his way over to the door. "My shift's about to start."

"You're staying?" Cole asked. "Like, *here?*"

"Why yes, naturally. The jackfish here is to-die-for. Right out of Silk River and onto the plate. Fresh as a daisy."

"But why would you—"

"I get free meals every shift. Silly boy."

Cole slept the afternoon away. When he woke up in the evening, the chest pain seemed to have lessened quicker than what seemed natural. He figured this, too, was a gift he had been given. He wondered, though, if he had held up his end of the bargain, then why did he still have these abilities? Was it something he got to keep? Now that he knew how to use his strength and speed, he wondered what good he could do. *The world's first Indigenous superhero? The world's first superhero, period.* He just happened to be Indigenous. He was day-dreaming about this, setting aside the hard days he'd just experienced and giving himself superhero names while simultaneously debating whether he was borderline appropriating his own culture, when Eva and Brady walked into the room.

"Wow," Brady said. "You're sure getting the hero's treatment. Hard to find a room without a bunch of beds in it."

"They're just making sure he's not exposed to the illness," Eva said to Brady. "It's okay, Cole, don't mind B."

"Hey, I think it's cool," Brady said.

Brady had come into the room with some levity, but Cole knew better. This was an act. Somewhere in the clinic, Elder Mariah was dying. Brady was trying to shield Cole. It wasn't necessary, but Cole didn't say anything. Cole shimmied to sit up, propped against some pillows.

"Easy," Eva said to him. "You just had a knife stuck in your chest. Dr. Captain said another inch and you would've been toast."

"It's okay," Cole said. "It must not have been that bad, really."

"Not that bad?!" Eva said. "Cole, he stabbed you with a fu—"

"I put some, uhhh…" Brady pointed at the wound. A spot of blood seeped through the gauze pad taped to Cole's chest. "Medicine on the wound when you were asleep. I guess it worked."

"Thanks, Brady," Cole said.

Eva was leaning forward in the chair. The ring was outside of her shirt, and she was twirling it around in her fingers.

"Where's Michael?" Cole asked.

"With his mom, I think," Eva said.

"How is he?"

"As good as you could expect? Both of them are. As good as you could expect."

Cole shook his head. "He must've *hated* me."

"He's fine now, I think. He'll be fine, anyway," Eva said. "He knows you didn't…" She trailed off, couldn't stand to say Alex's name right now. Cole just nodded.

"You saved me." Cole had his hand resting at his side. He moved it to the edge of the bed slightly, just in case she might get the signal. He opened his hand, palm up. She traced the scar on his palm with her fingertip, and then she took his hand and squeezed it.

"I guess that makes us even."

She let go of his hand, and for a moment, even though his two best friends were there, he felt alone.

"I just can't figure it out," Brady said. "Why did Scott do all those things? Why did he kill Ashley, Alex, Maggie? Why did he want to kill Eva?"

Cole looked back and forth, between Eva and Brady, and argued with himself how much to tell them. All he had were pieces, and he wasn't sure yet how they all fit together. What could he say to them that would make sense, if nothing made much sense to him?

"Do you know those files I told you about?" Cole asked Eva.

"Yeah," Eva said.

"Eva told me about them, sure," Brady said.

"It wasn't just a hit list or whatever. They were talking about an experiment or something. We were getting tested for a cure for a virus. They called it God Flare. I think…" Cole remembered what Choch had just said to him, about saving Elder Mariah's life. Could he? Was that what it meant on his file when it read "SUCCESSFUL"? "It's the same virus that everybody has now."

"That's why Ashley," Brady started, "that's why everybody was killed? Because of a stupid virus? Why?"

"A cover-up? I don't know," Cole said. "All I know is that kids were getting a placebo, or a real test that failed. Except mine. Mine said it worked."

"What, like you can cure it?" Eva asked.

"I don't know," Cole said. "Maybe."

Brady looked around the room. Cole did, too, out of curiosity, wondering what Brady was looking for. They were in a storage room with a bunch of things stuffed along the sides of the room—boxes, chairs, medical supplies. Brady saw what he was searching for. He walked to the back corner of the room and grabbed an old wheelchair. He unfolded it, brushed off some dust, and wheeled it up to Cole's bedside.

"What are you doing?" Cole asked.

"If you think you can cure this thing," Brady said, "Then you're going to start with my kókom."

21

HOW TO SAVE A LIFE

ELDER MARIAH WAS UNCONSCIOUS, a shell of her former self. Her hair, once mostly black despite her age, looked dead and grey. Her skin, too, looked pale, as though the grey had filtered down from her hair to her skin. Cole was rolled right up next to her. He took her hand, bony and cold, and watched as her chest moved in time with her shallow breath.

"Elder," Cole whispered, as though his voice alone was enough to bring her back to life, because surely this was what death looked like.

She didn't stir. He looked back at his friends and made eye contact with Brady. Their exchanged look said everything. She didn't have much time left. Brady went over to the side table, picked up the smudge bowl and the feather resting on the surface by its side. He walked to the other side of the bed, and then he meticulously smudged his kókom from head to toe, whispering a prayer in their language all the way. When he was done, he walked up to Cole and offered to smudge him. Cole didn't know what to say at first. He sat there, watching the smoke rise and the tiny ember within the bundle glow reddish-orange. He hadn't done this since leaving Wounded Sky. It felt foreign to him.

"It's okay," Brady said, as though knowing Cole's inner struggle.

Cole nodded. Brady raised the smudge bowl, and Cole, with two hands raised together in the shape of wings, collected the smoke. He brought it towards his body in fluid movements, first brushing it through his hair, then over his eyes, his mouth, and his heart and, finally, pushing smoke down over the rest of his body.

"Ekosani," Cole said, thanking Brady in Cree.

Brady replaced the smudge bowl and the feather on the side table, and then he pulled up a chair and sat beside Cole. Eva stood behind them, her right hand on Brady's shoulder and her left hand on Cole's.

"What now?" she asked.

Brady looked at Cole, then at Elder Mariah, trying to figure something out. Finally, he said, "I guess we have to get your blood into her. Simple. Right?"

"Makes sense, but how do we do that without Dr. Captain?" Cole asked.

Brady rubbed his chin as though he had hair there. To Cole Brady still looked wise, but it was Cole who talked first. The idea came to him in a memory. "You know that old Mustang in Ashley's driveway, the one that's been there for a million years?"

"Yeah, of course," Brady said.

"Okay," Cole said. "So one time, my dad was low on gas, and the gas station was closed. We went to Ashley's, and he took a garden hose. He stuck one end in the Mustang, sucked on the other end, and when the gas started to come out, he stuck the *other* end into his car. Voilà—we had gas."

"So you want to get a tube, suck your blood out one end, and put it in my kókom on the other end?" Brady tried to clarify.

"Something like that," Cole said. "Do you have any better ideas?"

Brady shook his head. "No." He got up from the chair, and went to the door. "Your room has a bunch of medical supplies. Maybe I can find a tube and some needles or something."

Eva cleared her throat. She'd been quiet until now. "Hold on, boys. I love the energy, both of you. But just to clarify: do you want to jimmy a tube with a needle on either end? Stick one end into Cole, the other end into Elder Mariah?"

"Yeah, 100 percent," Brady said.

"Absolutely," Cole said.

"I think if you stick a tube in the Elder's arm, the blood will just push out of her arm, right? And the blood'll push out of *your* arm too, Cole. Right?"

"So…" Cole said.

"So how's your blood going to go *in* her body when blood's coming *out* of her body?" Eva asked.

Brady and Cole looked at each other. They both shrugged at the same time. In Cole's mind, the idea was brilliant. Listening to Eva, there were some flaws.

"Why don't we get a needle with a syringe, okay, and take *your* blood out?" She pretended to draw blood out of his arm and then walked up to Elder Mariah. "And then use that to put your blood into Elder Mariah." She stuck the pretend needle into Elder Mariah's arm. "Like that."

Brady and Cole exchanged another look. "The Mustang was cool, though," Brady said.

"It was so cool," Cole said. They paused awkwardly for a second. Cole cleared his throat. "So let's get a needle and a syringe, then."

"On it." Brady ran off down the hallway. In the silence of the clinic, Cole could hear and feel Brady's footsteps leading away from the Elder's room.

Eva and Cole, alone, looked at each other awkwardly.

"Smart," Cole said to her.

"Your way was definitely more imaginative," she said.

"It was dumb. You're just being nice."

"It was dumb, *but* imaginative."

"Let's just hope it works."

Minutes later, Brady ran back into the room. He had a needle in his hand. He was holding it rather triumphantly. "Ready?"

22

AHEAD BY A CENTURY

"OKAY," EVA SAID, "MAKE A FIST."

Cole did, reluctantly. None of them knew what they were doing, but Eva was the one with the needle right now. He thought he would've felt a bit better if Dr. Captain was here, doing all this. But she couldn't be. She'd never let it happen. *Oh yeah, Dr. Captain, I might have magic blood and it could cure everybody.* They were left with Cole, Brady, and Eva, trying to work their way through this based on the knowledge they'd accrued from *Grey's Anatomy*. Eva had made a band out of tied-together hair elastics, and had fastened that around the top of Cole's forearm. She was pushing around at each of his blood vessels.

"Wow, you've got some good ones."

"Thanks, I think." Cole had never been complimented on his veins before.

"I think we're good," she said. "Are you good to go?"

No, he thought. "Yes."

Brady handed her the needle and syringe, like she was the surgeon and he was the nurse. She took a deep breath and moved it towards Cole. She did it slow enough that it gave him way too much time to think about it piercing through his skin and sliding into his vein. He pushed her hand away. "Isn't there any of that stuff that makes this hurt less? That stuff they give patients before sticking needles into them?"

"Alcohol?" Eva looked at Brady.

Brady just shrugged. "Sorry, my friend."

"Can you just run back and see if you can find—"

"Cole," Eva said. "Look, I don't want to argue with you, but I'm just saying, last night you took a huge knife to your chest. I mean, I don't know if you actually saw it, but it looked like a sword."

"A samurai sword," Brady interjected.

"Exactly," Eva said. "Now you're up-and-about like you got a scrape on your knee or something. So: knife, needle, knife, needle." She made motions as though she were weighing the two items.

Cole gritted his teeth. "Fine, just get it over with."

Eva nodded, and went in again with the needle. Cole looked away. He felt the sharp, cool metal press against his skin and then puncture it.

"There." Eva took the needle out, and with it came deep red blood. She handed Brady the syringe. He held it in both of his hands like a relic. He walked to the other side of Elder Mariah's bed, where there wasn't an IV line sticking out of her arm. He took the band that Eva had made for Cole and fastened it around the Elder's arm. With two fingers, he patted around at a few blood vessels. He took a long time doing this.

"Do you want me to do it?" Eva asked.

Brady shook his head. "I have to."

Eva pointed at one thick, blue vein at the top of Mariah's forearm. "That's a good one," she said to Brady. "Use that one."

"It'll work," Cole said to Brady.

Cole looked at the blood in the syringe. It looked like normal blood, nothing special. How was it going to save anybody?

"Okay," he could hear Brady say. "Here goes."

"What the hell are you kids doing!?"

Dr. Captain was standing at the door, her hands on her hips. Brady was frozen in place, the needle pressing against Elder Mariah's skin. Brady took the needle away and stood up straight. Dr. Captain rushed across the room. She held out her hand.

"Give that to me." Brady handed her the syringe. "What is this?" She held it out to the group.

The friends all looked at each other. It was a mix of confusion. Nobody said anything until Elder Mariah gasped for breath. It startled Cole into saying, "It's my blood, Dr. Captain."

"And why are you trying to give it to the Elder?" she asked.

"Because we think it can heal her," Brady blurted out.

"I'm sorry, what?" Dr. Captain said.

"It's true," Eva said. "We think."

Dr. Captain walked over to Cole. He was still sitting in his wheelchair. She sat down on the bed, right in front of him. She grasped the syringe tightly. It looked like the glass might shatter in her hand.

"Explain yourself. Now."

Cole took a deep breath and told the long story again. He told her everything he could.

"Where is this *file?*" Dr. Captain asked.

Great question. Cole thought. "I don't know where it is. But I read it, it was there, I swear to you."

"And so based off all of that, you want me to let you inject your blood into our Elder?"

It was clearly a rhetorical question, but Cole nodded his head weakly. It did sound dumb. And impossible.

"Dr. Captain," Brady said. "What's it going to hurt to try? Maybe it's horse crap, I don't know. I've seen some pretty amazing things, though, and most of them have involved Cole. If it doesn't work, she's going to die anyway, right?"

Dr. Captain nodded slowly. "Yes, that's right. I don't think she has much time left."

"And if it *does* work," Eva said. "If it does work, then we'll save her life."

"Maybe everybody's lives," Cole said.

Dr. Captain looked down at her hand. She stayed like that for a long time. Then, she opened her hand, and rocked the syringe back and forth across her palm. Her lips were moving as though going over all the options with herself. She shook her head. "Well, it's good that I came in here when I did, to stop you."

She wasn't going to let it happen. She was going to take the blood, remove them from Elder Mariah's room, and probably get them all locked up in a jail cell (that is, once they'd fixed it).

"If you'd have given her Cole's blood straight out of a syringe like you were going to, she would've died anyway, whether it was going to cure her or not. She would've stroked out gone into septic shock, had a heart attack…" She took a deep, drawn-out breath. "Any number of things, all of them bad."

She stood up, moved towards the IV bag, which was methodically providing Elder Mariah fluids. Dr. Captain paused there, like she was having second thoughts, then she took it off.

"You have to dilute the blood," Dr. Captain said. "What we can try to do is add some of this to her IV fluid."

She picked the bag up, and laid it down on the bed beside Elder Mariah's body. There was a port beside the one that was already feeding a clear liquid into Elder Mariah. Dr. Captain lifted this one up, then pulled an alcohol swab out of her pocket. She took it out of the package, wiped down the port, then pushed the needle into it. Ready to depress the plunger, she looked up at Cole.

"Are you sure, Cole?"

Cole wasn't sure of anything, but this—*this* felt as sure as he could possibly feel. "Yes."

"I hope you're right," she said. "God knows we need something good to happen around here."

Cole watched as her thumb pushed forward. The plunger released his blood into the IV bag. The thick fluid entered the bag in a cloud of red. Dr. Captain lifted the bag up, rotated it gently back and forth to mix it all together, and positioned it back onto the holder. She squeezed the bag at the top several times, and they all watched as the drops of liquid trickling into the IV line turned from clear to pink. The solution, now mixed with Cole's blood, navigated its way down the line until it reached Elder Mariah's right hand, then entered her bloodstream.

"Now what?" Cole asked.

"Now we wait," Dr. Captain said. "For one thing or the other."

They positioned themselves around Elder Mariah. Brady sat to her left, holding her hand, whispering to her something nobody else could hear. Eva sat down beside Cole, and held his hand. And Dr. Captain stood at Elder Mariah's side, watching the Elder, unblinkingly. They were all waiting, as Dr. Captain said, for one thing or the other.

"I'm going to lose my license over this," Dr. Captain muttered.

It wasn't more than that first few minutes when Elder Mariah made a sound, a crackling kind of whisper that was as unintelligible as it was encouraging. Her eyelids flickered open.

"Nókom?" Brady said.

Cole watched as Elder Mariah's left arm tensed, and she squeezed Brady's hand. It was as though she squeezed tears out of him, because they came hard and fast, navigating around the largest smile Cole had ever seen on his friend, the only real smile Brady had offered since the night of Ashley's murder.

Elder Mariah nodded. "Nósisim. I'm thirsty."

"I'll get you some water." Eva got up from her chair. She reached over and grabbed a Dixie cup of water from the side table. Brady lifted her head for her, and Eva tipped the water into Elder Mariah's mouth. When she was finished, Brady helped lower her head back onto the pillow.

"Ekosani," she said.

During all of this Dr. Captain checked Mariah's vitals, over and over again, trying to make sense of what was happening. She checked the Elder's pulse, temperature, breaths per minute. Every sort of vital she could check, she checked. Finally, she turned to Cole and said, "I don't believe it."

"I don't think I really believed it would work," Cole said. "I just hoped, I guess."

"I'm going to need, uhhh—" she started. "More blood. Enough that I can dilute it into all the IV bags, give this to everybody. Now."

"Yeah, of course." Cole felt it then. He knew that this was why he was here. For all the pain, all the loss, the sickness, and the confusion, this moment, right here, gave it all purpose. "Take it all, whatever you need."

Dr. Captain smiled. Maybe it was her first smile in a long time, too. "I won't need *that* much. But we should get you over to—"

There was a knock on the door. They all turned to see four people standing in the doorway. At the front of the group was a woman in a white lab coat. She was white, with blonde hair tied back tightly into a ponytail. She had a clipboard that she hugged close to her chest. Another doctor stood beside her, with his hands behind his back. He was younger, white as well, with short, black hair. He wore a white lab coat and black-rimmed glasses. Behind the doctors were two men dressed almost all in black: black boots, black cargo pants, black shirts, black hats.

"Holy shit," Cole whispered to Eva. "Look familiar?"

"How could I forget?" she whispered back.

"Dr. Captain?" the woman said. She gave a quick glance over to Cole, her eyes widened for a moment.

"Yes, that's me," Dr. Captain said.

"I'm Dr. Ament," she said. "So nice to meet you."

"I'm sorry, I don't…" Dr. Captain started.

"Your office requested assistance for the outbreak?" Dr. Ament said.

"Yes, that's correct." Dr. Captain walked towards the door. Cole listened intently as they talked. They were trying to lower their voices so the kids couldn't hear them. Cole, though, could hear them as if they were standing right beside him. "I had asked the Department of Health a few days ago. I'm sorry, but usually when we ask for help we have to wait a hundred years. You can't be from the government."

"We're a…" Dr. Ament began "…private contractor."

"We pride ourselves on not making people wait a century," the man said with a chuckle and a snort.

"And you are?" Dr. Captain asked the man.

"Dr. Carmichael," he said, straightening his coat.

"I see," Dr. Captain said. "I hadn't received any notification of this. You'll have to forgive me, who are you with, then?"

"Uhhh, yeah, we're with Mihko Laboratories," Dr. Carmichael said.

"Mihko Laboratories," Dr. Captain said. "You mean the same—"

"One and the same. It helps to know the community. This will be of great benefit to you," Dr. Ament said.

"We're here to help," Dr. Carmichael added.

"And we know you as well, Dr. Ament," Dr. Captain said. "All too well."

Dr. Captain looked back at Eva, Brady, Cole, and Elder Mariah. She nodded at them firmly and quickly. Cole would spend a long time deciphering that nod. It felt like so much more than that. And it meant even more to him when Dr. Captain turned back towards the strangers, and he saw her slip the syringe that held his remaining blood into her pocket before leading the four new visitors out of the room.

23
ALL THE COOKIES

"COME ON, LET'S GET YOU IN BED." Eva helped transfer Cole from the wheelchair to the bed, and he dutifully pretended to need that help. She sat in the wheelchair herself and began to roll back and forth. Cole watched her for a minute, happy that they could be content with being bored. She continued to roll around on the wheelchair, and then got more adventurous. She started to roll all over the room, treating the bed and side table like an obstacle course.

Cole took the opportunity to look at his wound for the first time, curious as to how it looked, since he could hardly feel it anymore. He peeled the bandage away from his skin—this hurt more than the stab wound—and saw that the knife had left a scar. It was slightly raised, pink, and about an inch in length. He put his finger against it and poked around a bit. He didn't notice that Eva had rolled up to the side of his bed and was watching him.

"How is that even possible?" Eva stood up from the wheelchair and leaned across his body, trying to peek at the wound.

"What?" Cole covered it up.

"It looks like a…" she started to reach for it, but Cole held her hand to keep her from touching it, even over the bandage "It's a scar now? After a day?"

"No, it's just, you didn't see it well. I should keep it covered, it's gross, trust me, I—"

Eva's phone buzzed. "To be continued," she said.

There'd never been better timing in the world. Eva took her hand away from Cole's, and pulled her phone out of her pocket.

"Wait a minute," Eva said as she read.

"What is it?" Cole asked.

"It's Michael. He just told me to get your blood and give it to the people. He said his mom told him to tell me."

"She said what?"

Eva rolled her eyes. She repeated the text verbatim: "Mom says get the blood. Give it out like she showed you."

"Why can't she do it?"

"I don't know." Eva looked through her text again as though she'd missed something. "He doesn't say."

"Text him back," Cole said.

Eva's thumbs tapped away at her phone. He watched as she waited for a response that never came. She looked up at Cole, apologetically. "I think we should just do it. We don't know how long she's going to be. Somebody could need it right now."

"You're right. Screw it. I mean, you've already done it once."

"Okay, ummm…" Eva darted off, away from the bed to a counter at the side of the room, one of the areas that Brady appeared to have rummaged through. She tore through a bunch of stuff that was piled there. Boxes fell to the ground, along with a stethoscope or two, a couple of clipboards. Finally, Eva turned around to show Cole a handful of needles. Cole gave her a thumbs-up. Soon, Eva was back over the bed. She had all the needles with her, seven by Cole's count, and he counted very carefully.

"Seven?" Cole asked.

"Yeah, there are a lot of people sick, right?"

"Right…"

"Don't worry," she said. "When it's over, I'll find you all the cookies."

"Every last single one of them," he said.

Eva set to work, and Cole was impressed by how efficient she was. Before he knew it, all the syringes were full of his blood, lined up in a row. After she was done, she even found cotton balls and bandages for Cole to use.

"Not that you'll need them," she said, ensuring that Cole knew their conversation about his knife wound was far from over.

"I can't explain it," Cole said, as Eva placed a cotton ball over each place in Cole's arm that she'd put in a needle. She taped down the cotton balls with bandages. "I can't explain why it did that," he said, motioning to the stab wound. "But I'm going to try and figure it out."

"Are you going to do all that figuring-out way back in the city, or…" Eva gathered the needles carefully, so as not to stick herself with one of them, and she avoided eye contact with Cole just as carefully. He thought, he hoped, that she was trying to seem like she didn't care either way, which meant that she actually *did* care.

"I don't know," he said. "I should get back, you know. My grandma's down there and everything. My auntie. Friends, school."

"Right," Eva said. "Well…"

She walked over to the door.

"But I'd like to come back," he blurted out. "If that would be okay. I mean, with people in general."

"It'd be okay with me."

They looked at each other for longer than a moment. Cole couldn't tell how long it was. They got lost in time. He didn't want it to end, so his heart sunk a bit when she snapped out of it. "Well, I better get started."

"Are you going to be okay doing that?" he asked.

"Oh yeah. Everything's going to be okay now, Cole. Really. Get some rest," she said. "I'll be back in a bit."

"For more blood?"

"To bring cookies, remember?"

"Promise?"

"Yeah. I promise."

EPILOGUE

COLE STOPPED ONLY FOR A MOMENT, then walked off the pathway and into the field. One step after another, the school ruins drew closer. He didn't feel weak. His knees felt stable, his hands steady—heartbeat, too. No threat of fainting, no profuse sweating. His palms were dry. Maybe he had come this far in a short time. After all, so much had happened. The pill bottle holding his last two pills was in his pocket, but Cole wasn't tapping at it, wasn't endlessly deciding whether to take one or not. He wasn't thinking about it much. Maybe it was the tobacco bundle, held firmly in his left hand. Maybe he was drawing strength from it—from a medicine that he had neglected for far too long, medicine from the ancestors he was about to offer it to, from the Creator he was about to pray to.

He walked up the concrete steps, stopped at where the doors used to be. They were mostly gone now, burned into nothing. All that remained were the handles, resting on the ground by Cole's feet. He crouched down and picked one of them up. He thought about scars, and what Elder Mariah had told him. The ones on his palms, the memories they held, were important in their own right. But the scars were hard, and the memories were always conflicted. The one on his chest meant something else, and he hoped he could keep it. He wasn't sure how this particular gift worked, or if because he'd healed so fast, the scar would fade away. But it would remind him of something... good. He stopped the killer. No more people were going to die. What's more, Eva was talking to him now. Nicely. Maybe people would stop talking about him, too, in the way they had. Thanks to Choch, Cole didn't even have to address the bent prison bars. Choch fixed them, good as new.

Cole put the handle down, and opened the tobacco tie. He spread the tobacco across the steps, and closed his eyes. "Creator. I...I don't really know how to do this anymore. It's like I'm learning how, all over again. It's weird, too, knowing that you're actually listening. I guess I was never really sure. After the fire, I thought you weren't there at all. I don't know what to say. I guess I just want you to keep them safe. I want you to welcome Ashley and Alex and Maggie, everybody who got sick and didn't make it, home. Just, you know, don't let Choch keep them waiting, or whatever. And I want you to protect everybody else too. Protect Brady. Eva." Cole opened his eyes. He placed the red cloth down, moved the handle over it to hold it there. "That's it. That's all I have to say. Ekosani. Thanks for bringing me here."

"Uhhhh, to be fair, He didn't actually bring you here. I did."

Cole shook his head and let out a breath. He didn't get up. "How long have you been standing there for?"

"It's just that, I'm not one to complain, but don't you think little old me deserves *some* thanks? I mean, what did He do, anyway? He's probably binge-watching *American Gods* or something."

"*Fine*. Thank you for fixing the prison bars, and for making everybody think they'd just forgot to lock me in."

"Oh, and don't forget—"

"Don't push it." Cole got up now. He got to his feet, turned around, and faced the spirit being. "You look the worst I've ever seen you."

Gone were the bright suit, dress shoes, and top hat. He wasn't wearing his outfit from the diner, either. No, today he was wearing a Nickelback t-shirt, a backwards baseball hat, black Converse sneakers, and blue jeans that hung below his ass. To top off the outfit, he had a backpack slung over his shoulders.

Choch plopped down on the steps facing Blackwood Forest. He dropped the backpack, which landed heavily on the ground. He patted the concrete to his side, and Cole begrudgingly sat down beside him. The sky was pretty in the early evening, painted in autumn hues. Cole thought he could feel the warmth from it, as though Jayne were sitting at his side. He almost felt like he could tolerate Choch.

"Dude," Choch said, "my outfit is on fleek, bruh."

"Fleek? Bruh?"

Choch took a deep, exaggerated breath, and rolled his eyes slowly, making sure that Cole saw it. "I am being," he said dramatically, "Collo—"

"Kids don't talk like that. *Ever.*"

"What, really? They don't?"

"No, they talk like regular human beings. This isn't a teenage drama on the CW," Cole said.

"Well, it's not *quite* like that, anyway," Choch grumbled, looking off somewhere. Cole snapped his fingers to draw Choch's attention.

"Also, you look like a *forty-year-old man* talking like a teenager on a CW teenage drama," Cole added.

Choch leaned back and looked Cole over carefully, paying special attention to Cole's chest.

"So, how are you?"

"Fine," Cole said. "Really good, actually. I feel like Wolverine. But generally, yeah, just good."

"That has to be a nice change of pace, hasn't it?"

"Yeah, it is."

"You're less confused than you were before, then?" Choch asked.

"A little bit, yeah," Cole said. "I can connect most of the dots. I mean, I'd like to know about what happened to the folder…" Choch nodded throughout Cole's answer, like a psychologist. It looked extremely odd to Cole, watching Choch give all the psychologist vibes while dressed like some weird teenager. "But I'm guessing Jayne's already, you know," Cole motioned up to the autumn sky with his finger, even made an odd spaceship-taking-off kind of sound, "up where she's supposed to be. It's not a big deal, really."

"Actually, I just can't seem to tear her away from her friends over there at the cemetery," Choch said. "She's a stubborn one, her. I mean, cute as a button, but you can just *imagine* trying to get her to eat her Brussels sprouts, am-I-right?"

"Why are you even giving her a choice?" Cole asked. "Just put her where she's supposed to be. The deal's done. The killer's caught, people are going to get the cure…forget I even mentioned the file, okay?"

Choch took a good long look at Cole. He picked up the backpack, and placed it on his lap. He began to tap at it thoughtfully. "Here's the thing, Coley-B—sorry, CB. Do you like CB?"

"Whatever, sure."

"Here's the thing, CB. Jayne's kind of, sort of, not quite able to go home *just* yet. And you never know, the whereabouts of that folder might come in handy."

"What? What are you talking about?"

Choch took a bunch of textbooks out of the backpack and placed them in front of Cole, one by one. Cheerfully, Choch asked, "Did you hear they lifted the curfew? School's back on, starting Monday! I took the liberty of getting *exactly* what you'll need. And I'll even arrange a tutor for you. Except in math, of course, Mr. Eighty-seven percent! *Eva*, anybody? Huh? She'd for sure get you an *A* in Land-Based Education."

Cole picked up one of the textbooks, entitled *Canada: A Country of Change*, and dismissively fingered through the pages before placing it back on the pile. "This is such a load of shit."

"Come on! It'll be fun!" Choch said excitedly. When he saw Cole's reaction, though—shocked, disgusted, angry, take your pick—he added a *very* weak, "Yaaaaaay."

"I'm going home. I'm done. I did everything I was supposed to do," Cole said.

"Oh no, my dear child. I'm afraid you're only getting started."

To be continued…

ACKNOWLEDGEMENTS

THIS NOVEL STARTED ABOUT TEN YEARS AGO. I was talking to my friend Jeff about stories. That conversation gave birth to The Reckoner. Since then it's been this weird little kid I've raised. Like a kid, it's annoyed me, challenged me, and brightened my day. It has grown, matured, and, ultimately made me better.

I've had help along the way. Jeff Ryzner brainstormed with me, acting as my sounding board. David Jón Fuller read a very old version of the novel, and gave me some needed feedback. *(Very old version is right. Mr. Robertson here wrote this novel like 43 times before it was any good.)* There were others (not Choch), too. Sara Snow, who loves this world almost as much as I do. Scott Henderson helped me envision some of the characters and locations early on. Debra Dudek and Doug Whiteway took time to read over story concepts and offer their thoughts. Warren Cariou, my friend and mentor.

There are the usual suspects too. My parents have been there with me, and believed in me, since the beginning. My wife supports this little habit of mine in so many ways. My children motivate me in everything I do. My brothers, in-laws, friends, have all pushed me forward and lifted me up when I've needed it. And, of course, HighWater Press is like a second family to me.

But there is one person I want to thank most of all, and that's Desirae Warkentin, my editor. Yes, she made me rewrite *Strangers* at least twice (not 43 times), but whether it was offering up her expertise in the YA genre or taking phone calls from me to vent or toss around ideas,

I know this book wouldn't be what it is without her. We get to do this two more times! Thanks so much, Dee.

Sorry if I've missed anybody, but... *(please, I'll just say it: Mr. Robertson is a scatterbrained idiot. Honestly, if you ask his wife, she'll tell you. He forgets everything. I mean, this one time—)* ...sigh. You get the point.

Ekosani, Dave